HEROISM OR SUICIDE

When a routine orbital flight is interrupted for no reason—and at a tremendous cost to the nation—official excuses are too lame to satisfy the press and the public, and too mysterious to satisfy a crew brought back to earth for no apparent reason.

But one of the crew members does understand—and he knows that his long-awaited moment has come.

"Searls has a fast, punchy style ... neither slick nor predictable."

—*The New York Times*

Books by Hank Searls

The Big X
The Crowded Sky
Pentagon
The Pilgrim Project

Published by POCKET BOOKS

THE PILGRIM PROJECT

HANK SEARLS

A KANGAROO BOOK
PUBLISHED BY POCKET BOOKS NEW YORK

POCKET BOOKS, a Simon & Schuster division of
GULF & WESTERN CORPORATION
1230 Avenue of the Americas, New York, N.Y. 10020

ISBN: 0-671-81416-8

First Pocket Books printing January, 1978

Trademarks registered in the United States and other countries.

Printed in the U.S.A.

To my Dad, who encouraged me to hazard scientific waters, and to those in the space program who, unafraid to rock the boat, helped me chart the course.

FOREWORD

It is June 19, 1962. It has not yet become fashionable politically or scientifically to deny that there is a race for the moon.

The Institute of the Aerospace Sciences is sitting in the Los Angeles Ambassador. The engineer from New York reads his paper in an academically proper monotone; the point is comfortably wrapped in pounds, cubic feet, and degrees centigrade. But the point is there: to win the lunar race it would be feasible to strand a human being alone on the surface of the moon for a year or two, awaiting rescue when means were available.

In a few minutes, when the speaker has concluded his paper, some of the members will smile quietly and murmur something about "Project Kamikaze" as they file into the lobby.

The men are working scientists and engineers from IBM or Rand Corporation or Space Technology Labs or NASA; here, too, are self-employed engineering consultants, and astronomers from Cal Tech and Harvard.

John Cord of Bell Aerosystems in Buffalo (a Textron Company) drones on: "It is sincerely believed that capable and qualified people could be found to volunteer for the mission even if the return possibilities were nil." The speaker takes note of the moral and ethical consideration: "The fact that a man is willing to go does not alone justify our sending him." But he reminds his audience of the enormous leap forward a one-way, one-man mission would be in the race against time and the Russians.

He approaches the end of his paper: "The significant area of how to insure survival and return of the one-way spaceman to earth is a fertile field."

"You can say that again," whispers a young physicist.

The speaker concludes: "If this can be demonstrated, the One-Way Manned Space Mission becomes a two-way mission, and not only a feasible concept, but one which we can and should use."

The Russians have put cosmonauts into space for over 400 hours. U.S. astronauts have logged 50. Soviet cosmonauts have effected an exquisite near-rendezvous. The U.S. is nowhere close. Russia has photographed the back of the moon and impacted it where planned. The U.S. hit it but cameras failed.

NASA's present Project Apollo may yet put two Americans on the moon for a few hours before 1970. If America had moved to send one of the two men alone, he could have landed a year or so before. Perhaps before the Russians. If.

"Why the great hurry to get to
the moon?"
Dwight D. Eisenhower

"We have vowed that we shall not
see it governed by the hostile flag
of conflict."
John F. Kennedy

"Of course, I want to be the first."
Alan B. Shepard

CONTENTS

PART ONE

The
First Week

1.

In the spring the Russians dropped all pretense and began their final drive for the moon. They launched a space platform into earth orbit and manned it. Over the months they began to fling toward it components of the Vostok they planned to use for lunar reconnaissance and, later, landing. The platform crew was apparently augmented but never relieved. For over a year men painfully mated engines to tanks to capsule a hundred miles in space.

The U.S. Apollo program, hungry for funds, awaited its giant booster. In a year or so, when the booster was delivered, it intended to place two astronauts on the lunar surface while a third waited in orbit around it. Meanwhile the U.S. Apollo crews were occasionally launched by smaller boosters to circle the earth on training flights.

Two of the three Americans lying side by side in the earth-orbiting Apollo Three slept as they soared silently through the Pacific night toward dawn and the North American coastline.

The third was awake and puzzled. He was a young man with a tooth chipped years before in high-school football and dark blue, reflective eyes; he lay strapped loosely in the right-hand couch facing columns of glowing dials. He had just had a call, premature and crackling with static, from Apollo Control in Houston almost 2,000 miles ahead. He had reluctantly abandoned the search that was fascinating him and answered, hiding his irritation at the interruption because the voice was a familiar one and he liked and respected the Navy commander, an astronaut himself, who called. There was an odd hesitation before the astronaut on the ground spoke again, tentatively: "Steve?"

"That's right." A short silence seemed to demand further explanation, although he could not have told why. "The colonel's asleep."

There was another uncharacteristic pause. Then the commander said: "Roger. Wait one." The man on the ground sounded confused, exactly as if he had called the wrong number on a telephone.

The young man in the capsule tried hurriedly to take up his search again. In a few seconds their squat 12-foot cone would catch the morning sun west of the California Channel Islands. An early rising amateur astronomer in Los Angeles or Santa Barbara might actually pick its minute unblinking gleam from among the pulsing stars and follow it until it was lost in the east. He wondered if any would bother to look.

He was floating weightlessly an inch or so away from his couch, anchored by a slackened chest strap and toe sockets large enough for pressure boots he was not wearing. His face was stubbled—to shave was to risk free-floating whiskers in an environment in which a speck of dust could clog a valve or short a relay.

He had adjusted the couch to a position almost flat so that his head would extend to the tiny forward-facing window they used in rendezvous and docking; he could see silhouetted against fading stars the conical nose of their capsule. Somewhere ahead, a 17-foot target orbited at their altitude, blinking in the darkness. Four times in the last seventy-two hours they had found the target in daylight, snuggled the nose tightly into its base, released it, and deliberately lost it again in a sweeping cat-and-mouse game.

The rendezvous technique they were learning was the reason for this mission; it would go on for the next three days. Early in the flight he had become enthralled with the problems of closing speed and angle of interception; he was deliberately allowing the others to sleep late so that he could retain the controls. He had wanted to find the target again before the colonel awakened; to find it in the dark, too, for nobody ever had.

But it was too late now. A brilliant ribbon was lengthening along the eastern horizon, silhouetting the Coastal Range of California. In a few moments the ride on the night-side would be through and he would be peering over the rim of the globe, down at the blinding sun. Now that there was no more chance of saving his night vision, he pulled a pin in his couch, readjusted it to its normal, half-sitting position to watch the orbital dawn, which on his first flight, months before, he had learned to love.

The bright ribbon had already stretched a third of the way around the earth. It shone arc-light white where it touched the horizon, changed with Grand Canyon gaudiness to a layer of bright orange, then a line of red, then a thin, taut band of blue. The blue faded at its upper edge to the velvet daytime black which swallowed all but the brightest stars.

Awaiting whatever message Apollo Control had, he glanced across the slumbering navigator at the colonel. The spacecraft commander lay with an arm behind his head. He had been sleeping restlessly. His earphones hovered weightlessly from a strap above his balding head. His face, which could light boyishly when he smiled, was suddenly not the one the public knew, but that of a man with all the aches and pains of forty-five.

Steve felt a pang; the colonel might realize his dream of a lunar landing, if their crew was among the first, but after that the rest of them would learn the strange world without him. He would be simply too old.

The rising sun had crept through the window. Before it reached the colonel's eyes, Steve eased the capsule's nose almost tenderly to the left. The slash of sunlight moved from the colonel's face. Steve yawed the craft a little further so that the white glare fell on Rick Lincoln's eyelids. The navigator's pale eyes snapped open.

"Thank you, Mother," he commented. "I was so afraid you'd let me sleep in."

There was no waste motion in Rick Lincoln. His mind worked like the computers at Houston and Goddard, which continually predicted the point at which their capsule would impact the earth if everything went wrong and they had to abort. He was always a few moments ahead, a slim young man with a sharp face and light build, nicely coordinated. Whether you liked him or not he was a pleasure to watch on a tennis court or moving at zero g. And he always awakened awake.

Now, without a yawn or a stretch, he flicked off his chest strap and tugged lightly at the side of his couch. He floated weightlessly down its length, stopped himself at its foot with a finger crooked under Steve's toe strap. He twisted suddenly and finished erect, his velour-padded feet sticking to the velour-carpeted deck as a velvet letter sticks to a velvet bulletin board. He supported himself with his hands, and with one foot slid his empty couch under the colonel's, clearing a working space between Steve and the spacecraft commander.

"You spot LEM?" he asked without much interest. "LEM the Gem" was the target, named for the Lunar Excursion Module it duplicated in size and shape. Steve shook his head. Rick jabbed a button on the colonel's panel.

"Civilians," he commented, waiting for the radar screen to light. "You have to do everything the hard way." He studied the screen. "Fourteen miles," he announced, "bearing one-three-zero."

Steve shifted uncomfortably. For half an hour he had avoided the temptation to turn on the radar, because he was eager to know if they could spot the target by eye. A year from now, on the lunar mission, the radar beacon on the real LEM could, after all, fail when one of them was circling the moon alone in Apollo, waiting for the excursion module to return. Failing, it would leave him with nothing but his naked eye to find his two crewmates.

On the other hand, Rick was right. The less time they spent in searching and rendezvous, the more dockings they could make; the more dockings, the further ahead of rival crews they would be. Steve said nothing, but skidded the craft into position for the tiny orbital shove that would speed their interception.

Rick Lincoln characteristically checked the change in heading before moving forward to break out their breakfasts. Then he squatted under the docking hatch in the nose and took the top three packets of frozen, dehydrated food from the lockers under his navigating window. He straightened, brushing aside the leg of one of the pressure suits hanging in the exit tunnel above him. He had slept in his own, except for the helmet, apparently enduring the discomfort for the extra seconds of safety it would give him if a cabin leak occurred.

Perhaps, Steve thought, he should wear his own suit more. Their pressure suits were life-jackets in a sea of vacuum. The cabin was jammed with equipment, and the picture of three floating astronauts trying to fight their way simultaneously into suits at the same time was a tragi-comic scene that Steve did not like even to envision. But there were other factors, he decided. You have to take it off to use the john. Besides if you wore it all day you might snag it; then if you needed it, it would be useless.

Rick attached a tube to the top of the food packet and squirted water into it. "You raise Guaymas yet?" he asked, swishing the package.

Steve nodded. "Houston already, too." He paused. "In fact they didn't wait, they raised us. They were calling us blind."

The pale eyebrows shot up. "What was wrong?"

Steve shook his head. "I don't know. Cap Com told me to wait." Feeling a little silly, he added: "It sounded like he wished he'd called person-to-person."

"IBM's going to split. Millionaire's Club only—the Mercury Astronaut Chapter."

"Very funny," said Steve, hoping the colonel was really asleep. For a regular officer, Rick continually teetered on the edge of insubordination. Steve himself had been only a reserve. He had left naval aviation for civilian testing after Korea, reluctant to dedicate his life forever to non-constructive goals. He had emerged with a faint distaste for military life, but he found himself irritated at Rick's abrasive, stinging treatment of the colonel.

To Steve the First Seven, the Mercury men, were unique in testing. They were hardheaded, trained to demand facts before deciding, and each had a family besides. But at a time when there were no facts they had dived into Mercury in the dark. He respected the colonel's self-discipline, liked his clear intelligence, loved his warmth, and sometimes marveled at his courage, too. He wondered if Rick, or he himself, would have fought for a seat in Mercury. Rick's problem, he suspected, was jealousy; he probably felt himself unappreciated or underpaid.

"Or you know what?" Rick went on, unwilling to drop it. "They found a new motel for sale at the Cape and they need the colonel's power-of-attorney to get the *Life* magazine dough.''

"*You* know what?'' the colonel asked startlingly, adjusting his couch to the sitting position.

Steve winced, but Rick Lincoln glanced at the colonel blandly. "What, oh Leader?'' he smiled.

The colonel smiled back, but his eyes were rather cold. "When we land I'm going to give you a crack at some of that dough.''

"How?'' Rick asked, handing him a packet of food.

"At five bucks a game, I'm going to run your young ass right off that handball court. Unless . . .''

"Unless what?'' the navigator asked.

"Unless you'd rather not.''

The colonel attacked a handball opponent in a dogged, lung-searing style that sometimes exploded into physical danger. When you thought you had him beaten, the ball became a blurred meteorite ricocheting around the court.

"Tennis anyone?'' Rick Lincoln suggested to him softly. "Instead?''

Rick Lincoln had been a top tennis player at the Naval Academy; Steve was sure that the colonel had not been behind a net for years.

The colonel regarded his navigator. "You're sure it would be fair? I mean, I'm taller than you and all.''

"I'll spot you two games a set,'' Rick offered.

"How generous.''

"Unless,'' Rick grinned, "you'd rather not.''

He knew his man. The colonel nodded. "Give me two weeks,'' he said. "Steve, did you say we had a call?''

Steve nodded, squeezing food from his packet into his mouth. He chewed it without enthusiasm. Chicken and rice stood dehydration well, but the life-support people were straining the astronauts' tolerance of it to the breaking point. "They're going to call back.''

The colonel raised his eyebrows, called Houston himself instead. The commander's voice came back immediately with an odd, false levity: "Good morning, Old Buddy, sir." But then he added: "Steve?"

There was much less static now. Steve knew that if he opened his louvers he would find himself in sight of the Houston area on the Gulf ahead. "Steve, aye," he answered, perplexed. "Go ahead."

He heard the commander clear his throat. "Steve . . ." He faltered as if reluctant to continue. Then he went on in a rush. "What's your oxygen state?"

Startled, Steve glanced at his panel. A section was devoted to his Environmental Control System—ECS, the complex that permitted them to work in shirt sleeves three hundred miles in space. If there was a "no-go" system anywhere in the craft the pointer on its errant bar-gauge would sink or rise above the others like a sore thumb. Besides, a red light would show. All of the pointers were at equal height. No red light shone.

He shrugged and answered Cap Com. "Ninety hours oxygen per man. Cabin pressure normal. What do you show?"

In Apollo Control, he knew, the commander was sitting at a console in the rear of a circular green amphitheater. Each of the tracking stations behind them had electronically felt Apollo Three's pulse as it passed. From Grand Canary Island and Woomera and Hawaii and Guaymas, telemetry had sped the tiny bits of information to Houston. One face of the commander's console exactly duplicated the copilot's panel before Steve. On it, up-to-date to a microsecond, was the oxygen information.

Steve was sure he heard the commander sigh. "Colonel, we think you've got a cabin leak. Recommend you consider an abort on your next pass."

Steve readjusted his headset, not sure that he had heard correctly. They were on a six-day mission. The cost of putting their capsule into orbit was astronomical—$600 per pound. Apollo weighed 5 tons. It had cost six million dollars to launch them for six days of training and they were being asked to quit with the job half done.

"Did you say *abort?*" he asked incredulously.

Next to him the colonel jammed his earphones tighter, as if they had betrayed him. Methodically, but very swiftly, Rick Lincoln began to stow the food containers.

"Affirmative," replied the commander. "We are recommending an abort at—"

"Just a second," Steve said heatedly. "I said I showed ninety hours oxygen remaining per man. What do you show?"

"A little over two."

Two hours of oxygen would barely get them down, but the whole idea of Apollo Control panicking without a proper checkout was unbelievable. The copilot—"Systems Manager" officially—was the spacecraft's engineer. Steve's competence was being challenged from the ground.

"Cap Com," the colonel said mildly, glancing at Steve's panel, "I suggest you look over your circuitry."

Over the miles the commander's voice came back with a curious, formal emphasis. "We have checked our circuitry already, Colonel. We recommend an abort. *I* recommend an abort. Request you stand by to copy retro-fire times for Areas Golf, Hotel, and—"

Steve tore off his headset and slid from his couch. "Listen, Skipper, this is ridiculous! Don't let them stampede us!"

"They won't stampede us," the colonel said tensely. "I'm running this flight."

Steve eased past Rick and pulled a quick line check. He found no evidence of a leak. He passed a thumbs-up signal to the colonel, slid back in his couch, and slipped on his earphones.

"There's nothing wrong with the oxygen supply," the colonel was reporting. "I intend to continue the flight."

Steve, relieved, flicked open his rendezvous window. Within seconds he spotted the high-intensity light he had searched for all night. It was winking from the target, at this distance a tiny orange cylinder against the midnight-blue sky of daylight. He was about to report it to the colonel when a single word came over his headset. He did not quite catch it because he was busy and the voice of the commander in Houston was low-pitched, and very soft. It sounded like "pogrom" or "program." Or perhaps "pilgrim."

The colonel had found LEM too, was still watching it with his face turned to the window, but Steve sensed a sudden rigidity in his posture.

"What did he say?" Steve asked him curiously.

The colonel turned his head. For a fleeting instant the face seemed five years younger. Then the expression was bland again. "I didn't hear anything." The grey eyes were unwavering and impassive. Steve looked at him uncertainly. But if the colonel said he had heard nothing, he had not. Steve turned back to the window, easing the capsule toward the target with infinitesimal pressure on the control. He felt the colonel's hand on his arm.

"I've decided," the colonel said gently, "to take their recommendation."

"What?" Steve demanded. "What are you talking about?"

"I've decided to abort it."

The colonel had an impish sense of humor, but it announced itself through a twinkle in his eye. There was no twinkle now.

"For God's sake, why?" Steve cried.

"Safety," the colonel said without emotion.

Steve stared at him. He believed himself as cautious a test pilot as any in the profession, more cautious perhaps than the colonel. And the colonel knew it, damn it! His throat began to ache like that of a child who could not convince an adult of a great and evident truth. There was a nightmarish unreality about this decision that shook him to his core.

"You're kidding!"

"No."

"Skipper," Steve said intensely, "we're OK on oxygen. Believe me!"

"I'm going to suit up for re-entry," the colonel said. "Would you copy the retro times?"

Steve could not give up. "How are we going to justify it?" he asked fiercely.

This was no test flight of a jet at Edwards; the world was watching the race for the moon. American anger at being fooled by Khrushchev had cooled to apathy, but too much was riding on each Apollo mission to test public tolerance. No one in the Mercury or Gemini or Apollo had ever aborted before. The colonel himself had been in trouble on a Mercury flight; he had not been hasty then. The panic button and chicken switch were there, but you didn't jab them lightly. You worked out a problem logically and calmly, not on guesses, but on facts.

"The retro times, Steve," the colonel said flatly.

Still Steve could not accept it. He asked Rick Lincoln what he thought. The young lieutenant, fastening on his pressure helmet, paused to check the ECS panel himself.

"Skip it," the colonel snapped. "This isn't really subject to democratic processes, is it?"

"I guess not," Rick Lincoln admitted, a thoughtful expression on his face. "Besides, I somehow don't think I have all the facts. So I guess I'll have to go along with the boss."

"No truer words," the colonel agreed, "were ever spoken."

A wall arose for the first time between Steve and the two military men. The colonel had selected him because he trusted his judgment and now he was betrayed. And a sudden aching thought hit him as well.

Between the time that the wives below heard that they were landing under emergency conditions and the moment they knew they were safe would come hours of torment. Mickey had been through it once before. Quite literally it had almost killed her. She was not strong enough yet for them frivolously to put her through it again—she might never be.

Sick at the torture she faced, he cast about for another argument. Near Washington the huge computers at Goddard continually monitored Apollo's telemetry, backing those at the Integrated Mission Control Center at Houston. A quick request for a read-out from them might settle the argument.

"Goddard, Skipper!" he blurted. "Get Cap Com to ask them for an analysis!"

The colonel did not even answer. He seemed a million miles away. He got up and began to don his pressure suit. Blindly, Steve began to copy the retro times the Navy commander transmitted from Houston.

Once he looked up. The colonel was watching him while he fastened his helmet. The other man started to speak, changed his mind. Steve, numb with shock, went back to his copying.

2.

At the rear of the great green amphitheater in Houston the astronaut at the Capsule Communicator's console found a lull when he had finished transmitting the retro-fire times.

He was a Navy commander with humorous eyes and a monkey grin that belied his IQ. The flash of his smile was more familiar to a certain portion of the TV audience than that of most entertainers. The smile was missing now.

There was a sour taste in his mouth. The message was through to the colonel, who knew of Project Pilgrim, but now he faced the prospect of more evasions, more lies, if the colonel's two crewmen were to be kept from the truth. He glanced from his console to an enormous transparent map which dominated the front of the room. Across it crawled the black cone representing Apollo Three, drawing a graceful track behind. Fifty other sinuous lines crisscrossing the equator showed prior orbits. This was its last swing; the next fifty tracks would never appear. The commander sighed.

During a mission Apollo Control always smelled of sweat and heated relays and stale air conditioning. It could also smell of fear, he knew from experience. Never before had it smelled of deception.

Sy Larson, a lean, handsomely tanned young man with an easy grin, slid into the vacant seat beside him. He noted the new time to retro fire which denoted that the abort was in progress and nodded approvingly. He was not an engineer, the commander suspected, but he had learned enough technical details to pass as an assistant to Archy Gorman, Operations Director of the Apollo Project. He was a CIA man assigned local responsibility for Project Pilgrim. The commander did not particularly like him.

"It's done," he said without enthusiasm.

"It can't be that bad," Sy Larson smiled.

"Look, Sy," protested the commander. "Do you really think that Steve or that Lincoln kid are going to accept a half-assed apology instead of an explanation?"

Sy Larson winced and looked around. The commander shifted impatiently. The leather chairs in the glassed VIP gallery behind them were filling now for the recovery phase; he began to get the familiar feeling that God and a dozen Senators were watching every time he had to scratch his ear. He shrugged. Obviously no one could hear through the window, but the commander obligingly dropped his voice. "Neither of those two guys is an idiot, Sy."

"No."

"I like to think they won't believe we panicked."

"They better pretend they believe it," Sy Larson said, "if they expect to get another flight in Apollo."

The commander shook his head. "They won't pretend to believe it if they don't. Steve Lawrence, anyway. 'Sorry, Steve,' I tell him. 'You were right. I screwed-up. Tell the press you think I did it for your own safety.' Sy, he'll flip his lid!"

"No he won't. Not to the press. Look," Sy Larson

suggested reasonably, "why don't you just insist there *was* an oxygen leak? Say his gauge was wrong and yours was right! Who's going to know?"

The commander looked up at him resignedly. "Everybody monitoring a console at JPL in Pasadena. Everybody with a front-row seat at Goddard. Every scientist in the world who gets a read-out on this flight."

"Classify the tapes."

"We can't. It's too big. Besides, you just don't hang an abort like this on the wrong guys. How can we blame it on a North American capsule that functioned perfectly?"

Sy Larson shrugged. "In the national interest?"

"Tell North American Aviation that, Sy," the commander conceded, "you were right at first. We couldn't describe Pilgrim on an open circuit with half the hams in the country listening in. And there's probably no way to tell them via the recovery people. But we can sure tell them before they meet the press!"

Sy Larson spread his hands. "*I* don't care if you tell them or not. I told Archy that. They're both cleared top secret. One hundred and eighteen other people in NASA know it. And six outside, if you include the President and Vice-President and all. Hell, I don't care if you have to tell two more! But as Archy says, there's a quarter of a million dollars, times two, wrapped up just in ground-training those guys. Not including flights. They're your best copilot and navigator, but go ahead!"

The commander did not answer, thinking more of the shock to the men if they could no longer fly than of the funds involved. Sy Larson went on, his voice very low: "Suppose it's a false alarm, though? Suppose we don't go on it? Like last time?"

The commander rubbed his eyes again. "I just don't think we have any choice."

"Since you've decided that," Larson shrugged, "you might decide what you do with them after you cut them in.

Ground them until the President decides to go ahead with Pilgrim? Three months? Six months? Ever? Or drop them from the program to save money?''

"Their boss was cut in," the commander flared. "The colonel's in that capsule. He hasn't been grounded.''

"If we don't go this time," Sy Larson said softly, "when your *own* next flight is scheduled you may find out why.''

Inexplicably, the commander chilled. "I don't like mysteries in test work, Sy," he muttered. "Anyway, with or without knowledge of Pilgrim, I don't see why Steve and Lincoln can't continue to fly. With our flight paths, the odds that they'd land . . .''

His voice trailed off. Sy Larson was grinning at him, shaking his head almost sympathetically. "If you tell them, Commander," he said slowly, "then no matter how loud you, or them, or Archy, or the colonel, or your whole frigging program screams—believe me, those two guys will have made their last orbital flight."

The commander found that he needed a smoke. He got up to leave the console. He paused. "I almost forgot," he asked Sy Larson. "What of our Russian friend?''

Larson smiled grimly, "Goldstone Deep Space has him at 190,000 miles. Goddard Center says he's running sweet and true.''

"Oh," the commander sighed. "Oh, my aching ass."

3.

The hotel dining room in Huntsville, Alabama, was awakening reluctantly when Doctor Franz Ludwig of the Marshall Space Flight Center took his usual table, an hour early. He was a balding, slim man with gentle blue eyes, alert at fifty-eight. But he was so puzzled by the pre-dawn call from Washington that he almost forgot his morning smile for the sleepy girl at the cash register.

He studied the glossy menu, noticed from a grease spot that it was the one he had had yesterday morning. He turned it over. Sure enough, on its back were the equations and diagrams and celestial charts that he left everywhere nowadays—doodles they called them. He regarded the hen tracks sadly. Every day he seemed to burrow more deeply into little havens of formulae or to lose himself more gladly in the sweep of the stars.

His wife would not have liked it. At Berlin University and

at Peenemünde and in Texas she had always giggled at the bumbling, preoccupied *Herr Professors*. He must learn to fight the void in another way. Baseball helped on TV and he was even learning to like American football, but it was hard not to scribble when you had always to eat alone. At least in Washington he would have company, Max and Lisa and the kids.

He beckoned a young Negro standing by a fieldstone waterfall with which the hotel had tried to modernize the dining room. The young man darted over.

"You're early, Doctor."

"I'm going to Washington, Bill," he said as the waiter took his order. Then he remembered that Max had advised that he not mention the trip. It was only a suggestion from his son-in-law, a former assistant who was often overcautious, but it was odd. Since the shift with van Braun from the Army to NASA he had worked in a heaven of unclassification. Except for that one damned study his cursed, restless brain had conceived, and happily shattered just before Max had deserted him for Washington, he had not had a secret project in five years.

Strange that he should think of that study now. It had fascinated Max: "A mathematical evaluation of a one-man mission to the lunar surface in a non-returning capsule; probabilities for the continuing supply of the occupant thereof . . ." It had fascinated others in NASA, too, who lost sight of the man among the equations.

The waiter came back from the kitchen with coffee and told him that the last American orbital flight was landing early. Startled, the doctor took his coffee to the radio at the cashier's counter. The girl yawned but found a newscast and he learned that Apollo Three would not start its re-entry for twenty minutes. He would be on his way to the airfield by then; he decided to call for a cab with a radio instead of a NASA car without one.

He returned to his table, murmuring a silent prayer for the boys in the capsule. He had briefed all thirty astronauts at one time or another, standing in his most professorial manner before the blackboard in his office. He remembered this crew: the colonel, of course, and Lincoln—that was the name of the navigator—very young and assured, with a quick grasp of the trajectories they had discussed.

He had liked the copilot, Lawrence, best of all. He was a quiet, interested man who had asked only two questions, but the doctor felt that he would delve more deeply into astrophysics when he returned to Houston and would not forget what he learned. He swirled his coffee. Now the colonel and the two young men who had sat in his office were whirling above the thermosphere. In twenty minutes they must face the awesome heat of re-entry that lurked in the cushion of air below.

He had always described the heat as a benevolent but treacherous beast, protecting men on earth from meteors but waiting to pounce on those who left it when they wished to return. Absently he sketched a skimming trajectory on the back of the menu. His hand trembled. He stopped himself.

Over thirty years ago at the *Raketenflugplatz*, in Berlin, before the accursed days of Peenemünde, even, they had known of this particular predator. Von Braun and Willy Ley and himself and the rest were considered madmen then, of course. But they had known that someday they would have to build for men the weapons to fight re-entry heat and the other beasts that roamed the universe.

The dream of men in space was a strong one. But now that the dream was coming true, now that they were no longer madmen or armorers, he had learned something. Equations might shield you from loneliness but not from fear. When others put their lives into your hands, the hands could grow clammy and shake.

Well, he thought, at least we have been cautious. No American has died in space. We will probably lose the race to the moon, but there are always the planets beyond. We have been true to our trust.

Max was sending Lisa to meet him at the airport in Washington. It would be impolite to miss the plane and make her wait. He pushed aside his untouched ham and hominy, and left.

The doctor's battered briefcase contained a slide rule, two white shirts, and his shaving gear. The cab driver slid it onto the seat beside him, then turned on the radio sullenly and eased into the early morning traffic. He was a handsome man with an ugly, twisted back. The doctor tried to draw him into conversation.

It was no use. The poor fellow was probably so sick of false pity that he couldn't sense another's loneliness. The doctor sat back to stare at the grimy early morning face of the city.

Huntsville had grown from 17,000 to 80,000 since the doctor had arrived with the von Braun team and installed Anna and teen-age Lisa in a little home near the Marshall Space Flight Center. "The Space Capital of the World," Max used to enthuse during the chamber-of-commerce phase of his self-Americanization program. But the streets were no broader than they were then and the traffic much heavier now, as any cab driver in town would be telling him except this one.

Poor, twisted man in an ugly, twisted town, thought the doctor. Someone had said of Cape Canaveral—Cape Kennedy it was now—that launching the space age from its cluster of motels and cafes was launching it from a billion-dollar junk heap. Well, at least the Cape had sunshine and salt air. Downtown Huntsville was Hamburg-on-the-Tennessee.

They were through the traffic now, joining the stream to the Marshall Space Flight Center and Redstone Arsenal. The doctor felt a familiar ache passing through this neighborhood, for here was the house Anna had loved so much, the tree he had scarred with the Plymouth's bumper, the old frame porch on which Max had courted Lisa.

He forced himself to look up the tree-shaded side street, because it was morbid and weak to look away. Besides, he loved the house; he had honestly felt loss when he gave it to Lisa and Max, wanting to be out of their way before the babies came.

He wondered who lived in it now. They passed it in the din of schoolchildren waiting for a bus where Lisa used to wait. The driver turned up the radio a little too loudly.

A newscaster chattered: ". . . A spokesman in Houston said that recovery forces have reported the capsule undamaged."

"Thank God," murmured the doctor. "They made it!"

"Goddamn fools," the cab driver said. "What they going to find when they get to the moon, anyway? Green cheese?"

"Russians, everybody says." And that is God's truth, he thought. Within the year, perhaps.

"Who cares? Ain't nothing there. You can see that."

"Well," the doctor said, "yes and no. Anyway, I have met those three and I was worried."

"You work at Marshall Center?"

"Yes."

The driver dropped back into moody silence. Once he aroused himself.

"What keeps 'em up there?"

The doctor broke out of his reverie. "Pardon?"

"No wings. What keeps 'em up there?"

He leaned forward. "You ever see little boys playing with . . ." He had forgotten the toy. "You know . . ." He demonstrated with his hand.

The cab driver actually smiled. He had clean white teeth. "A yo-yo," he said condescendingly. "You a Swede?"

"I am born in Germany. Well, if you take the yo-yo and swing it on the end of the string, it stays out there. Right?"

"Yeah, but there ain't no string on these capsules."

"No. You see, gravity is the string . . ."

He searched the eyes in the mirror. They were blank. The

driver shook his head and lost interest. But turning out of the Marshall Center and Redstone Arsenal traffic into Madison County Airport, the young man asked suddenly: "You say you met them guys. What kind of guys are they?"

The doctor smiled. "Just, well . . . just nice young fellows. Very smart." He was about to say athletic, but stopped short at the twisted back. "Just nice fellows."

The cab driver parked. He handed him the briefcase, took the fare without counting it.

"Goddamn fools," he said. He seemed actually angry, "Know what? They're nothing but goddamn fools!"

4.

Steven James Lawrence lay in his shorts on a medical examining table. Gus Scarbo, the astronauts' flight surgeon, pumped a bulb for his blood pressure and Steve felt the familiar squeeze of a rubber sleeve around his arm.

Outside the moist heat of the Texas Gulf washed against the massive Life Systems Building, but the examining room was a green oasis after the sweat and excitement of landing. Gus Scarbo read off his blood pressure, nodded, and unwrapped the arm. He began to put his instrument away, almost dropped the box, and banged his head on the table when he lunged to catch it.

Steve hid a grin. Gus was a bronzed Navy doctor with a greying forelock and shoulders like a rugged scarecrow. In action he was a clown—all knees and elbows. But behind his desk, mulling the health and safety of his charges, he was the Thirty-first Astronaut, a Good Troop, the Great White Father himself. And once he had saved Mickey's life.

Steve swung his legs over the side of the table and moved to the window. He peered through slits in the blind, spotted his battered station wagon in the parking area below. "She's here, Gus," he said. "Mickey."

He heard Gus leave the room to get her, was about to move from the window when he stiffened. Archy Gorman, the pudgy Operations Director, was crossing the lawn toward the Flight Simulator Building . With him, deep in conversation, was the colonel. Steve, who expected to spend half the night de-briefing into a tape recorder, wondered how the colonel had finished so quickly.

He climbed thoughtfully back on the table, sat swinging his legs. A mystery stalked the Manned Spacecraft Center; he had felt it since he landed. He had mentioned it to Gus, who agreed but couldn't explain it.

If someone in the program was playing with facts, was hiding information, it could be deadly on a flight. If the game he was playing had needlessly disturbed Mickey and the colonel's wife, and Rick's, nothing could excuse it.

The door swung noiselessly and she was suddenly in his arms, laughing like a child, cheeks wet against his bare chest. He took her face in his hands and looked into her eyes. They were pool-green, flecked with brown. She was holding back the tears, holding her lower lip with small, even teeth. But she had been crying, he knew.

"I'm sorry," he murmured. "God, I'm sorry."

She shook her head. "It wasn't your fault. I know that. What happened?"

"Nothing, damn it. That's just the point. When did they tell you?"

She swallowed, still caricaturing a smile. "About an hour before you landed. Cindy Lincoln called. She said if Rick was along there was nothing to worry about . . ." She took a long, shuddering breath and tried to grin. "So, of course, I didn't worry. Since Rick was along . . ."

He looked into the tanned hoyden face with the nose that

was just a little too broad for true beauty. He brushed a wild strand of copper hair from her forehead, touched the square little jaw that showed such strength, knowing that she was not strong at all.

She was a general's daughter. He had met her during Korea at the Yuraku Officer's Club in Tokyo; he was a carrier pilot on liberty. She had been drinking with a sodden Army captain; the boldest of the Navy pilots with Steve had enticed them to their own table. It was not until Steve had looked into the deep green eyes that he had seen the sorrow— noticed that, young as she was, she was as drunk as her escort.

Her bright smile was driving his normally reticent mates to the brink of heroism: "Honey, this gook battery was behind the ridge, throwing up everything but their mess kits . . ." "So this patrol takes cover in the paddy and—pow! pow! pow!" "I made a pass while they were smack in the middle of the Han River, and man . . ."

Only Steve had sensed that her eyes were blank with pain, that the girl was trying to make fools of them, not really listening at all. And then she spoke to him in a quiet voice; he had to strain to catch the sarcasm.

"And what about you, Lieutenant Lawrence, junior grade?"

He wished she had not drunk so much. He shook his head. "You're clobbered, little girl."

She ignored that, nodded toward the pilot who held the floor, flying with his hands. "It seems Fort Sumter has been fired upon," she remarked, her expression shrouded. "Doesn't *your* regiment ride tonight?"

Steve, who was certain that two weeks before they had mistakenly attacked a column of refugees, had spun his last war story. But the others were his friends. "They haven't been ashore for three months."

"That isn't what I said. Fly me a mission, sir. How many gooks did *you* get on your last strike?"

He had raged at the whole stupid strike for days. Now the anger was gone but the ache was still there, and for the hundredth time he was at mountain-top altitude over the wooded canyon north of Seoul. He banked steeply and dived into the valley leading to the River Han, flicking his arming switch.

For once he was cool in combat, searching too intently to worry, looking for the dingy tan column of infantrymen who had fired at the preceding flight from the canyon floor. They had scattered, though, at Catseye's first pass, so he held his fire and flung his Panther-jet around the wall of the canyon. He was suddenly flashing over the River Han spilling down from the mountains in the afternoon sun. Then, in precise double file, he saw the figures scrambling across the riverbed with Catseye's 20-mm. shells streaking about them, ricocheting into the pine-clad hills.

Instinctively he fired too, pressing the attack at 400 knots, but as he pulled up he saw with soul-twisting certainty the white tunic of a Korean peasant, the awkward gait, perhaps, of a running woman, a sprawled bundle of rags on the gravel rushing beneath his wing, a heap of rags that might have been a child.

Very carefully he put down his drink before he spilled it or crushed the glass.

"Maybe ten gooks," he said to the girl, his voice hollow. "Maybe twelve."

"How *marvelous*," she said distantly. "How utterly—"

"A couple of old men," he murmured, "a few pregnant women, a kid or two."

The words landed in a sudden silence; his flight leader turned on him in disgust. "Oh, for Christ's sake!"

But Mickey suddenly sobered, reached out her hand and took his. "I'm sorry. I am very, very sorry."

In that instant he fell in love. That night at her father's quarters they talked of his flying, and his unfinished engineering, and his crazy conviction that their own generation would send men into space.

During the long, cool dawn he had come to understand the pain in her eyes. She had had a brother a year older than she. Through their rootless Army childhood they had clung together like swimmers in a rip. Three weeks before, in a command post on Kelly Ridge, he had been caught by a North Korean bayonet. Her mother, a placid Army wife, had broken and had just been safely harbored at Walter Reed in Washington. They had talked until after dawn, and then, strangely nervous, Mickey led him through the foggy rock garden to catch her father before he left for headquarters.

The general had been tying his necktie in his straw-matted bedroom, a giant of a man who must once have been handsome. There was an open bottle on the dresser. The room was a jumble of military maps and PX purchases, of dusty combat gear and packing boxes. The general's bloodshot eyes passed over him; when Mickey left to call his staff car, he offered him a drink. It was 8 A.M.

"No, sir," he shuddered. His eyes strayed to the picture of a young Army lieutenant on the dresser. The general caught the glance.

"Own goddamn fault," he said, adjusting his tie in the mirror. "No pickets out. Spitted in his sleeping bag. He knew better." Steve stared at him. The general turned from the mirror. "Can't convince her of that."

"You haven't *tried?*" Steve whispered.

"Why crap her?" the general shrugged. "She's not a child. Her mother, maybe, not her. War's war—facts are facts." He smiled quite pleasantly. "*Sayonara*, Lieutenant. Come back and see us."

The general slid open the rice-paper door and was gone across the rock garden. Steve watched him leave, waves of nausea rising in his chest. He sensed Mickey beside him.

"He doesn't know it," he told her, "but when I do come back I'm taking you away."

"Why? Because you feel sorry for me?" The green eyes swam with tears. "Well, don't!"

"Because I love you very much already, and it's growing by the hour."

She was suddenly in his arms, and his life had changed forever. But hers had not, not then. At twenty, though Steve had not realized it, liquor was her haven from pain, and she had flown to it again and again for solace over the long, long years. Another few hours like today's abort and she might enter it once more. He remembered the night he had almost lost her in a tiny desert hospital; it was cruel to test her again and again. He resolved, as soon as de-briefing was over, to track the mystery of the needless emergency to its source.

He could not be home tonight; he had another six hours of dictation. He kissed her goodbye. As she walked to the door his apprehension made him say, "Mickey?"

She paused. "Yes?"

"It's been a rough day," he explained. "Ask Gus and Marion to come over."

She smiled her elfin smile. "I've told you, Steve. I'm a big girl now." The door swung silently behind her.

"Damn," he murmured, "damn."

5.

Doctor Franz Ludwig sustained the ache of disappointment and glanced at his daughter fondly as she swung off the Washington National Airport ramp into the traffic on Memorial Parkway. Her light gold hair shimmered in the wind. She shot him a quick look, half-loving and half-fearful, as she used to when she was a child and was afraid she had hurt his feelings.

"So do you mind, Daddy, really? Because if you do, I'll stay home with you."

He could not bear the pain in her gentle brown eyes when he showed hurt so he smiled: "With a Congressman and a Senator and all the NASA bosses going to be there? It would ruin Max's career."

Her eyes were just like Anna's; for an instant he felt the closeness they had known before Max had taken her away. But then her face was serious. "It is important to him," she affirmed loyally. "He's not a phony, Daddy."

"He's a very smart young man," he agreed, "and I miss him in Huntsville, and if he'll bring you back I'll give him his old office, you see, and even buy you back the old house?" The whimsy ended in a plaintive note. He saw the regret on her face and changed the subject. "I'd rather eat with Joey anyway."

"Oh, Daddy. No," she protested. "He's so much trouble, and even the baby's a handful now, wait until you see. We're leaving them at the nursery. That way you can rest up for whatever mysterious thing he has planned for you tomorrow . . ."

He had had a tiny stroke three years before. He would almost have risked another for an evening alone with his grandchildren. But he could not bring himself to beg for the privilege. Perhaps, once he learned why he was here, he could drag out the visit for a day or two.

He sat waiting for Max on the back patio while Lisa—Liz, he must remember to Anglicize it when Max appeared— mixed him a glass of lemonade in the kitchen. He turned on the portable radio to listen for news of the three young astronauts. He heard Max's car climb the driveway—a new one, from the muted engine. Every two years, he thought with amusement, Max must have a new car. He would plead depreciation, taxes, planned obsolescence, but really it was because everyone in Chevy Chase did the same thing.

Max arrived sweaty, still in coat and tie from NASA Headquarters. He gripped Franz Ludwig's arm tightly and looked dead into his eyes. "I'm glad you're here, Franz. I'm very glad you're here. Something's come up."

Franz smiled paternally at his son-in-law. Max was always too serious, always too theatrical. In Peenemünde, as a young technician, he had carried the whole weight of the Fatherland on his shoulders. Now that he was the most American of Americans, it was the same here. His office had doubtless run into a trajectory problem on Apollo, or a question on the Mariner Program, or a snag on Surveyor Eight, but it could hardly be the end of the world.

"Before we get to that," said Franz Ludwig, "let me tell you a cartoon I saw on the plane."

Max subsided, an automatic smile appearing on his face.

"You see," the doctor said, as Lisa arrived with a tray, "it shows these two spacemen. And they have landed on the moon. And they are standing in their pressure suits, all ready to raise this American flag, and you know what the one is saying to the other?"

"What?"

"The one holding the flag says to the other: 'Hans, these stripes. Do they go on top or underneath?' "

Lisa chortled delightedly, but Max hardly grinned. She winked at her father and, when her husband glanced at her significantly, made a face and left. Max handed him his lemonade and took a glass of ice water for himself. Dieting, thought the doctor, as always. Golf at Chevy Chase Country Club every Sunday, too, and still the tanned face beneath the blond hair grew heavier year by year. Strange that Max must fight weight, for his father had been small. The doctor remembered a mouse of a man with kind eyes who worked in the physics stockroom at the University of Berlin.

Mostly he remembered watching the little man's face light at the sight of Max, a new-caught *Frosch*, standing in line as his father doled out laboratory equipment to an entering class. *Ach*, well . . . Over twenty-five years ago. Max had a good mind. He would have gone far even without his own help. Max, suddenly alert, had turned up the radio.

". . . National Aeronautics and Space Administration spokesmen in Houston declined to state the reason for the flight's early termination. A press conference is scheduled—"

With a sudden motion Max switched off the set.

"I know why they terminated, damn it."

"Why?" For some reason, as he asked it, the doctor had a

premonition. He knew unexplainably that the answer had to do with this trip; more, that it had to do with an odd, almost tangible door that had closed between Max and himself in the past year.

"Franz," Max said quietly. "They've launched another one. The Russians."

Franz Ludwig put down his glass quietly and shivered in the heat. "Lunar?"

"Yes."

"I wonder," Franz Ludwig murmured, "if it's manned?"

"We think so," Max said. "So does Goddard."

Franz Ludwig had expected it for so long that he felt no surprise. He knew immediately how the Russians had launched it: from the space platform they had maintained in earth orbit since 1964. He could even have drawn a fair picture of the spacecraft's shape.

"Manned reconnaissance," the doctor stated flatly.

He had no thought that the Russian craft would land. It would simply swing past the moon and return to the platform. The Russians had no need to rush. It would be over a year before the new Saturn booster could do with Apollo what the Russians were apparently doing today.

The actual Russian landing would come later, but not much later. He remembered Max handing him a secret paper, when they were working on the ridiculous one-man landing study. The banks of computers in Santa Barbara and Pasadena and Goddard had apparently been whirling and squeaking, and the Rand Corporation had been thinking. All agreed that the Russians, when they tried, would home on a year-old U.S. moon probe, Surveyor Six, well placed with its unceasing electronic beacon in Oceanus Procellarum.

They estimated that once a Russian orbited the moon and surveyed the landing area near Surveyor, Russia would attempt an actual landing when the lunar dawn next crept across the site. Twenty-eight days. The doctor had seen no reason to doubt the estimate.

So! There it was, finally.

Twenty years ago he had stood in a shell-pocked farm-house in northern Germany not far from the sheltered V-2 base at Peenemünde. It was freezing cold; he could smell *ersatz* coffee on the wooden stove. And he could hear, too, the distant boom of Russian howitzers to the north. The assembled scientists shuffled, blowing on their hands, wait-ing. A driver in a leather coat entered, breathing steam. He murmured to Werner von Braun, handed him a pack of false identity cards that might help them get through the trigger-happy *Wehrmacht*. The choice was a hard one: to stay in safety underground at Peenemünde and surrender to the Russians or to risk a dash through the convulsed, Gestapo-infested Fatherland to American lines in Bavaria.

Franz Ludwig weighed the possibilities: eventual freedom in the west if they made it; quick death before a German firing squad if they failed; a longer intellectual death in a Russian laboratory or arsenal if they simply waited. And so he stepped forward, shuffled through the cards until he found his own, put it carefully in his wallet. He would never regret it. But now, after everything, it was a Russian rocket which hurtled toward the moon.

Scientific envy was despicable, but he could not help it. His teeth clenched in anger at the doubters in Congress, the dullards in uniform, the procrastinators in the White House who had blocked every step until it was too late; anger at those who had not been careful enough with the fine young mind that had seen the importance of winning and acted. Now, after everything, America would lose.

He forced a smile. "Well, there was never any question, was there, Max? And we must give them credit. They did it alone."

There was an odd American fable that German scientists were sparking the Russian effort. "Their Germans must be better than our Germans" was the joke. As if the Americans and Russians had chosen sides for a baseball game, he thought. The fact was that virtually every creative scientist at Peenemünde had followed von Braun to Bavaria and Texas and, finally, Huntsville. The Russians had found nothing at Peenemünde but technicians and hardware. They had used the technicians and sent them home; they had gone on by themselves.

"Yes," the doctor sighed, "they did it alone. And they are to be congratulated."

"We don't *know* it's manned," Max said tightly. "And even if it is, he hasn't made it yet."

"How far out is he?"

"Almost 200,000 miles, at noon."

The doctor translated the distance into kilometers and decided that for the optimum flight path the craft must have been launched some two days before. It would have another eighteen hours or so to go before it would pass the moon.

"And you have called me to evaluate the trajectory?" the doctor asked hopefully. There had been no public announcement. The Russians seldom broke silence until they had successfully completed a flight; we would never admit that we were tracking until after the fact. Perhaps that was the reason for the secrecy.

"Franz," Max said heavily, "it is not to evaluate their trajectory."

"What is it?"

"We are getting ready to do something," Max murmured. He seemed unable to meet his eye. "You remember that study we made two years ago? On alternatives?"

"Yes?" Franz Ludwig answered cautiously.

"Your concept—the one we argued about?"

"It was not my concept," the doctor protested. "Many people had that 'concept' before. I only showed that it might be done, perhaps."

"And how it could be done quickly," Max reminded him. "Very quickly. In a year."

"And why it should *not* be done! Remember that!" The doctor forced calm upon himself; he was supposed to guard against excitement. "Anyway," he went on more softly. "It is dead. It is laid to rest. Pandora's box is locked tight, *nicht wahr*?"

Max did not answer.

"It *is* locked, Max?"

Max Steiger shook his head. "No, It is not locked."

"Anyway, *das macht nichts*," the doctor smiled. "Such a project would be a little late now, don't you think? How long from a Russian reconnaissance to their landing? A month?"

"Yes," Max murmured.

"Why think of it? You and I—we cannot be concerning ourselves with what the other team is doing. It is not a race. Not anymore."

"But it is a race," Max said somberly. "It is, Franz."

"All right," the doctor conceded. "You are right. Not scientific, but right. To start, man must go first to the moon, so it became a race to the moon. But for years we have known that that race was lost. Now we still work for the moon, but only as a step to the planets beyond, you and I. Maybe that race we can win. Why have you been wasting time worrying about—"

"I've been trying to tell you, Franz," Max Steiger blurted. "I *have* to worry about it!"

The younger man's face had turned harder beneath the round smooth curves. The doctor remembered again the Peenemünde farmhouse, the crammed cars outside, the Russian artillery rumbling closer. There were not enough autos; some of the younger technicians, like Max, if they wanted to try, would have to go it alone. At the last moment Max had jammed his way into the front seat. The driver struck a shielded match.

"Out! There is no more room!"

Franz himself, in memory of the boy's father, had had to threaten to get out before the driver agreed. Franz had seen in the flare of the driver's match the same hardness that stiffened Max's face now.

"*Why* do you have to worry about the Russian time-table?" Franz Ludwig asked quietly.

"Did you ever hear," Max murmured, "of the Pilgrim Project?"

"The 'Pilgrim' Project? No."

"I'm sorry," Max said softly. "Because it is yours."

"*Nein!*"

His heart began to hurt him. Everything became clear: the gulf between them, odd silences when he had visited here last summer, a day when he had spotted Max in Huntsville at the center, unheralded and apparently avoiding him. Everything—even the Apollo abort. It fell into place as neatly as an equation in conics, yet he could not absorb it. "You've been working on this behind my back?"

"I don't work for you anymore, Franz," Max reminded him. "It's true you weren't told."

"But Max . . . For over a year you have worked on this?"

"Yes."

"But why?"

"I believe he'd have a good chance. I told you that from the beginning."

"How good a chance?" scoffed the doctor.

Max dove for cover in jargon. "It's not too susceptible to mathematical proof, but on the computers—"

"Damn the computers! Damn them! Would you do it yourself?"

"I'm a physicist, not an astronaut."

Franz Ludwig's head began to ache. "Why wasn't I told?"

"Not telling you wasn't my idea. NASA Headquarters insisted. The CIA insisted. Once we got a handle on the problem, nobody wanted anybody rocking the boat, so—"

"Max, Max, Max," the doctor groaned. " 'Handle on the problem'! 'Rocking the boat'! How far has this gone?"

A certain pride flashed on his son-in-law's face. "We're ready, Franz."

The doctor rubbed his forehead. "You are joking."

"No."

With an effort the doctor sat back. "I presume," he said acidly, "that the reason for the abort today is that one of those pilots is the man?"

There was a long silence. "Yes."

"Who is so fortunate?"

"The colonel."

"The colonel, *natürlich*. He has probably four or five children, but he was a Mercury astronaut, so—"

"The first two they asked, volunteered," offered Max. "The colonel and a back-up pilot. So you see?"

The doctor stared at him. "What do they know about it? Only that they have never done wrong to trust us. That is all they know!"

"They're engineers," offered Max Steiger.

The doctor felt that he was acting out a nightmare. "There are hardly twenty *astrophysicists* in the world qualified to judge this." In blind anger he added: "You are not one of them!"

Max Steiger reddened. "That's a matter of opinion. Up here they've bet a hell of a lot of money that I am."

The doctor tried to muster his faculties. He would need them, need all his calm and courage, too, if this project had come so far. What was its stupid name? "Pilgrim"? Why "Pilgrim"?

"You opened the lid," the doctor said heavily. "And now I must close it." He tried to build sense out of chaos. "Did you ask me here? Yourself?"

"Well, at headquarters we—"

"Don't tell me 'we'! Everybody up here who read my study knew how I felt about this two years ago. Before you got here. You said that yourself. Who calls for me, now, to 'rock the boat'?"

Max was clenching and unclenching his hand on his glass.

"Now, Franz," he murmured, "why don't we grab a bit of lunch here, and then we'll go down to NASA and—"

"I have asked you a question!" the doctor lashed out, as if addressing a student or a *Wehrmacht* ordnance lieutenant. "Someone here wants my opinion on this. To whom will I be permitted to express it?"

Max Steiger flushed.

"Apparently," he said heavily, "to the President of the United States."

6.

During the night Steven James Lawrence had shaved, showered, de-briefed from the flight, and slept six hours. Now he glanced at his watch and moved restlessly, full of dread, to the window of the Public Affairs Office.

The Manned Spacecraft Center on the shores of Clear Lake was less than five years old. Each building in the vast center was nicely air-conditioned against the moist Houston heat, but he found that his shirt was damp. The glass-and-concrete administrative structure in which he stood towered above the hangar bays, laboratories, and low-lying astronaut-training buildings. From the window he could see Clear Lake, mirror smooth across the lush Texas Gulflands, even spot their own housing tract on its shore. From the window too, unfortunately, he could see the center's auditorium.

In the past half-hour he had seen two network crews snaking TV cables across the lawn in front of it. He had lost count of the reporters entering the long, low structure. A group of photographers was lounging at its entrance now. He turned to the desk. "Joe?" he pleaded.

Joe Garcia, the swarthy marine aviator who handled astronaut press relations, was slowly hanging up his phone. He had intense black eyes and his civvies always seemed rumpled. He was savagely honest, a published writer of two war novels, more a poet than a military public-information man. But he was a combat pilot and solid under fire. He was trying to track down the colonel. "No answer at his home, either."

Rick Lincoln grinned from the *Aviation Week* he was reading. "That shoots my afternoon quickie theory. Well, maybe when you said 'press' he thought you said 'chess' and he's over in the recreation room."

"I wonder," Steve asked Rick sincerely, "if you'd be this damn flip if the word was out that we were off in our navigation instead of our oxygen?"

Impatiently he moved to Garcia's desk. He scanned a mimeographed transcript of the Apollo Three ground-to-air communications. He found the fiftieth and final orbit, and read the transmissions, searching for a clue to the colonel's decision to abort.

The transcript was always accurate and complete. Idly he noted that whoever had typed it from the tape had, like the colonel, now heard the portion that had puzzled him.

Pogrom . . . program . . . pilgrim?

There was something odd about it. The typists had sharp ears and plenty of time to run and re-run the tapes. He wished he had time to listen to them himself. "Has this been given to the press?"

Joe Garcia nodded. "This morning."

"They haven't been told about this Russian pass," ruminated Rick Lincoln. "What do we do if the Russians announce it in the middle of the press conference? Are we hoping he'll bust his ass?"

The Assistant Operations Director, Sy Larson, had told

them of the Russian reconnaissance mission, apparently moon-bound, possibly manned. He had warned them not to mention it until there was an official announcement. And there was something, Steve sensed, that he was hiding from them, too.

"Tell them the truth," suggested Garcia.

"We're disappointed, but we hope he makes a good pass," Steve decided. "We hope he gets back."

"Smile," murmured Rick Lincoln. "You're on TV?"

The phone on Garcia's desk rang. Joe looked shocked as he listened. The colonel was in the Flight Simulator Building, simulating a flight in the Mercury Capsule Trainer.

"In *what?*" Steve stared. He remembered an old one-man Mercury mock-up in a corner of the Flight Simulator Building, a relic of the first days of the center. Presumably it could still be hooked up to the Integrated Mission Control Center for a simulated mission, but why?

"They sold the movie rights to the first orbital flights," Rick Lincoln proposed. "They're using the original cast and the Flight Simulator Building as a set."

"Joe," Steve exploded. "The press knows there were three days' oxygen left. They're going to ask me a three-million-dollar question on TV and I don't know the answer, and the guy who does is down horsing around in the simulator building! What'll I say?"

Rick Lincoln said: "Whatever it is, you better not tarnish his image. It'd be better to come out against motherhood."

Joe Garcia glanced at Rick coldly and stood up. "Don't try to protect any images. Forget the loyalty crap."

"You have a great future in public relations," Rick Lincoln chuckled. "You better get back to flying."

Joe Garcia ignored him. "Because Steve, if you try to mislead these newspaper people, or bullshit them, you know what?"

"What?"

"With the whole country watching, including your wife and kid, they will tear you into little, tiny bits."

Steve followed the other two men from the office.

Somewhere in the middle of the conference, as the eyes of the TV cameras stared at him, Steve made a discovery. For the first time in his experience, astronauts faced a hostile press. Newsmen crowded the auditorium, an anonymous group of blank faces. All the rapport he had felt after their previous flight was gone.

Joe Garcia, sitting in the center of the half-empty table on the stage, had tried for a short time to protect him by calling on men from the contractors' organs, the military press, even the technical publications—men dependent on Joe for good will. But he had soon run out of friendly smiles.

Neither Archy Gorman, the paunchy Apollo Operations Director, nor the colonel had arrived. Archy's tanned, smiling assistant, Sy, was on the wing of the stage, talking on the telephone, but he might as well have been a mile away. The three accusing lenses of the TV cameras had hardly strayed from Steve, and his head was hot and his eyes ached and it took a real effort not to wipe the sweat from his brow before a million American taxpayers.

Phil Garrow, one of the first Washington columnists to resume sniping at NASA after Kennedy's assassination, was standing among the rows of blank faces. He was a skinny, bespectacled man with a disarming air and he was lacerating Steve.

"Well, Mr. Lawrence, let me put it this way. You knew more about the oxygen state than anyone else in the capsule. Did you talk him into aborting?"

"No," Steve said, fighting his anger. "No. I did not."

"I think," Rick Lincoln interrupted suddenly, "you may have the wrong idea on how our crew handles a flight, Mr. Garrow. The colonel's the spacecraft commander. We follow orders."

The reporter regarded him curiously. "If you had been in command, would you have aborted?"

"But I wasn't, sir," Rick Lincoln smiled. "I was the navigator."

The reporter returned to Steve. "Mr. Lawrence, what I'm trying to find out against heavy odds is whether you think that the spacecraft commander was right or wrong. He stopped a six-million-dollar bus ride halfway through. The public bought the bus ticket. It's entitled to an answer, right?"

There was a stir at the rear of the auditorium. Steve peered past the lights. His heart jumped. The colonel was coming down the aisle, his face alight. He spotted a friend, nodded, flashed a grin at another. One of the cameras swung away. Steve was so glad to see the taut, smiling face that he forgot his anger. He stared at the colonel in wonder.

As far as he knew the man had finished a three-day orbital flight with, for some reason, another day lying on his back in a cramped training device. There were faint shadows under his eyes. But he trotted up the stage steps like a teen-ager, winked companionably at Steve and Rick, and pulled a chair to the table.

"I'm sorry, I was unavoidably held up." He smiled ruefully at the press, ignoring the TV cameras professionally. "Mr. Garrow? Something about a bus ride?"

"Colonel, " said the columnist, unruffled, "now that you know there was sufficient oxygen to finish the mission, do you feel that you acted correctly in terminating it?"

"I was dead wrong."

There was a moment of crystal silence. Someone broke it with a cough.

"I see," said the writer. He fiddled with his papers but met the colonel's eyes coolly enough. "Would you say it was an expensive mistake?"

"Three million dollars," the colonel said bluntly. "Half the ride."

"Yes."

"When you took off from Washington this morning, though, Phil, your airline pilot might have made this same sort of mistake, say, if the tower operator up there thought he spotted too much smoke on take-off." The colonel grinned at him. "Would you have complained?"

There was a burst of laughter. The writer smiled placidly and stayed on his feet. "You were not always this . . . conservative, you might say, when you ran into trouble in Mercury. Is this new wisdom a product of . . . well, age?"

Steve felt a jolt of anger. He glanced at the colonel. He sat stiffly staring at the back of his hands, a red tide rising on his face.

"I don't feel," Steve flared, "that the colonel's age is at issue! I think Mr. Lincoln and myself are the best judges, of his competence and his judgment, and as far as we're concerned—"

"As far as you're concerned, then," Garrow suggested smoothly, "there was another reason for his decision. Right?"

Steve licked his lips, suddenly cautious. There was something he did not understand and retreat was best. He cast about for an answer, any answer that would fill up the ticking seconds. He noticed that Sy Larson had emerged from the wings, was in deep conversation with Joe Garcia at the end of the table.

"The colonel was alone in Mercury," Steve began. "There are two other men in an Apollo capsule! He has a responsibility to them, too. And—"

Joe Garcia had moved to the central microphone. "Pardon me, Steve," he cut in. "Ladies and gentlemen, I believe that you'll be more interested in this announcement than in pursuing Apollo Three any further. So, I'm sure, will the TV audience." Garrow seemed about to protest, but Joe Garcia went on. "First, our Deep Space Instrumentation Facilities have been tracking for the past twenty-four hours a large Russian vehicle on a trajectory which brought it within ten miles of the moon at about 10 A.M. Eastern Standard Time today—nine our time.'' A few of the reporters standing in the rear moved to the door. ''Item two: There are indications from intercepted radio transmissions that this vehicle may be manned. It did not land. It orbited the moon once. It's apparently now on its return trajectory. Goddard Center estimates that it'll rendezvous with the Russian space platform at around noon Friday. Assuming, I guess, that its return flight is successful.''

Joe Garcia carefully put away his notes, glanced at his watch, then at a TV technician wearing earphones. ''Gentlemen, we are running out of time. Thank you for your interest in the Apollo mission, and—''

''I have a question for the colonel,'' Garrow said. His voice cut across the hubbub. ''Did your decision to land have anything to do with this Russian attempt?''

The room was suddenly still. The colonel looked at him blankly. ''Sir?''

''Your facilities have apparently been silently tracking this target since yesterday, with their usual consideration for the press. I'd like to know if this Russian attempt caused your return.''

The colonel stood up to leave. He smiled politely at the columnist with a hint of the same pity that he might have shown an interested patient on a visit to a ward for retarded children.

''I landed because I thought we might be running out of oxygen, Mr. Garrow. Not,'' the colonel added gently, ''running out of space.''

7.

The President of the United States lay tense on the table in the steamy White House gym. The young Negro masseur sensed the stiffness in his deltoids and kneaded them more fiercely than usual. But when the President sat up he was not relaxed and cheerful as he usually was after his noon-time massage; he was frowning and preoccupied. I wouldn't trade places with this cat today, the young man thought, for all the tea in China.

He faced his young Vice-President across the desk which had once belonged to Abraham Lincoln. He had moved it from the West Wing Executive Office to the oval study overlooking the South Lawn when he found that he was escaping more and more to the sanctity of the second floor.

"Damn it, though," the President pointed out, "you said the same thing in January. Suppose I'd said 'go'? We'd have had a dead astronaut!"

He arose and moved to the full-length windows behind the desk. Through the spaces between the lush trees of President's Park he could see cars speeding up Constitution Avenue—civil servants who had dawdled too long over lunch. The Washington Monument towered in the foreground; the Jefferson Memorial shone whitely across the Tidal Basin.

"That's right," said the young man. "I did say it then. And you were right. One hundred percent."

The Vice-President was a tough, driving man, shrewd and hard in a fight. He found it difficult to be wrong but more difficult to be unrealistic. Six months ago he had come very close to persuading the President. The admission must have come hard that if he had succeeded it would have been tragic, that there had been strings still untied on Pilgrim. He went on with his argument, though; this time he seemed utterly certain that he was right. "Remember, whatever we were tracking in January hadn't made the turnaround. This Vostok is on its way back."

"If they aren't lying," mused the President. "If it *is* a Vostok, instead of a TV camera in a garbage can. I don't know. It'd be so easy for them to bait us without risking a thing . . ."

"To what purpose?"

"To find out if we have a hole card."

"Suppose the hole card is an ace? If they make us play it, they've lost the pot."

"Suppose it's a deuce?"

The Vice-President shrugged. The early afternoon sun slashed his face. It was growing hard; the lines were etched more deeply and there were creases under the square jaw. A brilliant man, the President thought—potentially great, perhaps, if he could only learn patience and resilience.

"Anyway," the President said flatly, "we decided it would be morally impossible to justify this until certain conditions were met. I don't want to go into that again."

The Vice-President's temper rose. "The first of these

conditions was met at 10 A.M. yesterday morning when that guy came within 10 miles of the moon!''

The President's eyes never wavered. ''We don't know that there is any guy.''

''We think there is.''

The President smiled. After election he had asked the Vice-President to oversee the space program as he himself had done. ''We?'' he asked gently. ''You're a lawyer talking like an engineer again.''

''You learned a lot,'' the young man said briefly. ''I'm a fast study, as they say on the Coast. I've learned a lot, too.''

''I know it. I've got more confidence in your advice on this thing than I would in the sharpest mind in NASA. That includes your technical judgment. Even secondhand.''

The Vice-President seemed moved. ''Well, thank you . . .''

''Knowing this, I'd like you to be as objective as possible,'' the President said, returning to his desk. ''Regardless of your personal feelings, now, do you still advise setting this in motion before the Russians tell us whether this thing is manned?''

The young man nodded decisively. ''Yes. They don't have to tell us, ever. And we only have three weeks. Astronomically. And our next chance would be a full month later. And that may be too late!''

The President sighed. Drifting across the South Lawn came the sounds of Washington traffic: a honking horn, a squeal of brakes, the low rumble of a sightseeing bus. ''I have some people coming in this afternoon, '' he remarked idly. ''Ralph Fellows, for one.''

The Vice-President became suddenly alert. ''It's too damn soon! Are you going to cut him in *now*?''

''Yes.''

''Look, I'm the one who has to handle him in the Senate Chamber!''

''You want to tell him?'' the President asked wryly.

The young man had guts. "If you want me to. But not now. Later."

"I'll tell him," the President said. "Now."

Senator Fellows was Minority Leader. It would be essential to tell him of the project, but apparently the Vice-President thought that delay might muffle the hue and cry; restrict the opposition to too little and too late. Well, the young man may have become an expert on space, but there was no doubt which of the two was the expert on the Senate. "His reaction will be one of the factors in my decision."

The Vice-President got up impatiently. "In other words, you *haven't* reached it yet?"

The President looked at him blankly. "Did you think I had?"

"No," the Vice-President admitted. For an instant he grinned boyishly. The President felt a pang. He had such charm when he let himself go and he smiled so seldom nowadays. "For a wild moment there, I had hopes, but not really, I guess."

The President winked and the young man left. When he had gone the President massaged his temples for a moment, then pressed a button and asked a secretary to send in the U.S. Ambassador to the United Nations.

Doctor Franz Ludwig waited tensely in the Treaty Room outside the President's oval study. Next to him, leafing elaborately through a *National Geographic*, sat Max. Once he grunted, showed his father-in-law a photograph of workmen mortising the last segments of Berlin's sturdy new Wall.

The doctor barely glanced at it. He had had little to say to Max all day. Besides he was marshaling his arguments. He wondered why Max, with so much at stake, was not deep in thought organizing his own. Maybe because he felt that the weight of NASA headquarters behind him made argument unnecessary. Or perhaps he did not really intend to take a stand.

The doctor found that his knees had begun to tremble. With an effort he made himself relax from his stiff posture. This was not the first head of state he had waited for. Twenty years ago, at Peenemünde, he had stood by a launching platform in the North Sea rain and waited for Hitler. Von Braun had been sloshing impatiently about and the generals had been complaining in the background.

He had survived that day. And surely to meet the President of the United States was a less harrowing prospect than to meet the intense, unpredictable Führer with his sudden enthusiasms and sullen silences. His chest began to ache, not with the new physical pain, but with an older one.

He had been as good a patriot as any of them, but random rocketing of London had sickened him. He had been young, his work little known, he had hardly ten words with Hitler, but that was no real excuse. They could have been words of discouragement: the proposed rockets were costly and their trajectories hideously inaccurate and he could have proved it mathematically. Instead he had held his peace. He seldom thought of it now. Once he had mentioned it to Anna, who had smiled away the pain. He had learned not to think of his silence as cowardice. But he had been silent once when with courage he might have acted for good. He would not hold his peace today. If only his hands—look how they were becoming mottled with the brown of age—if only they would stay still.

A rotund man with a beefy face stepped from the paneled door, carrying a dispatch case. His face was familiar and the doctor nodded, sure that he should know him. Max got to his feet, bowed politely. The man smiled back and left the Treaty Room.

"U.N. Ambassador," Max murmured. "You think we're next?"

"We are the only ones left in the dugout," the doctor said, taking comfort in the fact that Max had shed his casual air. "Why, Max? You have something else to do?"

His temporary calm left him when much too soon the secretary crossed the room and led them to the door.

They had been sitting together on a couch in the enormous oval study for half an hour when the doctor discovered that he was staring at his son-in-law in a kind of surprised awe. He had expected Max, if he made any real attempt at argument at all, to become involved in technicalities that would only confuse the President. But Max was sketching in stark clarity the theory of probability, the theory of games, the theories behind spacecraft and missile miss distances and reliability.

It was concise, simple, understandable to anyone. And the President, his elbow on his desk and his face half shadowed, was giving it attention the doctor felt as a physical force. He stirred uncomfortably. He had been following Max closely, searching for a flaw in his reasoning, but apparently there were to be no flaws. Now Max was approaching his summation.

"In brief, sir, here are the facts. Surveyor Six, as you know, is in very good position on Oceanus Procellarum east of Grimaldi Crater. Its solar-powered beacon has operated uninterruptedly for seventeen months."

He took a deep breath. "Here are the mathematical odds. If we were to launch ten capsules and they homed on this beacon, we should expect eight of them to land within the critical radius—the 5-mile walking range—I spoke of." He nodded toward the doctor. "These figures stem from Dr. Ludwig's study of over a year ago."

"I know," the President said.

The doctor looked at him in surprise, flattered but disturbed that anyone who had read his study could think of proceeding.

"Since," Max went on, "we have only one manned capsule to launch, a better way to look at the mathematical probabilities is that the man has four chances out of five of landing inside this area we speak of."

The doctor had hardly spoken except to acknowledge the secretary's introduction. Now he took a deep breath and addressed the President. "Mr. Steiger is right, Mr. President," he admitted bitterly. "Yes, with the Surveyor beacon, the odds on his reaching this flat, golden plain between Grimaldi, Flamsteed, and Hansteen craters favor him by a magnificent five-to-one."

The President chuckled. "I see."

"When I first made the study, I did not count on the Surveyor beacon. I didn't realize," the doctor added acidly, "how humane a project this could be."

The President was grinning at him, but the doctor had the impression that he was very worried. He felt a great pity for him, sensing the other pressures which must be acting on him now—Berlin and Thailand and the open sore of India. At least he could help him in his own field. He had always spoken better on his feet. Now he arose. "Mr. President, you know that I was not informed that this . . . this scheme was ever seriously considered?"

"I know," the President said. He suddenly moved to a steel cabinet, incongruous beneath a portrait of Thomas Jefferson. He extracted a red booklet emblazoned "Secret" and the doctor realized with a shock that it was his own study. "And I know that you ended this by making your brainchild an orphan."

"Then now I make it a bastard! It is not my brainchild! This mission was proposed before the National Security Council in 1959! In 1962 one like it was worked out by Mr. Cord and Mr. Seale of Bell Aerosystems! It is not my brainchild!"

The President sat down again. "I realize that, Doctor. But you have great imagination; everybody knows that. And I think it's a measure of your imagination and your dedication that even if you were against this, you were thorough enough to point out how it could be done with available hardware.

That's your contribution. It may turn out to be a very great, great service."

"No!" The doctor shook his head. "I cannot see how. Figures, equations, odds . . . what do they matter? This is not a horse race! We are talking about a human life!"

For a moment he thought he had gone too far. The seasoned face before him turned tense, the eyes narrowed. "I am aware of that, Doctor."

There was a long silence. "I'm sorry, Mr. President," the doctor said finally. "But I feel very deeply about this."

The President's face softened. "I wonder, Mr. Steiger, if I could have a word with the doctor alone?" When Max was gone the President offered the doctor a cigar. He seldom smoked, but for an insane moment he almost took it, thinking of the wrapping as a souvenir to give to someone. Then he remembered—to whom? According to Max he was not even supposed to mention the trip to Washington, let alone the White House visit. He shook his head. The President replaced the silver lid on the humidor.

"Cuban," he noted. "They stock them for my guests because they're rare; the stores are getting low. Ridiculous, isn't it?"

The doctor had an inkling of what the President meant, but he was not sure. "Pardon me?"

The President shrugged. "Progress. If President Grant discussed seriously what we're discussing this afternoon, he'd have been impeached and committed. But I doubt he ever ran out of Cuban cigars."

"That is very profound, Mr. President."

"It's this desk," the President smiled. "It gives you the large view."

The doctor said, "Take the large view of this, Mr. President." The President regarded him steadily. The doctor went on, choosing his words carefully. This powerful man was easy to talk to. He must not fail. "In 1975, again in '77 and in

'83 Mars will be right for a mission. And we will go, and then who will care about who was first to the moon?''

"But the moon is the first step, isn't it?"

"Yes," the doctor admitted. "But Apollo, not Pilgrim, that is the way to.get there! Look, Mr. President! You know Apollo well. They have set a goal in Apollo quality control of 9,500 hours between failures. For a 180-hour mission! You might have fifty missions, then, before a line leaked or an instrument failed, yes?" The doctor found himself leaning on the desk. "Apollo is careful and slow. It gives the men the choice to continue or return. When the new Saturn booster is ready for Apollo, with all that thrust, they can decide almost anywhere during the flight—"

The President cut in: "But Pilgrim has choices. Pilgrim can abort."

The doctor sighed. He was fighting phantoms. "In theory," he admitted. "Yes, if everything else has gone well and our poor Pilgrim astronaut does not like what he sees, he circles the moon. Yes, then he will fall back into earth's gravitational field. And he can perhaps re-enter. And he can perhaps land. And that night perhaps he can sleep in his home with his wife and his children. But Mr. President, the margin is zero! He must have a margin!''

His outburst had tired him, and he returned to his couch and sat down. My God, he thought, what a place to have an attack! If I died here how would they explain it? Would they drop me in the Potomac?

"Are you all right, Doctor?" the President asked.

The doctor mustered a smile. "Yes." He licked his lips and went on. "Mr. President, we must face it. The Russians are ready. We are not. I don't care what the others say—to try this now will hurt us more than it will help us. Economically, scientifically, and—"

"Politically?" the President suggested. "To try this and fail might be fatal to me politically. But I liked your concern for the man better."

"It is more honest," the doctor agreed.

"In Southeast Asia and over Cuba," the President said, almost to himself, "we have to ask men to risk their lives for the good of the group. This may be the same situation."

"But this is a fallacy!" the doctor protested. "It is war, yes, almost. We should have started earlier, yes. But what does it matter really who is first? We will get to the moon anyway!"

"Are you sure?"

"How can they deny it to us?"

"There's only a small optimum area, isn't there? To land on?"

"Well, yes," admitted the doctor. "For the best trajectory, very small. But why would the Russians try to interfere with a scientific landing? Only because they got there first?"

"What part of Germany were you from, Doctor?" the President asked suddenly.

"Berlin."

The President was smiling at him. "A small optimum area. They got there first. They interfere there."

Franz Ludwig blushed. "That is true, of course, but—"

"If they *wanted* to," persisted the President, "could they prevent us? That's the question."

"I would not know. I imagine it would depend on how long they preceded us."

"If we wait for Apollo, I'm assured, it'll be long enough."

"But they have been screaming for international cooperation in space."

"We offered it once, they agreed to a joint venture to the moon, we were ready to emasculate our own program, and what happened? They put a platform in orbit and we didn't know it until we heard it on Moscow radio!"

"They still claim they will internationalize it!"

The President smiled oddly and glanced at a report on his desk. He said nothing, so the doctor continued.

"Mr. President, your military advisors—do they talk of the moon as a military base?"

"The subject has come up."

"But we have both foresworn it as a military base! Weapons are banned in space."

"They foreswore their own lunar project once, remember?"

"It is a ridiculous military base!" the doctor said scornfully. "As a missile site, it is foolish. We can launch a ballistic missile to hit anyplace in Russia in half an hour; why should we move a quarter of a million miles and three days away? As an observation post? The Russian space platform is better to spy from today. So are our Midas satellites."

The President agreed. He moved to Jefferson's portrait, studied it for a moment. He turned and asked suddenly: "Are these the only military uses you can think of, Doctor?"

"Military technology," the doctor pointed out, "is not my interest. Not anymore, thank God. But are there other military uses than missiles or spying?"

"Today," the President admitted softly, "no."

"Or in the future," the doctor insisted. "Mr. President, you must not risk a life to slam the gate to an empty castle!"

"Believe me, Doctor," the President said gently, "if we took this chance, if we risked this life, it would be to set a precedent where the precedent would count, a quarter of a million miles from the U.N. It would not be to slam the gate on Russia. It would be to hold it open for everybody."

For a long while the scientist studied him. "I am glad, Mr. President," he said finally. "But still you must not do it."

They shook hands and the doctor moved to the door. He opened it and turned back. The President was reading the report on his desk. "Mr. President?" the doctor called softly.

The President looked up. "Yes?"

"Mathematics are unsympathetic. Good intentions do not change the odds!"

The President, dwarfed by the tall windows behind him, nodded thoughtfully and went back to his reading.

It was early evening. The President set aside the report of the U.N. Ambassador, rubbed his eyes, picked it up again. He found an obscure section submitted by the U.S. representative to a minor subcommittee of the U.N. International Law Commission. The President had often observed that the length of a subcommittee's title bore an inverse relation to its importance. This one was the Legal Subcommittee on the Peaceful Uses of Outer Space. The group had been deliberating for more than five years.

The weekly report of the U.S. representative to the subcommittee was pompous and stilted. The President guessed that the man was frustrated by an endless game of words, hiding his confusion behind his own verbosity. The President could not recall his name.

He dug through the section for a paragraph that had jangled his Ambassador's private alarm system:

The Soviet representative then replied that the principle that an uninhabited region may be claimed by the nation which first explores it, while imperialistic in origin and rather hastily rejected as not applying to celestial bodies by resolution of the General Assembly in 1961, had nevertheless historically lessened international friction and perhaps at times prevented war.

The Ambassador had encircled the paragraph in red. Beneath the beefy exterior of a Texas baron the U.S. Ambassador had an intuitive mind. The mind had been dedicated for years to a joyful series of cockfights with various Soviet Ambassadors. The Soviets came in a steady stream to the U.N., affable and glowing or sullen and sulky, but each left with his tail feathers drooping.

The public, Congress, itself, even the State Department, did not realize that the Ambassador was as good in his office as he was in the ring. The minor representative had apparently attached no significance to his own observation, but the Ambassador had spotted it and flown to Washington.

"To a wildcatter drillin' in the Gulf, Mr. President, offshore oil belongs to everybody. When he changes his mind, he's gettin' close."

Well there was no question of that. The Russians were very close to the moon indeed. Before he was President he had appeared before the U.N. and introduced the resolution now in question, on the peaceful uses of outer space. The Russians had signed. The President had once felt that they would hold to the agreement and internationalize the moon. He had had no illusion; it was only that, like Dr. Ludwig, he then could see no military advantage for them in a dog-in-the-manger policy. There would be political advantage in a grandstand play. The paper in his hand stifled the hope.

He looked at his clock. Senator Fellows would arrive any moment. He wished that the report from Rand had come early, so that he might face the Senator with a fact instead of a general's fear. Yet no one had promised him a fact. The computers were admittedly guessing because the men who fed them information were guessing. A weapon that could be based on the moon, if it would ever exist, would not exist for years. And then, too late, a successor might learn the fact in a quiet ultimatum or a blinding flash.

The light on his intercom blinked. The Senator was on his way in. With a sinking stomach he got up to meet his enemy.

The Senator leaned forward in the leather couch and stubbed out his cigarette. "Mr. President! What the hell are you talking about?"

Senator Ralph Fellows was almost seventy. He was a square block of muscle capped by a rowdy thatch of hair. He had fought his way from the 3,000-foot level of a Calaveras County gold mine to the University of California. He had battled through Hastings Law College, fighting middleweight in smoky Oakland clubs to earn money for food and books.

In World War I he had scorned a training camp commission and clawed his way to one in France. He had fought Harry Bridges and the Maritime Union as counsel for a San Francisco steamship company until the dock strikes broke the city and the company, and then he had slugged his way into politics. The President had never seen him wear a hat, even to an inauguration, or anything but a black bow tie and a black suit. His leathery face was quite bland ordinarily, but now the Senator was regarding him with undisguised astonishment.

"Would you repeat what you said?" Fellows asked sharply.

"I think you heard me, Ralph," said the President. Years ago in his first senatorial clashes with Ralph Fellows he had learned that a stiff posture was as good as any; at least one left the battlefield with pride intact.

"You said," the Senator murmured, "you've been funding a substitute program for Apollo? Surreptitiously?"

The President suddenly realized that he had never seen Fellows show emotion before, but there was genuine feeling in his eyes now. It had cost more than $2 billion to put it there, he thought, but the shock on the face was authentic.

"Not surreptitiously," the President amended. "Secretly. It was diverted from other NASA funds."

"Allocated to what?" the Senator asked.

He had recovered already; from now on every word and nuance would be recorded in a remarkable memory for possible use. Well, there was no reason to hide anything anyway. The Senator had sworn secrecy. He had promised reluctantly, to be sure, but he could be trusted.

"Allocated to a project they called 'Chuck Wagon.' Did you hear of it?"

It was an unnecessary question. The Senator heard of almost everything. "I wondered," he smiled grimly, "why that program was eating up funds like Apollo itself. 'Just a system to lob some supply capsules up there, Senator'—that's what some bright young kid at NASA told me. He said it was in case their damn fool landing bug couldn't get off the moon.''

"He probably didn't know himself.''

"Next time," the Senator promised, ignoring him, "I'll get the son-of-a-bitch under oath.''

"If he did know, he was acting on orders," the President flared. "My orders.''

The Senator got to his feet, moved to Jefferson's portrait. He studied it, rocking back and forth on his feet. He turned back. "All right, Mr. President. Let me see if I've got everything straight. You achieved office with the boast that, among other things, you had successfully negotiated an agreement for a joint moon venture with the Russians, saving untold money. The race was off.''

The President felt like a Teamster's official in a Senate hearing room. He did not like it.

"Ralph," he said, "I think you've got all the facts now. And I think you know it.''

"Let me check, please, Mr. President.''

The President nodded. To let him continue might conceivably blunt his attack.

"A little later the Russians knocked the wind out of the country by announcing that they had just begun to enlarge a space platform they had put into orbit. And that they would add to it, over the next year or so, six additional men—and women—and a couple of hundred tons of 'hardware,' as your space people call it. It was as unilateral, somebody said, as a bowl of borsch. You and NASA and the CIA heard about it on the radio.''

The President realized suddenly how very tired he was. Yet he felt that he would not sleep well. And by evening tomorrow at the latest he must decide. Fellows hammered on:

"Within a week, there was so much public reaction you

unloaded most of your top NASA people for mis-advising you. And at that time you instituted this Pilgrim thing?"

"That's right."

"For political purposes."

"No! As a back-up in case this meant a change in their tack on outer space! In case weapons were developed!"

"In case losing the race might be an issue in the next election?"

"I can't deny that," admitted the President. "We're the party pushing space exploration. But we think we're right."

"Over a year ago you started this Pilgrim thing," the Senator murmured. "Your security was very good."

"Only about a hundred and twenty people ever had to know. The rest thought they were working on Chuck Wagon."

"Like the Manhattan Project," the Senator recalled. "Except that that was war and there was a reason."

"This is war, as you often say," said the President. "And there is a reason. If the Russians knew about Pilgrim today, they'd knock the props out from under it just by moving up what we figure they've scheduled by two or three days."

"Did you have to hide it from the Minority Leader of the U.S. Senate?" the Senator asked harshly.

"*Didn't* I have to?" The President looked into the steely eyes.

Finally the Senator nodded. "I'd have fought it," he conceded, "from the beginning. It's too bad I didn't have the chance—we'd have a couple of billion dollars more in ICBMs and a couple less down the drain."

The President was slow to anger, but now he said bitterly, "You know why you hate the space program, Ralph?"

"Why?"

"It's geographical. Half of it's out of your state. The Manned Spacecraft Center is in Texas instead of California. The test facility is in Mississippi, where the economy needed it, instead of L.A., where the kids are driving Jags anyway.

Marshall's in Alabama instead of Sacramento and the Cape is in Florida.''

Fellows' eyes glinted. "Go on, Mr. President."

"We're armed to the teeth already! Do you think these billions would be any less down the drain if we'd sunk them in more missiles built in San Diego or extra Lockheed bombers built in Burbank? Or a few more pads at Vandenberg?''

Ralph Fellows' face began to glow with the joy of battle. "No, Mr. President. You can fling the coppers where you please. My concern is with the amount, not whose constituents get it. Not anymore. I'll be in the Senate until I die. You know it.''

He was right; the California voter realized that in Fellows' seniority he had an asset worth the gold of the Sierras. "Ralph," the President said tiredly, "this is stupid. I asked you up here to help me decide something, and we're ending up in a damn donnybrook.''

Ralph Fellows regarded him narrowly. "Are you asking for bipartisanship on this thing?''

The President's pride ached, but the stakes were high. "Of course.''

The Senator shook his head. "Mr. President, you were elected because your 'image,' as they say, was that of an experienced politician with a lot of guts. This particular music I'm afraid you'll have to face alone.''

The President leaned forward. "I'm not afraid of that. I just don't want to get stabbed in the back before I face it.''

"I already promised you secrecy," the Senator said stiffly. "I assumed, of course, you intended to discuss some question of national defense. I assumed too quick. But I told you that until it's public you have our silence. That still holds.''

"Until it's public," the President repeated. "Then what?''

"First let me ask you this. *Is* there, by any chance, national security involved?''

"Possibly. Anyway, there's national prestige."

The Senator regarded him coolly. "I wish you gentlemen would learn, Mr. President, that there is more usable national prestige in a B-58 over Moscow or a Minuteman in a hole in Kansas than there is in a whole squadron of Apollos circling the moon."

"I disagree."

"I've noticed," the Senator observed. He smiled almost paternally, got up, and stretched his square body. "In a fight in a mine shaft, Mr. President, it isn't the man with the degree in geology that impresses the neutrals. It's the son-of-a-bitch with the biggest shovel. Anyway, you say there may be a military reason for taking this risk. Specifically, what is it?"

The President couldn't honestly answer. "We're not sure."

"That's what I figured. After ten years of planning for the moon, nobody's sure whether there's a military use for it yet."

The President made a decision. "General Hollingworth's due in tomorrow, Ralph. To brief me on a report from Rand. Do you want to sit in?"

The Senator rejected the offer; he did not wish to be involved more deeply until Pilgrim was public. The President took a deep breath. "You haven't told me what then."

The Senator spoke slowly, almost with regret. "Mr. President, you've had almost a year and a half to decide how you might get the public to support this stunt. It looks as if we'll only have a week or so to make sure they don't."

"Why?" flared the President. "Why would you want to make sure they don't? Do you want to see us lose this race?"

"I think we've lost it," the Senator said flatly, "because, if you like, we refused to indulge in this sort of gamble with human life. I think this must involve great risk to the man and thus to the same prestige you've been speaking of."

The President wondered if the tough old Californian cared

in the slightest for the man. The Senator seemed to read his thoughts.

"Yes, Mr. President. I would be concerned for the man. This smells to me like a misbegotten patrol I went on in the Marne, or like the Rapido River crossing, or maybe like the Bay of Pigs." He smiled bitterly. "Potentially convenient for the brass, but ill-conceived, hasty, and pure hell for the guy that has to do it."

"There's a calculated risk," admitted the President. "But—"

"A calculated risk without a calculated goal."

"Well, what would your party consider an adequate goal?"

The steely eyes were narrowed. He is already planning his fight, the President thought, and he's deaf to anything else. He arose to show him to the door. But the Senator answered before he opened it.

"An adequate goal? Our national survival, Mr. President. Not one damn thing less."

After the Senator left, the President sat for a moment thinking. He turned the page on his calendar. Tomorrow at noon the colonel and the other two astronauts would be here for their medals—it was routine to award the NASA decoration in the Presidential study after every flight. He was sure that the Presidential presence was becoming an object of discomfort to the men and mirth to the press. Perhaps next time they could let the Vice-President handle it. But this aborted flight was no time to institute the change.

He was glad, anyway, to have a legitimate chance to talk to the colonel about Pilgrim. He wondered how the colonel really felt about the risk. He wished that he could consult the other astronauts. The new men were presumably ignorant of Pilgrim. But why should they be, really? He made a decision, picked up the phone and called the Vice-President.

"I want to talk to the other two astronauts—Lawrence and Lincoln—about Pilgrim when they get here tomorrow."

"My God, you can't just spring it on them!"

"Cut them in today."

"But the CIA says . . . does this mean you've made up your mind?"

"No," the President said, "I just want two fresh judgments, their judgments."

"All right." There was a pause. "Can I ask you why?"

The question irritated him because he really didn't know. "Because they're astronauts," he said. "Because they're coming to Washington anyway. Because I want to enlarge the sample of opinion. Now isn't that wise?"

Still the Vice-President seemed uncomfortable.

"Too big a sample confuses the issue!"

"To be frank," the President said, "I wish we could have a plebiscite. Cut them in."

He hung up and stepped to the balcony. The moon, quite full, was rising in the east.

8.

Steven James Lawrence sat trying to read his mail at his
front-row desk in the empty astronauts' office, but he was too
perplexed to concentrate. There had been an air of secrecy
about the First Seven astronauts all day: he had been on the
verge of confronting the colonel with it, but the colonel had
seemed to be on the run.

Lined up in the big room were thirty other desks. They
faced a blackboard flanked by training schedules and astronomical charts. He regarded the last envelope sourly. It
was a personal letter, for nothing else sifted through to him.
In the days of Mercury the astronauts had been swamped with
mail. There was much less now—what there was had the ring
of youth—but the mail-room girls still screened everything.
He picked up the letter and moved impatiently to the adjoin-
ing chrome-and-plastic lounge. He found change for the

Coke machine and stood reading the letter while he uncapped the bottle, restless, tired, and irritated.

It was almost dark and he had not yet been home. After the press conference he had had to spend the afternoon adding to his de-briefing. He had made the mistake of depending on Gus Scarbo for a ride back, but the flight surgeon was apparently still counting the colonel's corpuscles in the Life Systems Building across the lawn.

The letter was written by a squadron mate from the Korean days, still in the Navy and flying out of Norfolk. It was spiced typically with affection, envy, and reserve. There was a restrained postscript from the wife, sending Mickey her best. Steve wondered if any of his old friends would ever treat him again as a human being instead of an astronaut.

The phone in the office rang and he started back. He found the colonel standing at a desk, taking the call. He was leaving with Gus Scarbo when the colonel called after them. "Wait a minute, Steve." He spoke into the phone. "Gus is here, Sy. Isn't it time to cut him in too?"

Whatever it was, apparently the answer was no. The colonel hung up and Gus Scarbo whirled, his face set. In a few angry phrases, he let it be known that for months he had sensed that something was going on behind his back with the men under his medical and psychological care.

"I'm a Navy doctor. You tell Sy to tell his boss that if I quit NASA and go to sea, whoever relieves me can learn the Apollo medical statistics in a carrier sick bay in the Caribbean, between an ensign's genital problems and a CPO with the crabs! And I mean it!"

The colonel only said: "I'll drive Steve home." Steve, red with embarrassment, watched the flight surgeon leave the room. "I'm with him," he said briefly. "Whatever this is, I think we should all be told."

"Sit down."

There was an odd intensity about the colonel and Steve felt

that he was about to discover the real reason for the abort. He sat.

"Have you ever figured," the colonel began, "how easy it really is to get a man on the moon?"

"Yeah," Steve said grimly. "I've noticed."

The colonel got a Coke from the machine in the lounge. He returned, stepped to the platform in front of the blackboard. He looked down at Steve, smiling a little.

"I mean," he said slowly, "if you don't have to bring him back?"

For a long moment Steve studied his eyes. Somewhere in the building an air conditioner cut out. The clock on the wall clicked forward.

"Oh, no!" Steve breathed. "Oh, for God's sake, no!"

Early in the briefing Rick Lincoln had arrived. Now he sat impassively at his desk doodling on a scratch pad while the colonel went on.

"We called it Project Pilgrim," the colonel said, "and it's one man, all the way."

Steve had been grappling with the incomprehensible for the last half-hour; there was hardly any surprise left in him. The colonel moved from the board to his desk, sipped his Coke, and returned. Steve glanced at the clock. He should have called Mickey about dinner, but he was too fascinated to interrupt.

"Where was I?" the colonel asked.

Rick Lincoln said: "The week after the Russian space platform. They were mopping up the blood in Washington."

"Yes," the colonel said. He told them of meetings between the new NASA team and the Central Intelligence Agency. He told them of a trip by Max Steiger, Dr. Ludwig's assistant, from Huntsville with a study the doctor had made. "Ludwig had proved it could be done," the colonel said, "with stuff we already had." Then he admitted that the doctor had disavowed his own study on moral grounds.

Great, thought Steve. Use the man's advice where it suits you and throw it out where it doesn't. He commented on the logic. The colonel shrugged. "NASA bought it. The CIA bought it—"

"Sy Larson!" exclaimed Rick Lincoln. "To keep an eye on the troops. I thought there was something smelly about that guy."

The colonel smiled. "Yes. Well, the Vice-President bought it—"

"A great competitor," commented Rick. "On the other hand, he'd be on the bench, wouldn't he?"

"And the President bought it," finished the colonel. "Conditionally."

He told them that the program was an emergency back-up for Apollo. It was to be used only if the Russians seemed to be on the verge of a successful moon landing and only if conditions were right. But now that the hardware was ready, now that the plans were made, it could be launched three weeks from the President's nod. "He's waiting for the right sign of the zodiac, I guess," he commented, rather bitterly. "Sy Larson says you gentlemen are the new court astrologers."

"You mean in eighteen hours the President of the United States is going to ask us what we think of this?" Steve said.

"You better hope that's all he asks us," commented Rick.

The colonel looked at him oddly. He moved to the model case and opened it. He began to remove some of the scale-model missiles and boosters and capsules. He placed them on the reading table in the middle of the lounge.

"Either of you ever been in a Mercury capsule?"

Rick Lincoln had not; Steve had once climbed into the Mercury on display outside the Administration Building.

The colonel lined up the models carefully. "Were you comfortable, Steve?"

"No."

"A little snug for a trip to the moon?"

Steve studied the colonel's face, trying to decide if it was all an elaborate joke. But the colonel's eyes held no hint of it, if it was. "They're seriously considering," he demanded, "sending a Mercury capsule to the moon?"

"To the moon," the colonel smiled.

"Oh, for Christ's sake," exploded Rick. "Come off it! They don't have to listen to every half-assed NASA egghead who has an opium dream! Somebody might have sold the President, but how'd he sell Archy Gorman and the engineers?"

"Because it'll work," murmured the colonel. "It'll work, Rick." As Steve and Rick stared, he detached a tiny Mercury model, shaped like an inverted TV tube, from the top of the old Mercury-Atlas combination that had once sent him into orbit.

"Mercury was ugly," the colonel said fondly, "but it already existed. Outer space is outer space, on the moon or in orbit, and it was well tested in orbit. Hell, Cooper could have gone three days in it. It's only three days to the moon. You can spend six days in Mercury if you add a hundred pounds of water and a few pounds of food and twenty-five pounds more lithium hydroxide for your air."

"Mostly, though," Rick Lincoln said, "Mercury already existed. Right?"

" 'The uses of adversity,' " the colonel agreed. Out of U.S. poverty in booster power the Mercury had been born in 1959, a dwarf—light, miniaturized, rugged because the astronaut must ride it all the way down to a landing.

The Russians with giant boosters had built giant ships; presumably they had not yet landed on the moon because they lacked power until now to hurl them to escape velocity. Or perhaps their capsules had until now lacked structural strength—the cosmonauts seemed invariably to abandon them before landing. You had to ride your capsule to a landing on the moon; there was no atmosphere to support an ejection by parachute.

The uses of adversity, turning our necessity to an advantage, thought Steve. It might work, if they could find anyone heroic enough to try, or stupid enough.

The colonel told them that everything required by Dr. Ludwig's "proposal" had existed since 1963. Little modification of components was required. The whole system had been ready in ten months.

"Built," Rick Lincoln decided, "under another trade name. Chuck Wagon?"

"You should be a private eye," conceded the colonel.

"Anybody who considers this should be committed," Rick remarked seriously. "But go on. Tell us how you get it to the moon."

The colonel began to build a system. He stood the Saturn 1B booster topped by a Centaur third stage on the table. The Saturn 1B was the combination that had been putting their own 10-ton Apollo into low earth-training orbits while they awaited the advanced Saturn 5. It was dependable and well-tested, powerful enough to put three men into orbit, though too weak to hurl them free of the earth.

But the Mercury was much lighter. Suddenly engrossed with the engineering, Steve wondered if the Saturn could toss it to the moon. He had once calculated the weight that a Centaur-tipped Saturn could hurl to escape velocity. It was over 6 tons. Stripped down for landing the Mercury capsule weighed not much over a ton. If someone had devised a light enough rocket to brake the Mercury to lunar landing, maybe. Maybe not.

He leaned forward, fascinated. Rick Lincoln reached into his desk for a slide rule. The colonel was regarding the launch vehicle fondly. "That's the bird that gets it there," he said. "Now let's install the brakes." He picked up a Polaris missile and detached the second stage. The Polaris was a solid propellant rocket. The direction of thrust could be varied, but not its magnitude.

"A firecracker?" Steve protested. "You can't hover!

What happens? You shoot it off and if you're lucky you don't hit too hard?''

"Oh," the colonel said, "it isn't quite that bad."

"What's that Polaris stage weigh?" Rick Lincoln asked.

"About four tons," the colonel said, placing it on top. On the Polaris stage the colonel balanced the Mercury capsule with its escape tower capping it perkily. The base of the capsule overlapped the slim Navy rocket beneath it. "OK," he said to Rick. "How much more does that leave us, Einstein?"

Rick Lincoln made a few calculations on his rule. He looked up thoughtfully. "A little over a thousand pounds margin for oxygen, food, water, those sorts of non-essentials. And a prayer book."

"How many pounds of food, oxygen, and water will get you there—and back—if you have to abort and return instead of landing?"

"Quit saying 'you,' " Rick commented. "The sixty-six-hour trajectory?"

"It's the only way to fly," the colonel said comfortably.

The slide rule flashed. "Roughly 150 pounds."

"That leaves half a ton for extra fuel, altitude radar, and—" He smiled at Steve. "What else?"

Steve, his mind rebelling at the utter incredibility of the Project, was reluctant to reply.

"How would you use the weight, Steve?" insisted the colonel.

Steve gave in and wrestled with the problem. Solid rockets were simple, powerful, but headstrong; liquid ones were often heavier, more complex but controllable. Perhaps, since there was weight to spare, you could add a small liquid rocket to the brake. You might let the solid Polaris stage decelerate the capsule, let it fight most of the battle with the moon's gravity, and then touch down with a delicate hand and a little liquid thrust. The unmanned Surveyor probes were using a similar system to land; two of them had survived with their instruments intact.

"An auxiliary braking engine?" he proposed. "One you can throttle to hover?"

The colonel nodded. "Half the rocket companies already had throttleable engines that were light enough. On-the-shelf hardware. We picked three thrust chambers and a couple of propellant tanks. It brought the whole braking stage up to four and a half tons, loaded." He grinned at the model he had built up. "The tanks fit around the Polaris rocket. It even makes it look better."

The colonel had drawn the earth and the moon on the blackboard. Now he linked them with a sweeping figure eight. The earth lay in the center of the large loop, the moon in the center of the smaller one. Steve remembered Dr. Ludwig's office in Huntsville, with the doctor sketching the same trajectory. And he took the same odd comfort in it now that he had taken there. The laws of celestial mechanics might fill you with curiosity or great intellectual modesty or even reverence, but when your life depended on them they filled you with confidence. Especially those which applied to the moon.

The moon and the earth were very close, really, in their eternal waltz around the sun. They were a closed-body system, a very special case. The figure-eight trajectory the colonel had drawn took advantage of their celestial dance. The path he had sketched was a free-return trajectory. With one accurate burst of thrust you hurled your spacecraft into an unpowered glide which would curve close by the leading edge of the moon. No further power was necessary, theoretically. Trapped temporarily by lunar gravity, you simply swung around the moon at the top of the figure eight. Then, soaring back to the earth's side of the moon, you were clasped again by the earth's gravitational pull. Even without a pound of fuel in your craft, you would return to earth orbit.

You had merely joined the lonely waltz, and the earth had handed you to the moon and the moon had swung you once and relinquished you.

Of course, you didn't depend on completely passive flight. The mathematics of the perfect trajectory were too precise. You carried fuel for a mid-course correction and any other change in trajectory that was necessary. But in the main you substituted the laws of celestial mechanics for brute force. "You must join the spheres, not fight them," Dr. Ludwig had said once.

The colonel was tracing the path from the launching pad. "You separate from the last boost stage on command from Houston through Johannesburg. That leaves you with the Polaris braking stage and the liquid auxiliary."

"Also your parachutes, heat shield, everything but your escape rocket tower?" Rick Lincoln asked. "About 3,000 pounds worth of capsule and baggage?"

The colonel nodded. "And 9,000 in solid and liquid braking stages. Are you going to make it?"

The slide rule went into action. "God willing, as they say," Rick admitted, "you've reached escape velocity, on a trajectory toward the moon."

"God should be willing," the colonel remarked. "He wrote the book. OK. For hours after injection into your trajectory toward the moon you make your mid-course correction . . ." The colonel outlined the tracking procedures, voice communications, telemetry which would guide the astronaut on his way. The network, computers, and downrange personnel were simply those already being utilized for Apollo training. Steve wondered how many of the operators knew of Pilgrim, how many would have to learn, how long they had trained in secret. The chalk was approaching the moon. ". . . homing on Surveyor Six," the colonel was saying.

"Say again?" Steve asked.

"The whole mission is based on the Surveyor Six beeping for the next few weeks."

Surveyor Six was somewhere in the middle of a "Maria"—Oceanus Procellarum—the Sea of Storms. There were, of course, no storms and the moon's "oceans," so far as they knew, were vast, undulating plains covered by thin dust. The Ocean of Storms was broken only by sparse and minor craters; the moon's highlands, much older, had been scarred by thirty times as many meteors as the "seas." A dismal picture of a Mercury capsule hovering over a jagged peak evaporated from Steve's mind. To use the well-placed Surveyor Six as a beacon made the landing itself look almost feasible. But what then?

"Of course," said the colonel. "You don't land at all if things don't look right by here." He made an X on the incoming trajectory. "If they don't, you hang on to the chutes, the heat shield, and the braking rockets and fall back into earth orbit." The chalk continued along the figure eight around the far side of the moon and back to earth.

"You re-enter the atmosphere at lunar return velocity?" Rick Lincoln asked quickly. A body would return from the moon with a third more speed than the orbital velocity for which Mercury had been designed. The heat shield would burn away too quickly and then . . .

"Einstein," the colonel chided. "Haven't you forgotten something?"

"Yes," Rick admitted. "If you haven't used the braking stages to land on the moon, you can use them to slow down for earth re-entry."

"Right. Use them to ease into earth orbit and jettison them. Then the heat shield and chutes take over. From then on it's break out the whisky at Grand Turk Island."

"You make it sound so simple," Rick Lincoln said.

"An abort is simple," said the colonel. "So is a landing." He pointed back to the X. "The decision to land on the moon or return has to be made here," he said. "OK. Your decision is to land. But you're still a little heavy. What can you get rid of?"

There was much essential to an earth landing that would be superfluous in a lunar one. The parachutes in the neck of the Mercury capsule were no good in an environment with no atmosphere. A life raft was useless in a world with no water. There was no reason to expend fuel to slow dye markers, rescue beacons, and smoke lights to a soft landing on the moon when there were no rescuers.

"They could stow the rescue and recovery gear with the chutes," Steve found himself suggesting. "And you could leave the whole canister in orbit."

"Right," said the colonel. "What else don't you need?"

"Your capsule's still sitting on your heat shield," Rick said. "But you're stuck with that."

The heat shield was a heavy fiberglass disk at the base of the Mercury capsule. It was useless in an entry where there was no air, and, thus, no friction. But on the colonel's model it would obviously be sandwiched between the base of the capsule and the braking rockets.

"You're not stuck with it," said the colonel. "They designed you out of that too." He sketched a simple latch arrangement, unlocked by a switch on the instrument panel, which permitted the heat shield to be spun away by explosive bolts.

"Like a paper plate at a picnic," Rick Lincoln said. Steve wondered how the astronaut would feel as that particular paper plate went sailing into eternal orbit.

The colonel went on with his explanation. Having stripped the capsule for a moon landing, the astronaut would rotate it until he was riding backward. The main Polaris braking stage would fire on command from his altitude-marking radar. He would decelerate rapidly; at 30,000 feet above the moon's surface he would have slowed to 200 miles per hour before his solid propellant burned out. He would drop the burnt-out

Polaris case. His liquid engines would continue automatically to reduce his speed under the control of his radar. "By a hundred feet you're hovering."

"Flat on your back," Rick Lincoln reminded him, "looking straight up. Running out of fuel. How the hell are you going to see the surface to set it down?"

"Remember the periscope on the first Mercury flights?"

"Yeah?"

"It's back in Pilgrim One. A great view, straight down." With careful nonchalance he said: "It's been tested on one of the free-flight simulators at Edwards."

They had all trained in the desert on the "Bug-Eyed Monsters," as they called them. They were tall, half-jet contraptions built under a Lunar Excursion Module. Five-sixths of the landing capsule's weight was supported by a huge jet beneath the bulbous-eyed LEM; the force of the remaining gravity was the same they would find on the moon. The astronauts controlled the "lunar" gravity through jets, as they would on the landing.

"You mean," Steve demanded, "they've taken the LEM off one of those things and stuck a Mercury on it?"

The colonel grinned. Steve felt a surprising surge of hope. The insane jungle into which the colonel had led him was thinning. If they had given the astronaut a liquid engine to cushion his landing, a periscope to guide it, a trainer to practice it, perhaps they had guarded his survival in other ways.

But it made no sense to protect him. He might last for a few days in the capsule on the moon or a few hours outside of it breathing from a back pack, but then he would die anyway of thirst or heat or asphyxiation. Steve could not accept it. This was the United States in peacetime, not Shinto Japan fighting for its life.

The colonel continued. "You can hover and you can see. OK. When you're ten feet from the moon's surface you hover until you're out of fuel so you don't get your butt burned when you land. For the capsule it's a free fall from ten feet."

A ten-foot fall to the moon was no more of a jolt than a two-foot drop to earth. The Mercury capsule had been designed to strike harder than that normally, hanging from its parachutes.

But it made no difference how hard he hit. Unless the whole briefing was a bad dream or a bad joke, the astronaut would die anyway. Something was eluding Steve. There was an abort capability, the colonel had shown. If the man was to sacrifice himself, why provide him a way out in the first place?

"What's he looking for coming in on his approach?" he demanded suddenly. "What's he have to see to land?"

"Surveyor Six," Rick Lincoln suggested. "The whole project is to get it turned off. It's running up an electric bill."

The colonel smiled tightly. "I was getting to that. No. You don't have to see Surveyor Six." He sipped his Coke. "You have to see Chuck Wagon One, I guess you'd call it."

"What's that?"

"Your shelter capsule."

The two stared at him blankly. "I thought 'Chuck Wagon' was a cover-up," Rick reminded him.

"Not *just* a cover-up. It was developed to build shelter capsules and supply capsules. Project Chuck Wagon will land a shelter somewhere near Surveyor Six before the Mercury's launched."

Steve's relief must have shown. The colonel looked at him oddly. "Did you think this was some kind of a suicide mission, for God's sake?"

"I'm still not sure it isn't," Steve commented.

"I'm sure it is," Rick said. "Shelter capsule or not. But it's nice to know they've provided a coffin."

The colonel looked at him speculatively. "Keep an open mind on this, Rick. Stay loose. OK?"

Rick Lincoln nodded after a moment and the colonel sketched the shelter capsule on the board. It looked like a toppled GI can. It lay on its side, 10 feet in diameter and 12 feet long. There was an air lock at one end and a bunk inside. The colonel drew a stick figure standing on the flooring inside. There was barely headroom. It would be launched a week before Pilgrim. It, too, would use the present Saturn booster. Its control system was that of the Surveyor probes. Its guidance would home on the beacon on Surveyor Six. Ideally, it would brake itself to a landing soft enough so that the Environmental Control System inside the shelter would remain operable.

"It lands straight up for visibility," the colonel said seriously. "You unlock a landing leg to tip it over."

Rick Lincoln was watching him, shaking his head. "Straight up," he murmured wryly. "Aren't you a little brainwashed, Skipper?"

The colonel contemplated him coldly. "When you study the engineering behind it, you'll know. Straight up. *Will* you study it, Rick? Before tomorrow?"

"When the Commander-in-Chief can find time to give me a quiz," promised Rick Lincoln, "I can find time to study for it. Don't you worry, Daddy. I'll study!"

The colonel regarded him strangely, finally went on. But now he was straining like an insurance salesman with a reluctant prospect. He explained the shelter systems: those for maintaining a living temperature, regenerating oxygen, supplying power for the astronaut's radio. The shelter with initial supplies would weigh less than the Mercury capsule. In it was packaged a thousand pounds of oxygen and water, and two hundred pounds of food.

"Just a second!" Rick Lincoln protested. "Assuming the guy finds this thing and it isn't a pile of junk when he does, that'll only keep him a couple of months."

"He has to land at the beginning of lunar daylight so he can get squared away. It's two weeks before it's dark. In another two weeks it's light again. From that time on there's a monthly capsule launched. One-ton payload each."

Rick Lincoln sighed hopelessly. "That sewer pipe he's supposed to live in isn't much bigger than the Apollo capsule," he observed. "How long do you figure it'll be before he starts climbing the walls?"

"Admiral Byrd spent a winter at the South Pole alone in a 9-by-12-foot room," the colonel answered.

"And when the Saturn 5 is ready, the poor bastard's relieved by the first guy that steps out of LEM?" Rick asked.

"I like to think of it that way," the colonel said. "Maybe by one of you."

"What about you?" asked Rick. "You're in this crew."

Over the colonel's face passed the same look of youthful pride that Steve had noticed in the Apollo capsule at the garbled words on the air. A code, he knew suddenly, to which he had not had the key. Much became clear: the sudden abort, a few unexplained absences by the colonel over the last year. He remembered the colonel's session yesterday in the Mercury trainer.

"You're Lucky Louie?" Rick Lincoln whispered.

"I'm the one," announced the colonel happily.

"Jesus, aren't you getting a little old for these sort of heroics?"

The joy faded from the colonel's face; Steve had never seen his eyes so hard. Rick Lincoln flushed, began to put away his slide rule.

"The commander's my back-up," the colonel went on, ignoring Rick. "We're the first two they asked. The other five will be capsule communicators at the Instrumentation Facilities."

"They only considered the First Seven?" asked Rick Lincoln.

"Of course. Gemini and Apollo spoiled you . . . youngsters. Too much room. We're trained for Mercury; it fits us like a glove. You'd want to crawl out at the halfway mark."

"You do me an injustice," observed Rick Lincoln, "to assume I'd crawl in at the start."

The colonel did not smile. He leaned forward on the lecture stand in front of him. "I'm asking you, Rick, and you too, Steve. *Think* about this, don't prejudge it."

Rick Lincoln stood up. He seemed almost angry. "Don't prejudge it? Hell, Colonel, it's judged already as far as I'm concerned. All I have to do is explain the verdict to the man!"

The colonel's jaw tensed. "Steve?"

Steve's mind fuzzed. He had assimilated too much too quickly. All his training, all his conservatism shouted the impossibility of the project. It seemed incredible that they had attained the precision necessary to land a Mercury within sight of a shelter. And even if they had, radiation, meteorite penetration, extremes of temperature, the product of all the variables that they did not even know seemed to him intuitively to make the project certain death for a lone man.

But NASA could not have gone suddenly mad. The President of the United States had advisors. They were not murderers. Perhaps if one studied Pilgrim . . .

"Don't make up your mind tonight," the colonel begged him suddenly. "Sleep on it; study it tomorrow. I'll brief you on the plane."

"Why in the hell," Steve demanded, "weren't we told before this? All of us?"

The colonel looked uncomfortable. "That," he said briefly, "is a long story." He looked at his watch. "You're the guy who was crying to go home. Shall we?"

The colonel pulled into Steve's driveway. Steve opened the car door. A chill breeze from Clear Lake ruffled the tree Mickey and he had planted to hide the bare spot in the lawn. Its leaves shimmered in the moonlight. He felt the colonel's hand on his arm.

"Will you tell Mickey?" the colonel asked surprisingly. "Tonight?"

Even in the awful past the most deadly of military secrets

would have been safe with his wife, but to break security on this?

"You think I should?" he hesitated. "Why?"

"So tomorrow, damn it, Jean will have a woman to talk to. For the first time in a year."

Steve nodded. He began to get out, but the colonel spoke again. He was staring out over the lake, his hands tense on the wheel. Tomorrow, in that big oval room . . .

"Yes?"

"He's going to toss your judgment on the scale."

"Look," Steve said uncomfortably, "a couple of peons like me and Rick aren't going to affect—"

"I'm sure it's a very carefully balanced scale," the colonel went on, his voice hoarse. "Steve? Please?"

"I don't know," he whispered doubtfully. "I just don't know."

He went into the house.

9.

Steve let his hand brush his son's soft crew cut as he removed the last "trained" ant from the upper bunk. "The bailing can got lost," the little boy commented sleepily.

Steve decoded the information. It probably meant that the skiff they kept at their rickety pier had sunk again. The last thing he had asked Stevie before the countdown was to keep it afloat until he could calk it. He grinned. "How'd it get lost?"

"You were on TV."

Steve decided not to pursue the logic. "Of course," he agreed. "How else?"

"Tell me about the flight?" Stevie suggested.

It was a transparent ploy to ward off taps. Stevie was a naturalist, not an engineer. A housefly orbiting a bowl of cornflakes could fascinate him for minutes. Perhaps he had inherited the interest from Steve's own father, a professor of zoology at Berkeley.

His father had brought Steve up, with the aid of a series of superannuated housekeepers. He had a cloudy, baby memory of his mother, an impression of warmth and cigarette smoke and bobbed hair. She had been a graduate student who had, apparently in a gesture of emancipation, deserted his father for a Canadian stockman and then died in a plane crash in Ottawa. His father, immersed in science, may have driven her off, but he had never allowed his preoccupation to come between him and his son. When he had been a few years older than Stevie was now, his father had given him a BB gun. There had been no restriction, of course, outside of safety precautions. When, frightened but proud, he had brought back his first trophy, the professor had fondled the dead chipmunk and smiled.

"Steve, you're going to hunt if you have the instinct. Some of it's built into every man or we'd still be swinging from the trees picking fruit." Steve, who knew his father loved every feathered, furry creature that roamed the Berkeley hills, was surprised. But the old man went on. "However, Steve, there's more wonder built into the circulatory system and the little brain of our ex-friend here than you may realize. Scalpel, Doctor . . ."

Together they had dissected the little body. Steve had become utterly lost in the minute system and the symmetry of the animal. When they were done, when they had explored the last artery, he had a new and earnest awe of anything that lived. He had seldom hunted since. Until Korea, anyway. God, he wished his dad could have known Stevie.

"The flight," Stevie was demanding. "Tell me about the flight?"

"I'll tell you at breakfast," Steve promised. He kissed him and turned off the light. "All about the mouse, too."

"What mouse?" Stevie yelled. "What mouse?"

"The space mouse that tried to get into the capsule," Steve said casually. "Good night, Skinhead."

* * *

The breeze off the lake had made it cool enough for Mickey to light a fire in the living room. He poked it tentatively, noticed a crack in the fieldstone hearth. He would fix it this weekend, after Washington. It would be good to have a few days at home.

He stepped outside and crossed the patio, moved down the sloping lawn to the dock. Balancing himself, he walked along the planking. Sure enough, only the bow of the skiff showed over the slapping waves. He looked out across the lake. On a low-lying point a mile away he saw lights in the colonel's ranch-style home.

When NASA, reputedly swayed by the then-Vice-President, had announced Houston as the home of the new center, a developer had offered to give the astronauts free homes. The press—unreasonably in Steve's eyes—had screeched that the First Seven were exploiting their status. So they had acted in concert as always and rejected the gift, but most of them had moved swiftly to buy. For men on military pay they had done well. Clear Lake frontage had become golden. Steve's $17,000 NASA salary was undoubtedly more than the colonel's military pay, but by the time he had been sure enough of selection to move, his own slice of land had almost bankrupted him and it was a tiny slice at that. The colonel had spent no more than he had years before on a miniature estate that was a showplace.

The moon paved a silver path from the colonel's place to his own pier. Gus Scarbo's outboard bobbed at a buoy in the middle of it. The lights on the point began to go out. Steve wondered what the colonel and Jean had discussed at dinner.

Chilled, he went back inside to eat.

Steve finished his sherbet and looked thoughtfully across the candles at his wife. She was clearing the dishes, her supple body moving beneath the jade hostess gown she knew he liked. When she had finished he must tell her of the colonel's fantastic mission; there would be no more excuse to delay.

He lifted the split of welcome-home champagne from a red Navy fire bucket, relic of a squadron party a dozen years before. He had once given up alcohol, thinking that it might help Mickey. She had reacted violently, as she did often in those days. She was no freak, she insisted, no puzzle to be solved; he could forget his heroics, she would lick her problem alone. He looked at the dripping bottle: it was still half-full.

Drinking champagne alone was wasteful, but Mickey had deliberately served it tonight as she always did to celebrate homecomings, minor triumphs, and successful flights. And perhaps as reminder, too, of what they had been through. She noticed him looking at it and paused. "What, Steve?" He smiled noncommittally, trickling the wine into his glass. Her eyes were gentle. "You're thinking of steak night, aren't you?"

He nodded. They had been living in Palmdale, on the desert near Edwards. He had been flying production test for Convair, praying for a promotion to experimental work, when one blazing morning the chief had called him in and slid a contract across the desk. Suddenly, he was an experimental test pilot.

And so they had called Gus and Marion Scarbo down from the Navy's test station near Mojave and that night in the backyard of their squat, stucco home the old red Navy bucket rang with ice and the steaks sizzled in the desert breeze and the old flying stories were re-told. It all began quite happily, and then Steve reached into the bucket and pulled out the empty bottle.

Fifteen minutes before there had been a full magnum. Gus had had a glass or two, Marion Scarbo hardly drank, Steve had had just one. With cold apprehension he guessed at Mickey's drinks: a toast when he opened the bottle, one sneaked perhaps when he went for the steaks, another while he was busy seasoning them, maybe a fourth while he turned the meat.

She smiled up at him from the lawn, holding out her glass. God, he thought, couldn't they just once entertain someone without his having to carry her to bed? He jammed the bottle upside down in the ice. Surprise, than a kind of happy shrewdness, flicked across her face.

"Somebody around here drinks," she announced. She arose from the grass, smoothing her dress and weaving a little. "Scotch, in the kitchen—"

"No!"

She stared at him innocently. "No what?"

"The steaks are almost ready, Mickey. If you'll just—"

"Steaks, schmeaks," she sang, starting for the house.

He put down his long-handled steak fork and faced her. "No!"

Her eyes narrowed. "Experiment with airplanes, Steve. Not me."

He stepped in front of her. "I said no!"

For an instant everything stopped as if a motion-picture projector had broken. He heard Marion Scarbo draw in her breath, not in surprise but sorrow, heard the scratch of Gus Scarbo's match and the sucking sound of his pipe. He looked into her face. The full lips were moist, the upper one stiff as it always was when she drank. Her eyes were rock-hard. Two spots of scarlet glowed from her cheeks; a drop of spittle oozed from the corner of her mouth. Suddenly he was tired of analyzing her, entreating her, studying her, babying her. He grabbed her arm and the contact seemed to sober her for an instant, for he had never touched her in anger. The instant of shock turned to hissing rage.

"Take your goddamned hand off me!"

She had never sworn before. He slowly relaxed his grip. "I'm sorry," he grated. "I forgot you were a general's daughter. You pick that up around the barracks?"

Her hand flashed in the light of the kitchen window, his cheek stung wickedly, and before he could stop her she was running across the lawn, crying. He started after her.

"Steve!" Gus Scarbo's voice cut across the lawn. "Hold it!" He turned. Marion was up, following her, and Gus was watching him coolly from across the ruddy coals. "That's not the answer, Steve."

"I'm going to lay her over my knee," Steve promised softly, "and I'm going to beat her tail until it's black and blue!"

"And tomorrow," growled Gus, "she won't even remember it. If she isn't ready to learn to swim yet, you can't beat it into her."

"What the hell *can* I do?"

"Be there, in case she wants to learn."

"I'm going to leave her," Steve said, sick at the idea.

Gus Scarbo regarded him across the glowing bowl of his pipe. "Push her off the life raft to lighten ship?" he meditated. "No, Steve, I don't think you could."

Gus was right. He could not leave her, that night or any night. He had put her to bed. At midnight he had awakened and found her nude in the kitchen, pouring a drink of Scotch. She had shrieked and clawed at him until a neighbor pounded on the door. At dawn he had found the bed empty again and discovered her asleep on the living-room rug, with an incoherent note in her palm addressed to him and swearing abstinence.

It had been the worst of her drunks until the accident, but bad as it was, thank God, he had not been able to leave her to face the aching, raw aftermath alone. Or perhaps he had been unable himself to face the animal fear in her face, the dread of loneliness. For she loved him as much as he loved her; it was herself and the fear of solitude that she hated.

The accident later had almost killed her, but she had not had a drink since. If she had not weakened yesterday, he told himself, she was safe. And yet the aching doubt hung on. Last night, halfway through his de-briefing, he had thought of her alone at home, with the strain of the day suddenly easing and the temptation growing. He had panicked at her danger and phoned.

She had answered late, breathless but absolutely sober. She had gone next door to the Scarbos' to watch a re-run of the press conference. Maybe she had after all felt the need to use Gus and Marion as props.

Then he set aside the thought. You have licked it, my darling, he told her silently, and I love you for it. She finished clearing the table. He blew out the candles and led her to the living room, and then he told her, moving about the room while she sat crosslegged staring into the fire. He explained Pilgrim in all the detail he knew. She had made herself knowledgeable about space; at first she could not believe that he was serious. But she accepted it, finally, and when he was through she began to poke viciously at the embers. The firelight touched her hair with bronze.

"A year on the moon," she murmured.

"If he survives."

She and the colonel's wife had been very close at first. She told him now that last spring Jean had become morose, touchy, and nervous. And they had drawn apart. "My God, Steve. No wonder! How's she going to stand it?"

"You can help. Until it's released you'll be the only woman who knows, I guess."

"Me help?" she smiled. "Because I'm so brave myself?"

"You're brave," he answered her. "You're braver than you think." Together they turned off the lights in the living room. On their bedside clock radio he heard that the Russian probe had completed 40,000 miles of its homeward trip and was on a good course to rendezvous. He groaned and flicked off the set.

Before the Apollo launch he had been three weeks at the Cape; he had spent hardly five nights with Mickey in the last month. All evening he had been longing for this moment.

Now, easing into bed, he found himself so heavy with fatigue that he could hardly move.

She lay on her side, the sheet following the gentle curve of her hip and flowing over her breasts. She was gazing into his face and her eyes were wet.

"I'm sorry," he whispered angrily. "I don't know why . . ."

She kissed him lightly. "It's not that. Oh, Steve, I'm *not* brave. I'm no damn good!"

"For me," he murmured, "and to me, you're perfect."

"I ought to feel sorry for Jean, but all I can think of is myself."

"Yourself?"

"Myself and how lucky I am. Suppose it was you?"

He took her into his arms and clicked out the light, and after a while she slept. But he thought of the colonel alone on the vast grey plain, of the brutal cold and crushing heat, and he did not sleep for hours.

10.

The President stepped reluctantly from his air-conditioned study to the balcony. It was sultry outside, but preferable to the strain within, where the Vice-President and his Greek chorus of NASA scientists hung on an open line from Goldstone Deep Space. The Vice-President had gathered them ostensibly for the award to the colonel and his crew. But he had brought them early to sweat out news of the Vostok's rendezvous with its platform. Actually, the President realized, they represented a subtle pressure group to push him to a decision.

Well, he would not be pushed. Even assuming the rendezvous was successful he would wait for the Rand report and consult with the one military mind he really trusted in the Pentagon. And he would talk to the colonel and the two others. He wondered whether he would get honest opinions from the colonel's crew. Their desire to please their pilot might sway them to argue for what he obviously wanted. On the other hand, their concern for the safety of a friend might cause them to be too cautious.

He must accept their judgment with reservations, weigh it as he would weigh the rest of the advice he would get on other matters today, measure the guess of a State Department Thailand expert against the hopes of a Bangkok business-man, balance an opinion on Polaris funds by an admiral against the decision of the joint chiefs.

But on Pilgrim there was so little time to steady the scales. He looked with envy at the Vice-President, who was com-pletely immersed in Pilgrim and had probably not another problem on the day's schedule. He stepped inside the room as the young man thanked an unknown voice on the Goldstone line and faced him. A muscle twitched in his jaw. "Rendez-vous," he announced gruffly. "A hundred miles over Hawaii, 11:04 our time."

The President's Special Scientific Advisor was in the room. He was a young radar specialist, an electronic genius, and now his sensitive black eyes were alive with excitement.

"Irv," asked the President, "is there any question that they did it?"

"Mr. President, they were tracked by the most precise network in the world. If that Vostok and that platform merg-ed on the screen, it's either a rendezvous or a mid-air colli-sion. We have to assume a successful docking."

Ned Mooney, his Press Secretary, lumbered into the room with a clipboard and a quick instinct for the President's need. He was a solemn giant, built like a milk bottle, with sloping shoulders, wide hips, and battleship feet. He was 6 feet 5. Surmounting the mass of him rode a patch of strawlike hair. The face was chalk white, but then it always was. Two dull eyes, forever red, glowed from it.

"Morning, Ned," the President said. "Well, they rendez-voused."

"I figured they'd be getting close," Mooney murmured.

He had a beautifully modulated voice. Where you expected a growl or a squeak, out flowed music. Where you expected inanities, out came fact. You expected delays from a man so deliberate and he was always ahead of you.

"Ned," the President said, "I think you'd better prepare a statement . . ."

Ned Mooney showed him the top two papers on the clipboard. One was a message of congratulation for use if the Russians admitted their probe was manned, the other for release if they didn't say. The President smiled at him gratefully, made a minor change, and then it was time for the award, and the colonel and his crew and their wives were filing into the study.

Steve sat next to the colonel on the leather couch. He felt the weight of his second NASA Distinguished Service Medal on his lapel. It seemed somehow ludicrous and almost Russian to be wearing a medal in civvies, but he took a certain pride in it, too. He wondered if the colonel and Rick, also in business suits, felt the same way.

Anyway, it would hardly be appropriate to slip the medal off in front of the President. He was busy on the phone, but in a moment he would return them his attention. Steve had not decided yet what he would tell him. He wanted sincerely to help the colonel, but he could have no part in risking his life. The colonel was a close friend of the Vice-President's family. He wondered if personal likes and confidence had entered the equation, wondered whether a man of the colonel's age, no matter how skilled, was as good a survival choice in a lunar environment as Schirra, Shepard, or Cooper perhaps.

But this was a problem for the aeromedics; at least he knew that he himself could never bring it up before the President of the United States. His mouth was dry. He envied Mickey at the buffet downstairs, hoped that she would not pick up a martini to ease the tension, dismissed the thought as disloyal.

The President hung up the phone and announced that Radio Moscow had confirmed a successful docking.

"Sir," the colonel said vibrantly, "we have to go on it! Now we have to!"

The President studied him for a moment. "That's what we're here to discuss, isn't it?" he reminded him mildly. "We were already assuming a successful docking. And a manned vehicle, which we still don't know."

"Yes, sir."

"Then nothing has changed, has it?" The colonel shook his head. Steve glanced at the President. He felt better. Here was a man who would not be budged. "Before the call, you were saying, Colonel?" the President said.

The colonel leaned forward. "I had no doubts last January. I'd have gone then. Gladly. It was marginal maybe, but—"

"Very, very marginal," the President cut in. "It would have been fatal, I've since been told."

Steve had heard today that false news of a Russian manned probe last January had almost triggered Pilgrim, that later tests of the capsule's radar altimeter showed that it would have failed, crashing the colonel onto the lunar surface.

"Not fatal, sir," the colonel protested. "More marginal than we figured, that's all. The human mind can cope with sudden emergencies; I might have made it with the human back-up. Not necessarily fatal."

The President drummed a pencil on the desk. "Well," he admitted, "you gentlemen should certainly be the authorities on survival. Mr. Lincoln?"

Rick Lincoln's face was set and impassive. "Yes, sir?"

"Now that you know about this, how do you feel?"

Next to him, Steve felt the colonel tense; he was staring at Rick as if trying to hypnotize him. Rick Lincoln avoided his eyes and spoke to the President. "I'd prefer to make a more detailed study before I give an opinion, sir."

The President sighed. "Since there isn't time for that, what do you think?"

Rick Lincoln met the colonel's stare. He shook his head sadly. Then he spoke with heavy emphasis, in clear, concise layman language. He spoke of computers and the tiny initial navigational error which, undetected, could grow in a quarter of a million miles to a fantastic miscalculation and turn the whole attempt into a monstrous joke. "Your fuel is marginal. Do you use it," he demanded, "to correct your course and then have to crash on the moon? Or do you save it and end up as another asteroid?"

He listed communication failures which could leave the world in doub for years of the colonel's fate, described supply-launch problems which could doom him to asphyxiation, starvation, or death by thirst. He spoke of solar flares and reminded the President that they were approaching a very hot cycle in cosmic radiation.

The colonel had been listening rigidly. Now he cut in: "It might even be better to subject one man now to this supposed danger than to wait for Apollo and risk three. Has that occurred to Mr. Lincoln?"

"Well," the President said coolly, "it occurred to several of my advisors. But since the first Apollo expedition has never been envisioned as spending more than a few hours on the moon, I think it's a fairly poor argument. Don't you?"

The colonel didn't answer and Rick Lincoln continued. He spoke of the chance of the advanced Saturn booster slipping behind schedule, stranding the colonel on the moon. He was an expert on lunar topography; he spoke of gaps in knowledge of the moon's surface, warned that the first Apollo operation sent to rescue him might initially fail, and that the second might, and the third. When he was through, the Pilgrim Project lay in shambles in the President's study. The colonel was glowering silently. the President seemed genuinely impressed.

"Thank you, Mr. Lincoln." He thought for a moment. "I

was going to ask you a rather important question, but I think you've answered it.''

"What was it, sir?'' Rick Lincoln asked.

The President looked up. "Whether in the colonel's place, you'd have volunteered?''

Rick Lincoln moved across the room to a TV set. On it rested a silver model of the X-15. He inspected the plane for a moment. "Volunteered? No, sir, I don't think so.'' He returned thoughtfully to his seat. "I'm a naval officer, of course. If I were ordered to go, I'd go. But . . .''

"But what?''

"I wouldn't expect to get back.''

There was a long silence in the room. An antique clock behind the President chimed disquietingly. The President studied the colonel. "Colonel,'' he said, "I've never asked you your motivation. Why do you have such a drive for the moon?'' He smiled. "Are you like the mountain climbers? Is it because 'it's there'?''

For a while the colonel didn't answer. "No, Mr. President,'' he said finally. "I'm just a military man. I want to win. The Russians are 'there,' almost. I want us to beat them.''

"Do you think,'' the President asked carefully, "coming in second would be really that bad? Militarily?''

The colonel shook his head. "Maybe. But I don't mean militarily.''

"I see . . .''

"We've slipped, Mr. President. I want us to stop slipping and win this. I want the flags to wave and the people to cheer. I want the teen-agers proud of something besides the new Impala the old man just bought them.''

"Yes . . .''

The colonel sat back. "I think that to lose this will be absolutely fatal. Spiritually.''

The President nodded. He moved his shoulders as if to

loosen them. To Steve he seemed tired. "Mr. Lawrence?"

Steve found that his breath was very short. "Yes, sir?" he managed.

"What do you think of the colonel's chances?"

Steve was abruptly aware that with a little of Rick's foresight he could have organized his thoughts, presented a smooth argument, impressed the President with his objectivity. Instead he had let the jumble of detail on the Washington trip distract him.

"I trust the engineers," he began, "and the scientists . . ." (But hadn't the colonel admitted that the best of them, the man who had engendered the very idea, had disinherited it?) "Instinctively, I like the trajectory planned for the flight. I think it affords him a chance to second-guess." (And how long to second-guess? A few minutes or a few seconds with the moon rushing closer and the world watching?) "I've worked out the thrust-weight relationships myself and I feel that there's some margin for error in launching and enroute . . . " (But this was out of his province: he was an aeronautical engineer who happened to fly, not really a propulsion expert. And the President must know it.)

"The lunar housing concepts," he went on, "seem logical, especially if there are unlimited launch facilities available for re-supply . . ." (Last year they had lived for twenty-four hours under vacuum in the giant lunar-surface environmental chamber at Houston, but it hardly qualified him as judge of a year's exposure to the blazing heat, the unspeakable cold, the insidious part-weightlessness of the lunar void.) "I agree with the colonel that a trained astronaut will be able to improvise in emergencies . . ." (But how could you improvise, say, if a meteorite punched a hole in the steel womb that held the only environment you could stand?) "And I agree with the colonel that getting there first is worth almost any sacrifice." (Now he was a flag-waver, too, a pseudo-political expert. And the sacrifice was not his own, but that of another man with a wife and children.) He was finished now, uncomfortable at the way he had presented his opinion, not even sure that it was an honest one.

"Thank you." The pencil drummed on the desk. The ultimate test of his evaluation was coming—would you have volunteered? The President said nothing. Perhaps it was because he thought he had answered already.

But that was not right; he had not answered really. He thought of the colonel's wife, and he thought of himself and of Mickey and Stevie, and he looked up. "But Mr. President," he continued desperately, "I can't deny that this project shocked me. I'm still shocked. It may be the only way to win, but it's a very, very risky way."

The President nodded. His eyes were on Steve's; now the question was utterly unavoidable.

Steve licked his lips. "I don't know, sir, that I'd have been dedicated enough to volunteer. I'm afraid not."

In the silence which followed, Steve heard the colonel's breath go out in a long, low sigh. The President seemed lost in thought. Finally he smiled tiredly. "That's very honest, Mr. Lawrence. Thank you."

The conference was over. Steve could hardly meet the colonel's eyes as they left the room. In the Treaty Room, Rick Lincoln paused to light a cigarette. "Enough to separate the men from the boys, isn't it?"

The colonel glanced at him coolly. "There's no doubt about the group you joined, Buster." He glanced at Steve, flicked his dangling medal. "About you, Steve, I'm not so sure."

They started downstairs for the buffet. Steve slipped the medal from his lapel. He wanted a martini himself very badly now.

11.

The President's desk was almost cleared. He had sidestepped a minor decision on Thailand, preferring to wait for more facts. A small U.S. convoy was stalled at a Russian checkpoint on the autobahn; he had okayed a stern protest and there was nothing to do but wait. Now, for a few hours at least, he could concentrate again on Pilgrim. He looked across the desk at his favorite military advisor with affection and admiration.

General Clair Hollingworth was a trim, bespectacled man with an ascetic face. He held an MS in nuclear physics from Massachusetts Institute of Technology. He had served on MacArthur's staff in Korea. He was the absolute opposite of the hardheaded, conventional Army general; his mind ranged sometimes so far ahead of present weaponry that he embarrassed his staff.

He headed the Intelligence Evaluation Center in he Department of Defense. He was the foremost U.S. authority on Russian military hardware, policy, and strategy. Now that he had finished summarizing the Rand report he lit a cigarette. Holding it delicately, he began to tick off the main points: "All right, sir, what've we learned? First, any attempt to land men on the moon against the will of tenants who'd occupied it for a year seems as close to impossible as any operation ever undertaken. It'd make the Dardanelles look like a rock fight."

"Yes," said the President.

"Second," the general went on, "assume a hostile military base on the moon. Or even a scientific base under military control. Do we have to land to take it? Can we knock it off from the earth with missiles if it seemed to threaten us?"

"Apparently not, if they keep the location secret," the President said. His head ached; he had been sitting at his desk without a break for almost seven hours. Outside, the sounds of afternoon traffic had almost dissipated. There was no one for dinner tonight; just himself and his wife. Thank God this was the last appointment.

The general was continuing: "That's right, sir. A moon base will be almost impossible to hit. You're fighting the earth's gravity, as with a spacecraft. A missile would take three days. During that time they might evacuate to another base if they wanted. Even on the far side, maybe. But why evacuate? They're already underground to protect themselves from random radiation."

The President nodded. Nothing in the report had really changed what they already knew, because it had all sprung from known facts.

"So much for getting rid of a hostile base," the general continued. "What about the future threat a lunar base might pose? There, things seem somewhat brighter if you stay away from the crystal ball."

But can we? the President wondered. Eisenhower stayed away from it once and we have not caught up yet.

"First," General Hollingworth said, "there's no lunar-based weapon that we can conceive of today—and I emphasize today—that wouldn't be more effective closer." He paused. "With the possible exception of the laser."

Laser . . . When he had headed the Armed Services Committee the scientists and generals had been picturing the earth prostrate beneath a nuclear base on the moon; that was passé now. This was the year of the sting from the laser. The President hated the sound of the word. Westinghouse, American Optical, Hughes, NYU, had been working on government studies of the laser as a weapon for years. An Austrian engineer thought that as a weapon it would never be anything but a laboratory toy. Others saw it on the moon as a gigantic death ray straight from Buck Rogers. Some perceived it as a finger of doom. Others touted it as the light of Providence, harmless to men beneath the atmosphere but picking off ballistic missiles as they entered space like ducks in a shooting gallery.

He sighed. "*You* crystal-ball it for me, Clair. That laser animal?"

The general shook his head. "I can't, Mr. President. It may revolutionize warfare, it may not. Whether man will ever find a lunar use for that particular weapon, I don't know. Intuitively, I just feel that, unchecked, he'll find some military use for the moon."

Whether it was the laser or another weapon didn't much matter, thought the President. If in five or ten years free men noticed their children shivering at the rising moon, it would not be the general or the scientists they would damn. The President had almost mired in high-school science, but it would be him they cursed. For an instant he felt closer to Eisenhower than he had ever felt before.

General Hollingworth took off his glasses and inspected

them. "I know one thing for a fact, Mr. President, " he said softly.

"Yes?"

"Men learned it from the apes, the Khyber tribesmen taught it to the British, and the North Koreans taught it to us all over again. The Air Force generals quote it at the drop of a budget, but it takes a dogface really to appreciate it."

"What's that, Clair?"

The general breathed on his glasses and polished them. He looked up. His eyes were dark brown and very soft. "Take the high ground," he said, "or they will bury you in the valley."

At 4:30 P.M. the Vice-President strode into the Presidential study with a teletype torn from the White House pressroom. It quoted an intercepted Russian broadcast: the circumlunar vehicle had indeed been manned. It even gave a totally undecipherable name for the cosmonaut. The President called Ned Mooney and had him make public the appropriate statement; he thought for a moment and added his personal congratulations to the Russian pilot.

Very quickly information began to flow to the study from more official sources. The CIA called with news that the Russians had announced good pictures of the optimum landing area. NASA informed the White House that the Russian trajectory, plotted out, showed that they undoubtedly used the beacon on Surveyor Six to guide the reconnaissance run. Proud of its tracking or its beacon, NASA wanted to announce the fact. It was, after all, a scientific contribution to the flight. The President wished that he could feel pride in the donation; instead, all he felt was a dismal foreboding.

"I wonder," the Vice-President grated, "what Ralph Fellows would do with it if he found out? 'How much of your tax dollar went to help the Russians to the moon?' Jesus . . ."

"What were we supposed to do?" the President snapped. "Turn it off?"

"If I weren't hanging on to the forlorn hope that we'll need it ourselves," the young man said significantly, "I'd find out if we can."

"Never mind," the President said. "And let's announce that they used it, too."

"Why?" the Vice-President demanded.

"A number of reasons," the President said wearily. "The most practical being that it'll leak out to Fellows anyway. Let the Russians deny it if they want to."

"They will," promised the Vice-President, "which ought to cinch the voter's belief that we helped indeed."

The President shrugged and moved to the balcony. For a long while he looked over the city, thinking. A few hours ago the colonel had stood before him and the President had murmured a few stock phrases and pinned a bit of silver to his lapel. And afterward, while the party stood chatting self-consciously in the study, he had watched the colonel's wife. She was a tiny, dark-eyed woman with streaks of grey in her hair. She was older than he had remembered her and her eyes were shadowed with a hint of agony. But when once or twice she had glanced at the colonel, her face had come alive and shone with pride.

The President thought of the months of lonely fear to which he would be sentencing her even if all seemed to go well, at the lonely torture she would face if everything went wrong. And he thought of his own prospect too: the solitary days of wondering if he had done right or the wrenching certainty if the colonel failed that it was he who had sent him to die.

The evening traffic was picking up. All across the wide land, the millions were heading homeward: apathetic, tired, their minds focused on the brush with the boss or the kids' poor marks, while in China the giant stirred and iron spewed from the Urals and the Siamese prepared to learn that complacency must be earned. And a hundred miles in space men were working again to teach America the same lesson. He sighed and went back to the study. The Vice-President had been skimming the Rand report. He looked up now and for an instant the two were frozen in a shaft from the setting sun.

All the facts were in, all the conditions for Pilgrim were met. The Vostok had circled the moon, returned safely, and now they were told that it was manned. The President needed no more "inputs," as the engineers said, and yet he found a huge reluctance to proceed. He took a deep breath.

"OK," he said. "Let's do it."

The young man's face broke into a grin. He wrung the President's hand and was gone. The President sat behind Lincoln's desk. He felt very old.

The President lounged in his living room swirling a drink and waiting for his wife. Perhaps because the decision was made, he found himself hungry for the first time in three days. His secretary entered apologetically with news that the Vice-President was crossing the street to discuss plans to implement Pilgrim. And besides . . . odd things were accumulating. Could he take two calls? She was a girl who worked largely on intuition; he had learned to trust it. He had been away from his desk for less than two hours, but he followed her back to his study.

His U.N. Ambassador had phoned; another line was ready with a call from the CIA. He learned from the intelligence agency that they had been unable to find a record of the newest cosmonaut in U.S.S.R. military publications or dossiers. But their scientific extract section had discovered a paper by a well-known Russian geologist of the same name: Alexis Plekhanov.

The man was a selenologist, a specialist on lunar terrain. The President put down the phone slowly. He rubbed his jaw. Was it possible that they had trained a geologist as a cosmonaut? A civilian? He picked up the U.N. line. His Ambassador's voice was as jovial as ever, but all the news was bad.

"Mr. President, I feel they are arrangin' our funeral again."

The U.N. sessions were breaking up for the day. With precise timing the Russians had leaked the news in the cloakrooms. The newest cosmonaut was indeed a civilian scientist; more than a scientist, a symbol of peace.

"This one's no eagle, Mr. President. This one's Picasso's dove." The Ambassador predicted that if a Russian actually landed next month he would be a civilian, too. "But way down in that little old subcommittee, Mr. President, remember?"

"Yes?"

"Their delegate came out this mornin', real quiet, for the principle of national domain in space by right of discovery. First come, first served."

"I see," the President said bitterly.

"We pointed it out to the wire services and the Voice of America and the USIS, hear? But with this Russian bein' a civilian and a weekend comin' up, it'll attract about as much attention as a pickpocket at a cattle auction."

The Russians were missing no bets. The President felt trapped. He told the Ambassador that they were going ahead with Pilgrim.

"Good!"

A question had been nagging the President since the shock of finding that the Russian was a scientist. "Assuming the colonel makes it, George—"

"Yes, sir?"

"And assuming you're right about the Russians landing civilians—"

"They can't land military now, Mr. President. Not first off. Not the way they're spreadin' it around up here."

"OK. What will the neutrals do to our space proposals if the first American on the moon is a military man and the first Russian's a civilian?"

"I've been thinkin' of that," chuckled the Ambassador, apparently scenting lonely glory in a floor fight in which the Reds held all the weapons. "They will tear me apart."

"Those proposals," the President reminded him tersely, "mean a good deal to me. Doesn't it bother you?"

"I reckon, Mr. President," the Ambassador agreed cheerfully. "But I'd rather we got booed off the floor for sendin' a colonel than booted off the moon for not sendin' anybody."

The President thanked him rather abruptly and hung up. It was easy to be sanguine when you didn't bear the responsibility of losing. It was another thing to sit behind Abraham Lincoln's desk and see your dream threatened and know that there was nothing you could do.

He was mulling the problem when the Vice-President arrived, Pilgrim would be set into motion tomorrow, despite the difficulty of maintaining secrecy over activity on a Saturday.

"You think," the President remarked, "with the Russians eating black bread to get to the moon, NASA could keep the store open *every* Saturday."

"If we'd eaten a little black bread ourselves," the Vice-President suggested, "we wouldn't be doing this. But the store'll be open."

He went on with details. The President's mind wandered. He was toying with a wish, but an impossible one, and he knew it, really. There was no choice but the colonel or perhaps another of the First Seven. And the original Mercury astronauts, though they wore civilian clothes, were all military men. It was not even his own fault; the First Seven had been inherited in 1960. They had been picked entirely and shortsightedly from military ranks because, as a colonel on their selection board had once told him, "records on civilian pilots weren't complete." In Apollo, of course, there were four civilians. At last. Three of them had not yet even orbited.

And Steven Lawrence, the other? Well . . .

The Vice-President had finished. The President studied him. The young man and the colonel were good friends—skiing companions and golf partners, he knew, since the colonel's first emergence into fame. He might not give an objective opinion, but he had to be asked.

"Do you think," the President began, "we'll be showing the world we want to demilitarize the moon if we start to explore it with a military man?"

The Vice-President's eyes narrowed. "Maybe not. Why?"

"Do you think we're even showing common sense, when the other side's apparently going to colonize it with civilians?"

There was a long silence. The Vice-President understood. "I suggest you put it from your mind," he said, heavily and distinctly. "There are no other choices."

"Are you sure?"

The lined young face grew grim. "Are you suggesting one of the Apollo civilians?"

"Maybe."

"Who?"

"Lawrence."

"From what the colonel tells me, Lawrence just doesn't sound properly motivated."

"It took guts to admit his doubts. And it's got nothing to do with his being a civilian—the Navy boy felt stronger about it, even. Anyway, I'm asking your opinion on the technical aspects alone. Could Lawrence be trained?"

The Vice-President flushed. "No! He probably doesn't know the Mercury capsule from a can of beans. He's not going to learn it in three weeks."

"I see," the President murmured. He would get no valid answer tonight; the Vice-President was loyal to the core; he would fight for the colonel with blind, deaf stubbornness..

"The man we're really looking for," the Vice-President grinned, "is a test pilot who's a former president of the

American Red Cross. His hobby is spelunking and he campaigned for Stevenson. He pickets the White House when we schedule a nuclear test. He's a colored Jew with an Arab grandmother.'' He got up to leave. ''Until we find him, can we stick with the colonel?''

The President smiled noncommittally. When the Vice-President left he wandered to the window. The moon was just past full. It would grow slimmer night by night and vanish. Then the crescent of its next dawn would peek around its rim. That dawn would crawl across its face, painting it with light, and a few days before it reached the other edge they must launch a man to greet it.

He buzzed his secretary. ''Get Mr. Lawrence back, please? He's in Washington or on his way to Houston. Either way, I'd like him here tonight.''

Then he sat down to wait. He was no longer hungry.

12.

The cab pulled up to the somber grey front of Washington's Hay-Adams Hotel. Pretty Cindy Lincoln, putting on lipstick, tried to get Steve and Mickey to go on to the Statler. Steve was glad to feel Mickey squeeze his finger, a signal for retreat; Rick and Cindy were in their usual combat and a few more hours of bantering strain between them would have ruined the evening. Besides, he wanted to read the *Washington Post* he had bought outside the theatre:

"RUSS SAY COSMONAUT SCIENTIST."

He was helping Mickey from the cab when he noticed a chauffeur sliding from behind the wheel of a glossy limousine parked in the reserved zone. The car bore government plates, very low-numbered government plates. As Rick's cab pulled away the chauffeur approached. He was young, with a clean-cut air; there was an indefinable aura of power about him.

"Mr. Lawrence?"

Steve stiffened. "Yes?"

"I've been asked to pick you up."

"By whom?"

"Well," the young man said, almost apologetically, "it's the White House."

Mickey also tensed beside him. Steve looked at the retreating cab. "Don't they want Mr. Lincoln, too? We're together."

"Apparently not, sir."

Steve nodded and told the man to wait. He took Mickey across the deserted lobby to the elevator. "Steve? What do you think it is?"

"I don't know," he murmured. He fumbled in his pocket, found the room key, pressed it in her hand. "Maybe they found out I told you a top-secret secret. They're going to have me shot."

She glanced at her tiny gold watch. "Steve, it's past midnight!"

"Honey," he reassured her, "the colonel's in Houston. There's something technical they forgot to ask him. He'll need his sleep and they don't want to wake him."

It was transparently ridiculous, but it was all he could think of to tell her. She pointed to the headline. "You're sure it hasn't got to do with this? Steve, could it?"

It was exactly what he had been thinking, but he saw no need to admit it now. "I don't see how. I told you what I said in there this morning."

"But it's the first thing you thought of, isn't it?" she asked huskily. "Isn't it, Steve?"

He could not look into her eyes and lie. "It doesn't matter, Mickey. I'm not a red-hot. And I won't be pressured. OK?"

The elevator door slid open. "OK," she whispered. He kissed her lightly and stood for a moment watching the hand climb on the dial above the door. Then he went outside and got into the limousine.

"All right," he muttered inanely, "take me to your leader."

The driver smiled briefly. The car moved with slow dignity through the deserted streets, like a trundle in the French Revolution, Steve thought. He wished it would move more slowly yet.

The President regarded him from across the desk, his face half in shadow.

"Because the other civilians have not flown, I don't think we can consider them." He paused. "And so, Mr. Lawrence, that's it . . ."

Steve nodded. His brow was hot; his eyes ached. "I feel as you do, sir. It should be a civilian. I can't deny that conceivably I could train for this thing in three weeks. It's just that . . ."

It was just that he loved his wife, that he wanted to see Stevie grow, that he knew too much about space to enter it with poor odds, that not even the colonel knew enough about it to guess at the real chances. The colonel! He had been thinking only of himself and Mickey and Stevie, but if conceivably he could bring himself to volunteer, he would destroy the colonel.

"Sir," he said, "what about the colonel? He's been living for this for the last year. It'll kill him if . . ." His voice trailed off. The President was looking at him as if from a great distance. Steve blushed. The personal disappointment of an astronaut must seem trivial from behind the big desk. The enormity of Pilgrim for the first time really engulfed him. "I'm sorry, sir. It's irrelevant."

"Yes, Mr. Lawrence, it is." The President stood up. He seemed exhausted, much paler than he had been at the ceremony in the morning. But his voice was steady enough. "No one will ever know why I asked you here tonight unless you tell them," he promised. "Your status in Apollo will not change, whatever you decide. I do ask you to think it over, to talk it over with your wife if you'd like.''

Steven took a deep breath. The words were on his lips: *I'm sorry, sir. If I were single, maybe. I'm sorry . . .*

But the words would not come. Puzzled, he stood up. ''How long,'' he heard himself murmur, ''do I have to decide?''

''Tomorrow morning,'' the President said. ''If it's yes, I'd like to see you at nine. If not, give my secretary a call.''

Steve got up. He felt a little dizzy. He nodded and left.

He stood outside the hotel room, listening. He had forgotten to pick up another key at the desk and he hated to wake her. But that was silly; he must wake her anyway. He tapped at the door and it opened almost immediately. Mickey stood in her nightgown, a set smile plastered on her lips.

He walked in, sick at what he had to say. He told her. The green eyes stayed dry and never left his face.

''I knew it,'' she said softly, ''the minute I saw that car.''

''I didn't commit myself,'' he said weakly.

''I know that, too.''

She went to the bed, tucked her feet up under her. ''Cold,'' she announced. ''Oh, Steve, what are we going to do?''

With Mickey before him, the project became monstrous. ''The whole thing is ridiculous,'' he told her. ''Really ridiculous! There was never any difference between the astronaut program and any other experimental project, or I wouldn't have come into it! I wouldn't test a plane with a reliability factor of 80 percent! Nobody would.'' He sat down on the bed, began to remove his shoe, found himself staring at it stupidly. He dropped it, untied the other.

''But?'' she whispered. ''There is a 'but,' isn't there?''

He shook his head. ''No. This was big enough to snow me for a minute; the power in that place kind of hypnotized me, maybe, but it's too hairy. I don't feel right about it. There's you and Stevie and . . .''

She was still regarding him. He found that he had been

dangling the other shoe. He had once sat in a foggy cockpit on a catapult off Korea. He had watched the catapult officer making hateful little "run-up" circles in the air with his forefinger. He had obeyed like an automaton and fed power to the throbbing engine, dreading the moment when the finger would fall and hurl him through a grey limbo toward the misty canyon and crags ashore.

"Steve," she whispered. "What?"

He dropped the shoe, grinned at her. His face felt like a mask. "A strike," he said vaguely. "Off Wonsan. I was trapped then. I'm not, now."

She studied his face. "I think you are, Steve."

"No."

She smiled, a twisted smile. "You haven't really decided not to, have you?"

He could not meet her eyes. "No."

"It's funny," she said. "You'd do anything I asked you, wouldn't you? Almost?" He nodded. "And yet," she breathed, "if I asked you not to do this, it would just make it harder for you."

"Harder to decide?"

"No. Harder to go through with when you did decide."

His throat was so tight that he couldn't reply. She had never tried to sway him in his flying; now she was fighting not to. Her tears were rising, he saw angrily. Why couldn't he promise her a flat, irrevocable "no"?

She went on, softly. "So I won't ask that. But Steve?"

"Yes?"

"If you did this thing—"

"Damn it," he said hollowly, "they can't make me risk my little finger if I don't want to!"

She continued shakily: "But if you did it and somewhere along the line you saw that if you went on, you wouldn't come back to me . . . would you back out?" She tried a smile. "Turn tail and flee?"

He heard the elevator whirr outside. A car door slammed

three floors below. The shower dripped. He cupped her face in his hands and kissed the wide nose and wet cheeks. "I promise, Mickey. No matter what."

She rubbed her nose with the back of her hand like a child. He flicked off the light and took her into his arms. Together the warmth of their bodies kept the specter of Pilgrim at bay.

But when she had fallen asleep he was alone with it. It hovered nearby and would not go.

He woke up at six. It was chilly in the room; the air conditioner had run too high. Mickey seemed to be sleeping deeply. He was glad, for he had a great desire, even a necessity, to be alone. He wrapped a towel around his electric razor to muffle it, as he used to do when he had an early test hop in the desert. He dressed and wrote her a note. Then he left the hotel and began to walk.

When he was a student at the Test Pilot Training School at Patuxent River he had loved the capital: the Jefferson Memorial and the Lincoln Memorial, and even the Library of Congress. Now, crossing the Mall, he saw the Washington Monument, his favorite. Today it was a ribald finger pointing skyward, mocking the city: *They went that way. . .* He cut across the lawn and passed the Library of Congress. This morning it was a blank-faced vault of dead knowledge, dully facing another day.

Perhaps it was the Korean War that had vitalized the city in his Patuxent days; the people of Washington had seemed to move with the vigor you noticed on the streets of San Francisco or New York. This morning the people he saw—a janitor swabbing a department store entrance while a haughty mannikin stared, a newspaper truck driver, a moody soldier heading for the bus terminal—all seemed morose, withdrawn, intent only on bracing themselves for the heat. The charm of the city had fled.

He wandered into a tiny cafe on 14th Street, thinking of ham and eggs. The place smelled rancidly of frying grease;

he decided to settle for a cup of coffee. The waitress had lifeless red hair, a trim body but utterly blank eyes. She wore an almost transparent seersucker uniform, with coffee stains at counter height. A sexless bra and slip showed through. He hurried the coffee, left her the change as a tip when she rang it up. She pocketed it unsmilingly, and he stepped out, reluctant to face his thoughts.

Mickey had awakened to the faint snarl of his muffled razor; with all her heart she had wanted to talk to him. But to decide, he must have solitude, so she had feigned sleep until he was gone. Then she felt a bolt of panic, terrified that he might act on the spur of the moment, without telling her. He would not, though, so she lit a cigarette and crawled to his side of the mattress, to the warmth his body had left between the sheets.

If she could only pray . . . But she had prayed alone for her brother on the ridges of Korea and she had not been able really to pray since. If she could get sick, seriously sick; then, once Steve was out of it safely, get well. But she had been sick once, in a way, and he had stood by her, and she could not wish that on him again.

The shower was dripping, and she could not stand the steady *tik, tik, tik* any longer. She moved into the bathroom and twisted unsuccessfully at the knob. Starting back to bed, she noticed Steve's after-shave lotion in a bottle on the sink. It was liquid, it reeked of alcohol, and for a moment she almost lifted it to her lips. If he returned to find alcohol on her breath the problem would be solved. She stared at herself in the mirror: hair tousled, cheeks pale, eyes dark from a restless night: she could fool him easily. The lotion was ridiculous, of course, but she could ring for a bellhop; they knew where to get liquor any time of the day or night. She need not even drink very much; she could pour some down the sink to make him think she had.

The crushing truth was, she suspected, that she would pour

none down the sink. After six years she could still long for liquor at this unearthly hour. Sick with guilt, she went back to bed. Waves of fear began to wash over her. She fought them with a trick she had learned; she pretended that Steve had hidden, omnipotent eye and could watch her.

See, my darling, I am lying here being brave. The thought of drink has passed. In a few minutes I'll get up and pack for us, and wait until you've decided that you are not a suicidal hero like the colonel but an analytical civilian test pilot . . .

One evening a half-dozen years before, in the squat stucco house on the desert, she had tried to tell herself that. The phone rang while she was reading baby books, expecting Steve to call for a ride home from his afternoon flight and wondering whether there was enough loose ice in the re frigerator for his evening cocktail. She herself was on the third week of a teetotaling swing that secretly she knew would not last the month. She had answered. The Convai Project Engineer had told her in a falsely cheerful voice that Steve was circling Edwards, using up jet fuel, with a terrified technician in the rear seat who refused to eject. One whee was jammed down and the other up. Could she stand by her phone, in case there was trouble? No, she must please not come to the base; for he might land elsewhere, on Lake Muroc or Marine Mojave, or even try for Palmdale.

She found herself in the kitchen, yanking at the re frigerator door. There was indeed enough loose ice and the assurance, thank God, of a bottle of bourbon two-thirds full. She began to walk around the room, feeling the life inside her that was to be Stevie, the warmth of the bourbon, the glorious detachment, finally, of an Olympian goddess radiating for tune down on a mortal that she loved.

And when the phone had rung again and it was Steve, she had been so filled with the goddess-glow that she had ignored his plea to wait, had flown to the little MG, roared down the driveway, sped across the darkening desert like Juno on a Ovian date. And then, in slow, slow helplessness, she had seen the great, glaring headlights, fumbled with her own light knob, heard the air horn of a truck, and then there was blackness.

Gus Scarbo and Steve had appeared from nowhere, out of a white-tiled haze, talked to her as if they had been conversing for hours.

". . . So when Gus sees this surgeon's X rays, Mickey, we'll know whether they'll operate here or in L.A."

"Did I hurt anybody?" she blurted. Oh, God, if she had . . .

He shook his head. "Only yourself, darling. We think—"

She stared at him. "The baby?"

Gus Scarbo's hand was firm on her pulse. He shook his head. "So far, so good."

"Steve . . . I was drunk."

"Maybe you had reason," he said dully. "It won't come up again. It's too tough on you. I'm quitting."

She swallowed. God, she was thirsty, and now there was pain. "No! No, Steve, I am."

He smiled, but there was no belief in it, only love, and then he left for a moment, and Gus Scarbo was prodding her stomach. The hands were warm and gentle, and the eyes were gentle too, and the voice was low. "You're a lucky girl, sweetheart."

"I know."

"Lucky to be alive. Lucky to have Steve. Flying's his whole life, but he means it."

Somewhere she had found the strength to shake her head. "He isn't quitting, Gus. I'll lick this instead." She felt a stab of pain in her groin and winced. "Gus, if I live, can I lick it?"

For a long moment he studied her face. "You'll live. And think you can lick it. But if you do, if he keeps on flying—"

"Yes?"

"Never ask him to change his mind again. This is the last stop, Mickey . . ."

Al Shepard had ridden the first Mercury a hundred miles down-range on a puffing little Redstone; Steve was aflame with desire to be selected as an astronaut. "I'll never ask him to quit, Gus. I promise." Then they were wheeling her to the tiny operating room, and Steve was beside her, holding her hand.

"You are holding the hand," she told him, "of a brand-new girl."

He looked down and smiled. The smile turned puzzled, then suddenly some of the doubt left his face. "You know," he said, "I think you may be right."

Well, she had been right, six years proved she had been right, but this morning the brand-new girl was fraying at the edges and if he didn't come back soon or call, her stuffing might run out.

The *tik, tik, tik* still sounded in the bathroom. She got up to take a shower.

He wandered into a Negro district. It was past eight A.M., he had less than an hour to contact the President; still he had not cared to grapple in his subconscious for the answer. It was growing sultry and the effort of dredging up his decision seemed almost too much. He was passing along a street of shoddy row-houses. He clung to the shade of the trees which lined it, clung to their smell, really, for the street was beginning to exude the same odor of frying fat he had endured in the cafe.

An enormous colored woman sat on her steps, watching a tiny boy on a tricycle. Her eyes were veiled. When she looked up and saw him, he grinned automatically. She nodded and slipped back into her private world.

His feet were beginning to hurt. He must force his mind to the problem; he might have done better to study it out in the hotel room or the lobby. He passed an alley, a classic alley of grey mud and the sweet, dead smell of garbage. Two Negro boys—of eleven or twelve, perhaps—were tossing a softball listlessly. One of them leaped after a high throw. He missed and the ball rolled ahead of Steve. He was about to pick it up when the boy darted ahead of him and retrieved it.

The youth glanced up, started back to the alley, and frowned. "Ain't I seen you? On television! Yesterday, on television. Wasn't you on television?"

Steve nodded. The larger boy wandered closer, studying Steve.

"They said you been to the moon," he said. "That right?"

The smaller boy said: "He ain't *been* to the moon. They been in *orbit*. That ain't going to the *moon*, is it?"

Steve shook his head. The little boy began to finger the ball, all the while regarding him nervously. He was almost purple-black, with bright eyes and broad yellow teeth.

"Do you," Steve asked, recognizing symptoms, "want me to autograph that ball?"

"Yeah! Yeah, Mister, if you want to."

The taller one scoffed: "He ain't a baseball player, Leander, you stupid mother! Hey, you ain't a baseball player, are you?"

"No." He drew a pen from his shirt and signed the ball, inscribing it to Leander. The little boy jammed it in his pocket, ignoring the protests of the other. It was apparently out of play forever. Steve squeezed the skinny shoulder and started down the sidewalk. He had gone ten yards when he realized that the boy was following him. He waited at the curb.

The youth looked up at him in studied nonchalance. "Hey, Mister?"

"Yes?"

"How you come to be an astro-naut?"

Steve said: "Well, first I learned to fly and . . . then they picked me for an astronaut."

"Man . . ." said the boy. "Man, I sure would . . ." The voice trailed off.

"You sure would what?" Steve asked gently. Far down the street a Good Humor truck chimed. Steve pointed toward it, tentatively. Leander shook his head.

"I sure would like to be an astro-naut."

"Well," Steve proposed, "you go heavy in school on math—you know, arithmetic and all . . ."

The shining eyes turned marble-hard and the smile on the little black face was not young at all anymore, but rather old and wizened. "Shit, Mister," he drawled. "Shit . . ." Then he grinned again, a little-boy grin this time, and ran back to his friend.

Steve watched him go. He wanted to protest— there was, after all, a Negro astronaut in the Air Force Gemini program. He had a feeling that Leander would only laugh. He stepped into a phone booth in a filling station and called Mickey.

"I'll go back to the hotel if you want," he told her. "But . . ."

Her voice trembled the tiniest bit. "You've made up your mind."

"Yes, Mickey, I have." He took a deep breath. "I don't want to, really . . ."

"I know." She was fighting the tears. "It's just that you're trapped, and I know that's all it is, and it ought to help . . ."

"But it doesn't?" he prodded gently.

"I love you," she said suddenly. "When you've seen him, hurry back."

He signaled a cruising cab. Inside, he settled back into dingy grey cushions. The cab exuded the same frying grease smell that had sickened him all morning, but it bothered him no more. His heart was drumming wildly. He was no longer tired. "The White House," he said.

He was surprised at how firmly he said it.

PART TWO

The Second Week

1.

In Johannesburg, South Africa, a NASA down-range communicator awakened with a headache in an air-conditioned hotel room. It was well past noon and his phone was ringing. He was an aging bachelor who considered himself rather exciting in the Humphrey Bogart tradition; it went with his footloose life. He had been up late the night before on a bar tour of the city; he let the phone ring for a full minute before he picked it up. It was NASA in Houston. The chance of their calling on a Saturday was minuscule; for a crazy moment he wondered if he had slept the weekend away.

The voice, ebbing and flowing with distance, was very casual. It was Sy Larson, Apollo Assistant Operations Director, whom he thought of as politically adroit to have gotten the job, but technically incompetent. They had never spoken together on commercial long-distance but only on the air in Apollo network checks. They discussed a few minor communication work orders while the Johannesburg man fumed, waiting for a chance to ask why he had been disturbed on his day off. But before the chance came Larson said offhandedly: "We're starting Phase I of Pilgrim at 1400 hours Zulu." There was a short pause. "And let's see . . . Oh, I never got your acquisition times on Apollo Three. Well, Charlie, I guess that's all. Any questions?"

The communicator had a question. Pilgrim? Pilgrim? What the hell was Pilgrim? Through his sleepy fog he sensed that he should know the answer. Then he remembered a red top-secret manual in the recesses of his safe at the station: The Pilgrim Project. He had been called to Washington a year ago to pick it up, had been briefed swiftly with two dozen other incredulous communicators and a down-range Base Operations Manager. Outside of the BOM, he was the only man at Jo-burg Deep Space that knew anything about it. Long ago the two had decided that it was another headquarters pipe dream.

He was suddenly excited. He arose, still on the phone, and lunged for the cigarettes on the bureau. "No questions, Sy," he said, keeping the emotion from his voice, as Bogart would have. "No questions."

"Everything OK, then?"

"I've been Boered to death," he said, "but it looks as if things will liven up." He wished immediately that he had not said it, not hinted at Pilgrim's importance on the phone. It was topsecret; presumably overseas lines could be tapped. There was a brief silence. "Boered?" Sy Larson said without humor. "Yes. Well, go to it."

They hung up. The communicator found that his headache was gone.

In a cavernous, deserted hangar bay at Cape Kennedy an annoyed security guard looked up from a magazine he was not supposed to be reading on duty. Footsteps sounded across the vast concrete floor. He had already been disturbed from his science fiction once this morning by a bespectacled young engineer clutching a thick red manual. The young man had been wearing the necessary green badge so he had passed him into the precincts of the Chuck Wagon Project beyond the sliding door.

It was Saturday, the guard thought angrily, slamming the desk drawer on his magazine before this second visitor could spot it. He had been looking forward to eight undisturbed hours. Chuck Wagon should require no overtime engineers. It was, so far as he knew, only a program to prepare a supply capsule, or living shelter, or some such emergency lunar foxhole, to launch if Apollo astronauts were ever stranded. Not even the maintenance crews that worked on the shrouded capsules and boosters behind the closed doors had ever wanted admittance on a Saturday.

The second young man was in a flight suit, and familiar: Rick Lincoln, he knew, one of the astronauts on the last Apollo flight. He checked his pass just the same; if the astronauts had to upset things on a weekend, at least they could be shown that security was still in force. He passed him in politely enough, but with secret amusement.

He had heard that the Apollo flight had aborted unnecessarily. Crash Craig, the Mars-bound hero of the story he was reading, would never have panicked at an oxygen shortage. He was sliding the drawer open again when he heard other footsteps. Livid, he looked up. A half-dozen technicians from the maintenance crew were crossing the bay now, followed by some rather important and well-dressed project engineers.

It was Saturday, damn it! Nothing happened on the Cape on Saturday! He slammed the drawer shut again and glared at the first ID card, hoping that it might have expired.

Rick Lincoln moved slowly along one of the two Saturn boosters lying in the guarded bay, looking up at the vast white skin, at the enormous nozzles in which a man could stand erect, at the glittering hydraulic veins ready to be sutured to those of the second stage. It was a twin to the booster which had sent them into orbit a week ago, but here on its side under a roof it looked much bigger. He continued along the big Centaur second stages that would inject both Mercury and shelter capsule into lunar trajectory, past the Polaris braking rockets that were the only components standing erect, around a covered Mercury capsule, then to the shrouded cylinder that he assumed was the shelter.

A young engineer stood smiling at it in the vast emptiness of the hangar, his glasses glinting. He recognized Rick and seemed to need to talk to someone.

"I was a pretty small cog—I designed the heat exchanger in the living compartment here—but I kind of wanted to get here before the crowd. You know, to kind of think over the philosophy of the thing. Is it this important or isn't it?" His face turned anxious. "What do you think?"

"Frankly," muttered Rick Lincoln, "I think it's a lot of crap."

The engineer seemed shocked. "Do the rest of them feel that way?"

Rick shrugged. "Apparently not the colonel, anyway."

The young man, more soberly now, handed him a red booklet and began to unsnap the shrouds. Rick leafed through it, impressed despite his dislike for the whole project. It was a countdown manual combining Pilgrim and its Chuck Wagon supply launch. In it in miraculous detail—"Check fingernail scissors operable"—were a hundred pages devoted to shelter check-out, beginning with a subsection for the Environmental Control System. Leading the parade, ahead of simultaneous tests of the shelter recirculation fan and the urine-and-condensate evaporator, was encircled a test of the system that the young engineer had apparently fathered.

The young man seemed to have regained his fervor. He

glanced at his watch. "I'm not supposed to start for five minutes, but it might be the only time we're ahead of schedule from now on." He grinned and began to peel off the covers as if he were unveiling a painting in the Louvre. "Let me take you inside. It might change your mind."

Rick Lincoln shook his head. He found that he did not want to see the interior of the shelter at all, or inspect the modified Mercury, or watch the preliminary mating steps. Just because other men had turned the ridiculous dream into titanium and plastic and stainless steel, written a manual complete to a count of the astronaut's spare toothbrushes, it didn't strengthen the victim's chances. He had figured the odds without seeing the hardware. He was right and he didn't want his convictions shaken by gleaming valves and eager engineers who would watch the colonel safely from the ground.

He turned away. He did not know why he had come. Cindy had been peevish all the way to Houston yesterday because Steve and Mickey were mysteriously staying in Washington an extra day. Maybe it had been to get out of her range this morning that he had risen early, checked out one of the F-100s, and whisked down to the Cape; maybe he had felt the tug of some motivation he couldn't explain to himself. For an instant he thought he had the answer: a cocktail waitress at the Missileer Lounge who didn't work Saturdays; she was a beautifully constructed creature, nicely astronaut-oriented, who lived alone at Cocoa Beach. If he could sneak out to her apartment without some local gossip spotting him, the trip might not be wasted . . .

Men were pouring into the hangar now, swarming over the boosters—excited, enthusiastic men like the young engineer. He thought of his own probable job in Pilgrim: briefing the colonel on lunar terrain. His slides and maps were here at the Cape; it might not be a bad idea to spend the morning putting them in order. There was less than three weeks.

He decided to arrange the maps and then return like a

docile husband to Houston. Feeling strangely alone, he bucked the tide of men and left.

Steve Lawrence sat with his wife in the coach section of the noon Eastern flight to Houston as it soared away from Washington's Dulles Airport. He glanced out the window. Grey clouds whisked past the heaving wing. They whitened suddenly and the aircraft was climbing past snowy pinnacles, over glacial cloud valleys, shafted with golden sunlight.

When he was ten or eleven a former student of his father's had come to breakfast, a tanned marine lieutenant ferrying an ancient Stearman biplane somewhere for the wartime training command. The professor—what courage it must have taken—had shrugged after breakfast. "If you can risk a court-martial, Ace, I can risk my flesh and blood . . ." In a daze Steve found himself goggled and lost in a sheepskin flight jacket he could smell yet, bouncing down the Naval Air Station runway in the open rear cockpit of the glistening yellow plane, with the chill bay wind whipping his cheeks. In an incredible moment they were free of the earth, snarling over the fog-shrouded hills of Marin, with San Francisco sparkling across the bay. They crested massive cloud banks guarding the Golden Gate, sliced over pink-tinged canyons, banked through crags and peaks, "landed" on plains as endless as the Pacific below. Then they climbed and climbed toward the rising sun.

When they had returned Steve was very quiet. That night, on the porch clinging to the Berkeley hills, he had told his father of his new dream.

"Testing airplanes, Steve?" His father had always wanted him to study medicine or teach or go into research. Now he looked up at the stars. "Well, a chipmunk's nervous system or the laws of flight—maybe it's all the same. There's a frontier there just as much as there is in a lab." Obviously his father had been thinking only of faster, higher-flying aircraft, not, in those days, of space. Or perhaps, at that, he had seen further than Steve dreamed, for he had viewed history as the story of an intelligent animal's inevitable triumph in the search for truth. "The moon, someday, Steve! Within a hundred years, maybe. And then the planets, and I'll bet someday the other galaxies. Don't quote me to the Regents, but it's bound to come."

Steve wondered if he would have found Pilgrim an example of the hasty, wasteful experiments he hated or if he would have approved. He had died while Steve was a freshman at Cal. An old ache, a void Steve had thought somehow filled, opened suddenly. If only he could talk to his father now, see his quiet grin and expose the project to the clean, uncluttered mind.

He sighed and peered out the window. The picture clouds had turned to dirty scud below. There would be little scenery on the way to Houston; perhaps it was just as well: he could study without distraction. The weight of what he must absorb in the next few weeks was staggering. His excitement had sustained him all morning, but now it left him and he was grey and depressed. Before his mood turned darker, he opened the beautiful leather NASA dispatch case they had given him at headquarters. He liked the newness of it, but he hoped that if they were going to treat him as a sacrificial offering they did not try it in front of Mickey.

He drew out the thick red countdown manual. While icy rain rattled against the windows, he studied, visualizing the effort that must have greased the skids to the Cape. He could see engineers at McDonnell drawing boards in St. Louis sweating to cram a week's supply of oxygen and water into Mercury. He could imagine Polaris men at Lockheed's California plant grinding in secrecy at what must at first have seemed the impossible requirement of turning an underwater rocket into a moon brake. He could see NASA technicians in Mississippi wrestling with the problem of barging two mammoth boosters, noticeably modified, to Florida under wraps.

And what had been done in the last year was only the

beginning. He thought of what must be finished in the next three weeks: the erection and check-out of the supply capsule on the pad, then its tracking; the mating of his own components and his own launch; and all the while, until the very last moment, his own training. The more you knew, the more impossible it seemed that nothing had been forgotten, or would be, and yet all morning long they had been telling him that this was so.

He went back to the countdown manual. He had finished the first fifty pages and he had not yet made his appearance as the star. That was something to be grateful for, because he would be busy with the training outlined in the green manual still in the dispatch case. When he did enter, it was without fanfare: "T minus 71 hours: Pilot installed in capsule mock-up at Hangar S for the first launch communications drill." Steve smiled wryly. "Pilot installed . . ." To engineers a test pilot was a component. He went on: "Installation under supervision of back-up pilot." Steve groaned aloud and Mickey put her hand against his cheek. The back-up pilot would be the colonel, of course; Steve would have wanted no one else anyway. He would not really be a substitute, but a teacher. And he must have him as coach all through the next impossible weeks. They had offered to phone him from Washington, everyone had, from the President to the director. But Steve had shaken his head. He must tell him himself if their friendship was to sustain the shock. If the positions were reversed, the colonel would have told him.

He had no more desire to study. He sat despondently and looked down at the grey clouds.

She sat in the hateful, lurching cabin fighting tears. All day yesterday in Washington she had moved in a silly haze of hope like a child in a dentist's office, dreaming of things that were bound to happen to change it all. Yesterday some sense of the unreality of the project had cast a soft light upon it, as if she were watching an amateur theatrical production in which Steve had been cast as a joke.

But from the moment he had taken the horrid red manual from the shiny briefcase—now why after two years had they seen fit to give him a briefcase like that?—the reality of it all had burst upon her.

He never wasted his efforts. Therefore, the thing he was studying would come to pass. Therefore, she would see him hurled into space alone, therefore she would face a year of loneliness, a year or an eternity, therefore . . . Panic tore at her and she drew in her breath. He turned from the window.

"Mickey?"

She nodded, afraid to trust her voice.

"Are you all right?" he asked.

She plastered on a smile. "A little airsick, maybe."

"Dramamine," he decided, craning for the stewardess. She shook her head and took his hand. There was a cleatmark on his wrist from a high-school football injury. She found herself committing its shape to memory. She shuddered and leaned back, eyes closed, holding his hand and feigning sleep.

Maybe the Russian platform would fail. Maybe Pilgrim would fall behind schedule and they would cancel it and wait for Apollo. Maybe the colonel would convince the President that he should go after all.

By the time they landed at Houston, she had almost persuaded herself that he was safe.

2.

Steve stood in the afternoon sun at the end of his shaky pier. Gus Scarbo's little outboard was slapping a golden wake across the lake with Stevie on the foredeck. Steve motioned them in. As always, Gus cut the engine too soon and paddled to the landing. Steve lifted his son out. He always seemed after a visit with the Scarbos to have put on weight; traces of chocolate lay on his cheeks.

"He'd really prefer to live with us," Gus said, "wouldn't you, Tiger?"

Stevie nodded, definitely. "Your boat floats."

"Thank you." Gus winced. He shot a glance at Steve. "I thought it was because we shared the innocence of the uninformed."

"The colonel home?" Steve asked, to change the subject. He was; Gus gave them the boat to take and cast them off. He was smiling but his face still held the bitterness of the evening in the astronauts' office.

"Don't decide to cut *him* in," he warned, nodding at the boy. "There are no secrets between us."

Without knowing quite why, Steve dreaded the moment when Gus would be told. More violently than he intended, he yanked at the starter cable and pulled away from the pier.

The colonel sat at a desk by the window of his den. Before him lay the red countdown manual for Pilgrim; next to it lay the green training book. He was penciling notes. When he looked up, an oddly anxious expression crossed his face, but he smiled politely. He nodded at the stacks of publications on the desk. "If I stop to tie a shoelace in the next three weeks, I'll miss the launch."

He moved to his tiny liquor cabinet in the bookcase, took out a single glass. "Last night I took the vow," he said. Most of the astronauts began to abstain two or three weeks before a launch; the colonel seldom indulged anyway and normally stopped before anyone else.

"None for me," Steve said. The colonel raised his eyebrows, replaced the glass, went back to the desk. He leafed through the countdown manual. "If you ever forgot a can opener on a picnic you ought to read this."

"I've been looking at it," Steve said softly. His mouth was dry. The colonel put the countdown manual carefully in the center of his desk. He seemed to be studying its cover. After a long moment he looked up.

"Why?"

"Skipper?"

The colonel's grey eyes held his. "Yes?"

Steve took a deep breath. A frog croaked from the lake front; he heard Stevie croak back. An outboard droned distantly. "They want me to go. Instead."

The colonel's jaw twitched; otherwise he showed no sign of emotion. "Who does?"

"The President."

The sound of the outboard faded. The frog was silent. For

perhaps half a minute the room seemed suspended in a vacuum. Steve cleared his throat; he had been told to explain it carefully. "His reasons are—"

"I know the 'reasons,' " the colonel said harshly. "I get the paper." He straightened suddenly. "OK. He wants you to go. What about you?"

"I volunteered."

For just an instant the colonel's eyes closed. "Did he pressure you?" he asked softly.

Steve shook his head. "Of course not."

"Then what made it look safer? Why'd you change your mind?"

Steve, not truly knowing, shrugged. "He asked me. I thought it over. I volunteered. That's all."

" 'Mustn't send the colonel,' " the colonel murmured. " 'The Watusis and the Vietnamese'll think he's up there building an H-bomb. Send the civilian. The hell with his qualifications—' "

"Skipper, you're better qualified," Steve said miserably. "Everybody knows that."

"I am," the colonel agreed. "I am indeed. What *is* this? The goddamned Russians send a so-called geologist and all at once our goddamned image is more important than whether we make it or not? Bullshit!"

Steve didn't reply. The colonel shoved aside the two manuals.

"My country," he said between clenched teeth, "is turning schizo. It is run by adolescents who mistake shadow for substance, for children so busy with toys they don't care."

"I think," Steve said carefully, "the image is important."

The colonel regarded him speculatively. "Yeah," he said, "I guess you do." He moved to the window, looked out at the sunset. "The question is whether that would sustain you, come hell or high water. I want to go with every cell in my body." He turned back. "Do you?"

"As long as there's a fighting chance I'll get back," Steve

said evenly. "Isn't that enough? I do have a wife and kid."

The colonel didn't answer. He picked up the training manual, riffled through it. "What makes you think you can learn the capsule in three weeks?"

"I think I can. With your help."

The colonel stared at him. "With my help?"

Steve nodded. "Somebody has to do what the back-up pilot did for Mercury: I can't train alone. I want you to coach me."

The tiny muscle in the colonel's jaw was working again. His voice was strangled. "Jesus Christ, Steve! Have you got any idea what this meant to me? Do you know what I've given up for it? I could be a vice-president of Sperry-Rand right now, did you know that? I might have run for the Senate like Glenn! I could be sitting on my ass in Florida making a hundred thousand a year endorsing wrist watches and jock-straps!" He shook his head incredulously. "Help you? I could break your goddamned arm! I could see you drop dead and not make a move!"

Steve licked his lips. It was worse than he thought. "Believe me, Skipper, it wouldn't matter. They are not sending a military man. Period."

The colonel moved to the liquor cabinet, poured himself a drink. As an afterthought he offered a glass to Steve. This time Steve nodded. The colonel sipped his bourbon thoughtfully. "The commander knows the project. Use him for an instructor. For your own good. For the good of the mission."

"If you're thinking of the mission," Steve said, "think of me sitting in that paperweight at T minus ten seconds wondering if there's anything *you* had figured that the commander didn't, or that isn't in the book, or that I never thought of. Does that jeopardize the mission less? Or more?"

The colonel slammed his open palm on the countdown manual. "Well then, goddamn it, why send a substitute in the first place?"

"It was never up to me! If the mission means anything to you, you'll help!"

"If it means anything to you," grated the colonel, "you'll quit!"

"It wouldn't make any difference!" Steve cried. "There are four civilians on Apollo. They'd train one of the others!"

"Quit," the colonel said tightly. "Try them and see."

Steve looked into the steely eyes. He had never bucked the colonel before; he would have followed him to hell. With all his heart he wanted to surrender. And yet . . . he thought of the greying man behind Lincoln's desk, and he shook his head. "No, Skipper. I'm not quitting. As long as they want me to go, I'm going."

The colonel seemed years older. He tapped the training manual. "I was supposed to start lunar landings tomorrow at Edwards. Take the commander. Start with a clean slate. I'll coordinate communications, or anything else you decide. But I won't—I can't—hold your hand. Take the commander. OK?"

Steve swallowed. "That's it?" he asked tightly.

"That's it, Steve."

Steve passed through the house and down the lawn, cheeks flaming and throat tight. On the way back across the lake his son suddenly, impulsively, threw his arms around him and squeezed. He had not done so for years. The smell of his hair was a blend of lake mud and chocolate and baby sweat. Steve throttled back to prolong the trip.

3.

Gus Scarbo, kneeling in his pew, felt a trickle of sweat run down his neck. *"Hoc est enim Corpus meum,"* chanted the wilted priest in a Southeast Texan drawl. Ten minutes to go, Gus guessed, if he could ease Marion out before Last Prayers. He shifted uncomfortably. He had been trying to sustain himself with the thought of the early phone call. He would learn in half an hour, he assumed, whatever dark secret had been tearing his charges apart. The briefing would be in the astronauts' office and the office was air-conditioned.

But the promise of coolness to come only made him sweat faster. He glanced at a white-surpliced altar boy. The youth had mild edema, probably nephritis. Gus wondered how the bloated tissues tolerated the humidity. He had willed him through Masses before. He stiffened suddenly. *"Hoc est enim Corpus meum?"* A cue for the bell!

He had been an altar boy in a Louisiana parish almost

thirty years before. He had clung to a certain respect for churchly ritual through medical school, through Tarawa, even in the ash of Iwo Jima. And then one night in a carrier sick bay off Korea a charred young Jew named Skip Gold-berg had begged for help and Gus had cut himself secretly adrift not only from the forms of the church, but from its soul with the greatest sin of all. But now he sent thought waves crashing toward the anonymous, dull-eyed youngster at the altar. Bell rings thrice! Bell rings thrice, damn it!

Woodenly the child raised his hand and jingled the bell. Gus let out his breath audibly. Marion, kneeling next to him, glanced at him from beneath her silken kerchief. There was amusement on her face at his concern, and affection, but a shade of impatience, too, for it disquieted her to sense that only through such distractions could Gus last the Mass.

They had wanted a child. Marion was no zealot, but even now, at thirty-eight, her religion kept alive for her a glimmer of hope. For that Gus was thankful. He would never, never tell her of the night he had cast the church aside. My darling, he thought wryly, ask not for whom I hear the bell tinkle. I hear it tinkle for you.

Gus had no desk of his own in the astronauts' office. When he saw that only the new men seemed to have come to the briefing he slid into the colonel's seat in the first row next to Rick Lincoln.

"What's the story?" he asked Rick. "Do you guys know?"

Rick flicked a thumb at the rest. "They don't, I do. I came because I want to see what the rest of these jokers think. Why, I don't know."

Archy Gorman, Apollo Operations Director, stood at the front of the room. His red, full cheeks were damp with sweat. Gus had never liked him particularly, but now he felt almost sorry for him. Whatever he was about to say was disturbing him deeply. His washed-out blue eyes were veined with red.

He looked once at Sy Larson, as if for support, took a deep breath and began.

"This is going to be a hell of a shock to some of you," he said, looking straight at Gus. "But it involves a mission that has to be flown. So there's no use discussing anything but its technical aspects when we're through. No time to, either. Everybody here?"

His tone was too brisk. Gus recognized the voice as that of a briefing officer afraid of what he must say. He had listened to the same timbre in a Marine major off Saipan and known that it was he who must clean up the mess that would bloody the beach. He had heard it again in the words of an air-group commander in a carrier ready room, and guessed that a large portion of his practice would return with shredded skin and shattered bones, if it returned at all.

As Archy counted noses Gus glanced around. Steve wasn't there; presumably his private briefing the other night had sufficed. The other Apollo astronauts lounged in various degrees of attention. A few were still reading mail; one was taking advantage of the lull to skim through a *Space Digest*. At Archy's words, his eyes flicked up; when he saw that he still had a moment, he went back to the magazine.

You were more likely, Gus reflected, to find an unoccupied medical student during finals than an idle astronaut. On the never-ending commercial flights between conference and symposium and inspection, from Edwards in California to Langley in Virginia to the Florida Cape, you found that when your seat companion was an astronaut, his head was buried in a manual from take-off to landing.

They were ambitious men, highly motivated—even Rick Lincoln, who seemed to learn by osmosis and had time for the stewardesses on the planes. While teaching at the School of Aviation Medicine in Pensacola, Gus had helped select the group. They were not supermen. Their IQs averaged above 140, but there were higher norms in scientific fields. Their endurance under 135-degree heat or in a high-altitude chamber was remarkable, but so was that of a Chilean Indian. Their reactions on a flashing light "idiot box" were excellent, but baseball players had been clocked with faster ones. Their cardio-vascular systems were normal—even Deke Slayton's, he suspected, despite the heart murmur that had so panicked the Mercury program. As a matter of fact, the very normalcy of the astronauts was the only thing abnormal about them.

He had always liked the well-functioning man, in a carrier squadron or on a test base. Perhaps it was because his own coordination was so ridiculous—as a medical student he had hysterically suspected locomotor ataxia—or perhaps the attraction was some sort of latent homosexuality, or perhaps he was big brother now because he had been big brother as a child, herding his mother's brood because his father was too busy to help.

Or perhaps, although he was no older than the colonel, he had become the Great White Father because he felt the lack of a son. Whatever it was, he was proud that they called him the Thirty-first Astronaut; that they accepted him and trusted him. He was sure that hardly an aspirin stood in the medicine cabinet of any one of them that he had not prescribed.

He was feeling better. If the wheels had rewarded his dedication by not consulting him on whatever secret Archy was going to divulge, at least he was about to find out now. He shifted in his seat and listened.

"OK," Archy said coolly. "We are going to beat the Russians to the moon."

There was an instant of silence. Then somebody in the back of the room laughed explosively. The astronaut next to Rick looked disgusted. "Oh, for Christ's sake, Archy! What kind of crap is *that*? I got to give a paper in L.A. tomorrow and —"

"We are going to beat the Russians to the moon," Archy repeated stolidly. "This is how."

He turned to the blackboard and began to sketch.

Off Wonsan, after the night that Skip Goldberg had changed his life, Gus had been plagued for months with a nightmare. In it he stood high on a carrier's superstructure next to a hawk-faced flight officer and stared in horror down at the flight deck. "Commence launching operations!" Below them a crazy procession of planes— Corsairs, Skyraiders, clumsy Guardians—began to roar past the carrier island.

From the wings of every one, even the stubby fighters, hung a ridiculous load of bombs, torpedos, wing tanks, and rockets. In the cockpits, intent on take-off and oblivious to everything else, were pilots he knew, men with whom he had played bridge in the wardroom or drunk in the clubs of Tokyo or Sasebo. Milligan bounced by, impassive in an AD, then Catseye, Muller, Rocky Kane, Tiny McGeorge.

The flight officer would not face the wind—only a damn fool would, 1 e had always said, aping Mitscher. So he could not see what was happening as his conglomerate force cleared the foc'sle, but Gus could. He screamed at the Flight Officer over the roar of the engines below, into the gale blowing aft. His voice was drowned; he could hardly hear it himself. He pointed forward but the flight boss only grinned and nodded happily.

Then Gus—and it would happen the same way in every dream—would take a last desperate look at the carnage ahead. As each impossibly loaded plane would reach the forward edge of the flight deck, it would dip below the level of his vision; after an interminable period reappear again, fighting for altitude. Then it would spin into the sea of flame left by its predecessors. From horizon to horizon the ocean was a hell of blazing Av-gas. He could smell it—why couldn't the captain or the admiral? And with it was the other smell that you knew instantly was burning hair and roasting flesh.

Then he saw Skip Goldberg grin up at him, his huge frame crouched behind the enormous engine of his Corsair. He saw that Skip had the greatest load of all. Suddenly Gus was stumbling down the ladders past the 02 level, the 01 level, into the mad jumble of the flight deck. But Skip was gathering speed, unable to see beyond the ear-splitting engine. Gus would start toward the center of the deck, but always he would trip on a pad-eye and watch helplessly on hands and knees as Skip took off, clawed for altitude, spun slowly, and cartwheeled into the furnace ahead.

And yet, it was all a nightmare. He had not even seen them launch that day; he was below in sick bay preparing for the results. Now, moments after Archy began to describe Pilgrim, the impossible truth dawned on him. Gus felt the same helpless rage that he had known in his recurrent dream. He was watching from his hands and knees as blind authority consigned human life to the flames.

He found himself on his feet, realized that he had knocked the colonel's prized Mercury model from his desk.

"What the hell," he demanded, *"are you trying to tell us?"*

Archy's face reddened. His mouth opened once or twice like that of a landed fish, but when he recovered his voice was quite cool. "If you'll let me go on, Gus, you'll find out."

Gus pointed to the diagram Archy had started on the board. "You're *serious* about this?"

"You think I'd ask you here on a Sunday if we weren't?"

"When do you plan this act of heroism?"

"Three weeks. I'll cover scheduling later, if you'll give me a chance."

"Who's supposed to go?"

Archy picked up his chalk. "Please, Gus?"

Sy Larson moved from the side of the room, replaced the Mercury model Gus had knocked down. He smiled at Gus, but his eyes were narrowed. "We figured it might sort of stun you, Doctor," he said softly. "But don't sweat it. It's past the discussion stage."

"Like hell it is," Gus said. "Like *hell* it is." But he sat down to listen.

4.

Beyond the locker room window at the center's airstrip Steve heard a gas truck move to the F-100F which would whisk him to California.

He regarded himself in the mirror inside his locker. He was sure that he had not changed overnight. But more people knew every hour, as the President's decision rippled over NASA, and their attitudes had altered toward him. He had called Archy Gorman early this morning, demanded that Gus Scarbo be told about Pilgrim with the other astronauts. "After all he's done for us, it's a slap in the face to keep him out."

"Steve, you don't have to bother about things like this. You've got enough to worry about."

"I want him cut in."

"The other aeromedical people think he'll raise hell."

"But Archy," Steve said patiently, "*I* want it."

It was amazing how much leverage a test pilot had. "OK," Archy promised reluctantly. "New subject: what flight are you catching to California?" Steve had a demand there, too. "I'm not going commercial. I want one of the F-100s."

He had studied the training schedule and decided that he could save six or eight hours in the next three weeks if he was flown in one of the fighter-trainers the astronauts used to keep up their hours. They were faster and if his back-up pilot handled the controls, Steve could study better in the privacy of the rear cockpit than in a commercial plane.

Archie seemed shocked: "You're supposed to be packed in cotton, damn it. If anything happens—"

Archy was irritating him. "Archy," he said wearily, "ask the commander to set it up, would you? He'll fly it. I have to pack."

"All right."

Now in the locker room, with the plane ready outside, he took his hard hat from its hook. He heard someone enter the door behind him. He turned, expecting to see the commander's monkey grin. It was the colonel.

"Are *you* flying me out?" Steve murmured, almost afraid to ask.

The colonel's eyes were tired and his face was drawn. "It depends." He hesitated. "I acted like a horse's ass last night."

Steve shrugged. "When you feel the way you do, why hide it?" His throat tightened. "Gets you ulcers."

The colonel sat on a bench, staring at the floor. "I still feel that way."

"I see," Steve said quietly.

The colonel looked up. "But I'll back you up. I'll coach you, if you'll understand one thing."

"What's that?"

"If it seems to me your determination is cracking, I'll go to the top. I don't know if it would do any good or not. But I'd go right to the top."

Outside the gas truck rumbled back to its parking spot. From the weather office Steve heard the clack of a teletype. "Good," he said softly, "because if you didn't, I would."

The two passed through the Operations Building to the blazing heat of the airstrip. Stevie and Mickey stood in the shadow. When Mickey saw the colonel she took both his hands and squeezed them. "Thank you," she said.

"If I don't think things are working out right, Mickey," the colonel said grimly, "you may be thanking me again."

She looked after him as he started for the plane. "What's he mean?"

"He's still in shock," said Steve. "Forget it." He hugged Stevie and kissed her goodbye. He would not see them for four days and then only for another five before he left for Florida. He decided to take Mickey with him when he went to the Cape. Even if she spent nine-tenths of her time alone in a motel room, she would be happier there.

Climbing into the cockpit he turned to wave goodbye. With the colonel's eyes on him, he hesitated. The colonel would not have waved; once committed, his whole mind was on the next step. The hell with that, he thought. He lifted his hand, swung in and opened a thick grey manual on the modified Mercury capsule. Before the colonel was airborne he was into its third page.

Gus Scarbo sat in the astronauts' office in a deep silence; he had been quiet since his first explosion. He marveled, as Archy's briefing progressed, at the energy that must have poured into the Pilgrim Project in the last eighteen months. He forced back the anger at a scheme so callously planned at the risk of a human life—a life under his own care—and tried to estimate medically the man's probability of survival.

It was impossible to evaluate. It depended partly on the

man and Gus still had no idea who was going. For a Mercury capsule they would select a Mercury astronaut, of course. The faces of the Mercury men kept getting in the way: Shepard and Cooper and Grissom and Schirra. And the faces of their wives and sons and daughters, too.

It was impossible to be objective, but it made no difference. There was one certainty. The chance of a man surviving on the moon for a year was less than that of his surviving for a few hours. Pilgrim was riskier than Apollo and that was all that really mattered. In peacetime you always picked the safest way and there was nothing else to be said.

Archy finished. The men around Gus were very still. Someone was drumming a pencil. "Who's the frigging guinea pig?" somebody asked from the rear. "The colonel?"

Archy Gorman seemed discomfited. "He was." A cold certainty grasped Gus Scarbo. All at once he knew. Steve, he thought. Steve! "Who is it now?" he asked softly. "Who is it *now*, Gorman?"

Archie Gorman took a deep breath, squared up his papers. "Steve Lawrence."

Rick Lincoln tensed beside him. Gus slammed his palm on the desk, arose slowly. "I figured! On top of everything else you pick somebody who doesn't even know the capsule!"

"Not us," Sy Larson said. "The President."

"In the sweet name of Christ, *why*?"

"Civilian," Rick growled from the first row. "Right?"

"Yes," nodded Archy.

"Glad you told me," sighed Rick. "I was hurt."

"Now you know," Sy Larson smiled. "Now you know everything."

"Not everything," Rick Lincoln said quietly. "Like I don't know why we weren't told about this eighteen months ago. Why not, Daddy?"

"I'll tell you why *I* wasn't told," Gus lashed out. "I wasn't told because it's my job to see that nobody puts you guys in an environment your bodies can't take. That goes for an airplane, a centrifuge, a capsule, or a year on the surface of the moon. I wasn't told because every goddamned time they forget there's a man in the system the flight surgeon screams like a wounded eagle. I wasn't told because they're afraid of the noise!"

Sy Larson's voice was very soft and he was smiling, but his eyes glittered coldly. "There'll be no noise, Gus. There'll be no noise at all."

Gus looked at him with distaste. This man was no engineering assistant; he was suddenly radiating authority that Gus had not noticed before. "Larson," he grated, "I don't know exactly who you represent in this murder mystery—"

"Good. Let's not worry about it."

"As to my noise, don't lay any bets on it."

Larson's smile became even wider; his eyes were distant. "Gus, you're cut in. The bet on your silence is already laid."

"If this is a safe program," Gus demanded, "why keep it top secret? Are you afraid of the public?"

"It *stays* top secret," Sy said. "That's all. Until the shelter's launched it's top secret."

"I asked you," Rick prompted, "why in eighteen months the *rest* of us weren't cut in."

"Oh," Sy Larson smiled. "Well, you were poor security risks. You fly."

"Do you mean," Rick asked incredulously, "they were afraid we'd land in Communist territory?"

"Yes."

"Russia?" someone scoffed. "From an equatorial orbit?"

"No," Sy admitted. "But what about international waters, with a few Soviet ships around? Or Cuba? Or an abort into North Vietnam or the South China Sea?"

"Are you serious?" Gus asked. "Listen, assuming they

got one of these men, if they so much as questioned him, world opinion would—''

''*If* the world ever knew, Doctor.'' Sy Larson spoke directly to Gus now and he had lost his smile. ''Get this straight, once and for all. The Russians cannot imagine a country as strong as this sitting around while they take over the moon. In our place they'd move. They'd plan a one-way mission. They can't believe we haven't. They want to know if we have.''

''How do you know?'' Gus Scarbo demanded. ''What's your authority?''

''We know,'' Sy Larson said flatly, ''that we can't send a scientist to an international convention without some Russian engineer pumping him on the feasibility or booster strength or morals of a hypothetical one-way mission.'' He moved to the desk, leaned on it, spoke very intently: ''If they question our engineers in public, what do you think they'd have done to two or three real live American astronauts if some junk picked them up in the China Sea?''

Gus felt as if the room were growing smaller. Behind Archy and Sy Larson loomed a shadow of power Gus had never sensed before in peace. His country, which had always seemed so solicitous of the individual, was playing heads and tails with a life. And he was powerless, a dwarf at a table where the giants had all the cards. Not all the cards, he thought suddenly. In a tiny desert hospital he had rung down the curtain on an eager butcher and brought in a surgeon to save Mickey's life. That was his card. He felt better.

Archy Gorman was picking up his manuals and Sy Larson was carefully erasing the board.

''Where's the victim?'' Gus asked.

Sy Larson sighed. ''You mean Lawrence?''

Gus nodded.

''On his way to Edwards. With the colonel. Why?''

Gus had a sudden black thought. ''Larson?'' he barked.

Sy Larson's eraser stopped. He turned patiently. ''Yes?''

"What *about* the colonel?"

Larson tensed. "What about him?"

"He knew about this. But you guys let him make flights. He was in orbit over Communist territory. How come?"

Larson was silent. Gorman began suddenly to leaf through the countdown manual, his cheeks bright scarlet.

"Did you figure he had a strong tolerance for pain?" Gus pried. "Did you figure he was old enough to keep his mouth shut?"

"He wanted to continue with Apollo," Archy Gorman blurted, "in case Pilgrim never went. It was his own choice."

Gus gripped the top of the colonel's desk. His voice rose. "Was he supposed to drop dead from fright if the Communists got him?"

"Forget it!" growled Sy Larson.

"From fright? Or a needle?" Gus demanded. His voice shook. "A needle or a goddamned pill?" There was deathly silence in the room. Gus, shaking with anger, started for the door, knocked the Mercury paperweight off the desk again. Nobody smiled. He paused and looked in o Larson's eye. "You bastards, " he murmured. "You cold, crummy bastards!"

Then he slammed the door, stalked blindly down the corridor. He found himself standing in moist sunlight. From across Clear Lake came the bells of ten-o'clock Mass. Gus climbed in his car, fumbled with the key, found that his hands were trembling too violently. "Mother of God," he moaned. "Holy Mother of God!"

When his hands steadied he started the car and drove home.

The last astronaut had left the room and Archy's manuals were gathered. Sy Larson felt a compulsion to continue to erase a board already clean. He was worried and irritated.

"It's just too bad we had to cut him in," he observed. "That's all."

Before the briefing, when Archy had phoned him with Steve's request, Sy had awakened the Assistant CIA Director in Washington. "He wants the flight surgeon briefed."

The decision had been flattering, in a way: "Sy, the way you've been running this we could probably cut in Drew Pearson. The President says give Lawrence what he wants. If this is what he wants, go ahead. After all, the doctor's a naval officer, isn't he?"

Now Sy Larson wished that he had the verdict in writing. The Assistant Director was an honest man, but memories could grow distorted under pressure. He put down the eraser thoughtfully. He had reached a decision, but there was no reason to mention it to Archy. He decided to phone Washington again. It would do no harm to send down a team to keep an eye on Scarbo, naval officer or not.

5.

With relief the colonel spotted the enormous hangars shimmering distantly in the Mojave sun. For a few minutes he could concentrate on landing and forget the turmoil he had known all the way from Houston across the Black Mountains and the Colorado to the baking California desert. He dropped his landing gear.

At least, thank God, he had been undisturbed in his agony; his passenger had asked only one brief question on Mercury voltages and remarked once on the complexity of its hydraulic systems, but seemed otherwise lost in study.

He felt another surge of rebellion and tightened his shoulder straps viciously. It should be him studying in the rear cockpit. He knew Mercury better even than the others of the First Seven. There were over six miles of wire in the capsule and a thousand relays, switches, and valves; it was unthinkable to saddle a new man with the task of learning them.

He called the tower and banked the Super Sabre gently, lining up with the runway. He took cold delight in the reluctant response of the heavy fighter at slow speed and his own mastery of it. He felt a swift lurch, as the wing dropped on a desert thermal, caught it automatically. There was nothing wrong with his reflexes at forty-five, he thought, wondering if his age had colored the President's decision. He hoped Lawrence had noticed the recovery; glanced into the mirror on his canopy. The battered gold helmet was still bowed; Lawrence had not even perceived that they were landing.

With savage intensity he began to feel through the jouncing air for the runway, sensing the thermals in the pit of his stomach before the plane felt them, anticipating the bumps, groping for the earth with the wheels. When they touched, it was with a gentle *tchk, tchk* that failed to disturb a pencil lying on his knee pad.

In his mirror he glimpsed Lawrence looking around in surprise. "Jesus, Skipper . . . we down?"

The colonel nodded and turned off the runway to begin the long taxi to the line. As they rumbled along he opened the canopy to a furnace blast of desert air, the squawk of his brakes, and the scream of his engine. He noticed suddenly that the helmet in the rear was bowed again. He closed the canopy, throttled back for silence, and let the plane roll toward the hangars with the jet whispering softly at idle.

The modified monster in which Steve would practice lunar touch-down techniques stood miles across the burning Mojave from the hangars. Steve and the colonel, still in flight suits, sped toward it in a NASA bus full of the monster's technicians. Steve tried to continue studying, but the page blurred. He had absorbed all he could. He must pace himself more slowly in the days to come.

He put his grey Mercury manual back into the dispatch case. At least, he reflected, the control panel was burned into his brain. He closed his eyes and called off silently from left to right, top to bottom, the two dozen lights, fifty switches, twenty dials he would see when he crawled into the capsule atop the monster. The switches: Emergency Capsule Separation Control, Emergency Escape Rocket, Tower Separation Control. The lights: Jettison Tower, Separate Capsule, Retro Sequence. The dials: Roll, Pitch, Yaw, the Eight-Ball . . .

The Mercury panel he found cruder, less organized than that of Apollo. Yet it was reassuring, too, when you thought of all the flights that had tested it, the six men of the First Seven who had trusted the blinking eyes and the gleaming, helter-skelter switches, and survived.

He had seen the colonel's Mercury launch on TV; the last glance at his booster in the pre-dawn glare of searchlights, the insertion into a spacecraft not really large enough for the man. Incredibly, impossibly, in less than three weeks the man would be he.

Archy Gorman had reminded him that he must give the capsule a name. His mind toyed with the spectacular: Peace One? No, too much like Friendship Seven. He found suddenly that he had always disliked the Madison Avenue ring of that. Pilgrim was good enough.

He peered from the bus window. He knew Edwards Air Force Base well. He had almost killed himself here for Convair in the F-106B. In Apollo's LEM capsule, perched on the monster, he had made dozens of landings last year with the colonel on the wide, flat Lunar Landing Area near the hangars. But now he looked at the landscape, puzzled.

They were leaving the flat country behind, heading for the parched Kramer Mountains, where the ballistic missile engines which had once seemed so big hung immovably over canyons and arroyos for test firings. As the bus began to climb the foothills, Steve heard a Titan start with a roar, cut out sharply, then catch and squeeze the bus in a crescendo of sound. When the test stopped sharply in a few seconds the silence was eerie.

"Where we going, Kit Carson?" Steve asked the driver. "Death Valley?"

The driver smiled, pulled up beside a sentry box set in a tall wire fence. A wizened guard climbed aboard. He checked the identification of every occupant. When he got to Steve he said, in profound respect, "Yes, sir!" The country beyond the sentry post grew even rougher. Magazine illustrators always mistakenly portrayed the first moon landing in terrain like this. The lunar highland, as a matter of fact, did not differ from it essentially, but if you were going to touch down on a maria, the desert below was a better training area.

Better and far safer. He was beginning to wonder if he could handle the monster in this region. Last year he and the colonel had had no trouble hovering and landing. But the glassy-eyed LEM, designed for good pilot visibility, was easy to land. He began to doubt seriously that he could land on this terrain, imprisoned in a Mercury capsule with nothing but a periscope to see through.

"I didn't know there was anything flat enough up here," he said. He wished he had kept quiet; his voice sounded positively plaintive.

The colonel regarded him speculatively. He had been very quiet during the flight out. "No sweat," he said briefly. "You'll see."

They lurched around a last dusty curve and Steve lost some of his apprehension. Before them lay a bowl ringed by the red-rocked hills of the region. Bulldozers had gnawed ugly gashes into the slopes, but the central terrain was flat and at least a thousand yards in diameter. Three Quonsets baked like loaves in the desert sun. A few jeeps, a fire truck, an ambulance, and a hook-and-ladder were parked nearby. The monster towered by a gas truck at the center of the flat.

It was a giant tubular tripod with landing pads on its feet. It squatted over a rotund jet engine; the engine's enormous exhaust nozzle was directed straight down. The jet had a constant thrust sufficient to cancel out all but the gravity one would find on the moon. The Mercury capsule capped the structure like a fez.

Smaller jets, pointed downward, duplicated the liquid braking rockets on the real Pilgrim. Steve would control his descent by throttling and swiveling them, hovering or even rising by pressing a button on the control stick. In space, the same stick would adjust his attitude through the tiny peroxide nozzles Mercury had always had on its skin. The monster could climb to 5,000 feet.

The reason that it had been hidden here was simple, of course. It was easy enough to pass off the Mercury training devices in Houston as sentimental relics, but this structure could exist for one purpose only: to train a man to land a Mercury on the moon. A dull ten-year-old would have gazed on it and understood Pilgrim, but hidden in this guarded, uninhabited hell the monster was safe. Even the sound of its jet could be explained as that of a test rocket. With LEM atop it last year, it had looked like a science-fiction bug with a bulging eye. With Mercury, it looked like a pot-bellied Turk with long legs.

The bus drove directly to it. Steve and the colonel waited while three technicians mounted the hook-and-ladder to unlatch the hatch. Steve found that his hands were cold in the blazing heat. He avoided the colonel's eyes, gazing up at the structure with what he hoped was a confident smile, until finally he was swinging up the ladder after him. When he reached the capsule he paused for a moment, looking through the open hatch.

It had been over a year since he had sneaked into the Mercury on display outside the Space Museum at Clear Lake. He had forgotten how tiny it was, how jumbled and coffin-like. He had a moment of panic. The colonel slid in to demonstrate. In three motions he had eased himself into the nylon couch.

"In a pressure suit," he pointed out, "it's something else.

But without one, it's easy: left hand on the hatch, left foot through, swing your butt, and ease down. Got it?''

Steve helped the colonel out and squeezed in himself, finally lay panting on his back inside. He felt a flash of fear. He could not stand three days in this—six days if he aborted —nobody could! But Gordo Cooper had spent a day and a half in this space, the size of a phone booth; Al Shepard would later have orbited for three days in it had it not been for a decision—could it have tied in with the birth of Pilgrim?— to cancel Mercury. The capsule was very, very tight, but he reminded himself that he had after all flown planes with hardly more room in the cockpits, and in a while the terror left and he studied the problem.

He was facing straight up; through the tiny window he could see only a slice of blue desert sky. He glanced through the periscope between his legs. Below, oddly distorted, he could see the metal hats of the technicians. He looked up. The colonel was silhouetted in the hatch against the blazing sun. His face was shadowed, but Steve knew that he was probing for a sign of weakness, so he began to check his familiarity with the Mercury panel. He asked the colonel to run through the starting procedure for the jet engines. Steve echoed them, pulled a communication check with the jeep on the ground, repeated the starting procedures to the colonel again.

The colonel nodded: ''You'll find hovering at ten, fifteen feet is so easy you won't want to climb. But by this afternoon, you'd better be pushing her up to one, two thousand feet, or you'll never get off the dime.''

Steve yawned nervously. The panic was returning; he had never been more unsure of himself in an airborne device; he was hemmed in, blind, restricted. Below him, dormant but waiting, slopped enough jet fuel to lift him bodily a mile into the air. He shifted his shoulders, mustered a smile. ''Are you sure you learned to land this thing?'' he asked.

''You want to trade?'' the colonel offered unsmilingly.

"Have them close the hatch," Steve said coldly. The hatch slammed. He waited for the colonel to climb down, flicked a switch, watched through the periscope as a technician below yanked the umbilical cord to the monster and trotted to a radio in his jeep. The man had reported the area clear by the time Steve really felt the pulse of the jet.

Dust swirled beneath the periscope. When he felt his vehicle lighten and sway, he fed cautious power to his rockets. With an eye on his radar altimeter, he hovered for a few seconds at ten feet. Then, thinking of the colonel's words, he gathered his courage and pressed his rocket button firmly. The monster responded much more swiftly with the lighter Mercury than it had with the LEM a year before. In two minutes he was hovering at a thousand feet.

Below him the landing area, the jeep, and the hangars rotated slowly. He used pressure on his stick. He heard a low hum as the engines swiveled; the rotation stopped. He braced himself and began to ease the monster down. From a thousand feet he sank slowly toward the red-brown sand. He stopped at ten feet, then settled softly until he felt the toes of the tripod drop with a bump in the minor cyclone below.

By late afternoon he was wringing wet, but he had made seven touch-downs. Tomorrow he would simulate landings without his automatic stabilization system, teetering in the air like a high-wire artist with trouble in his middle ear. And the third day he would try approaches from over the hideous mountains to test his ability to change landing sites.

When he climbed down the ladder he was weak. A technician pounded him madly on the back; another cut loose with a Rebel yell. They were all grinning broadly with a great and secret joy. The capsule had been warm, but the desert heat was a hammer blow. Steve's knees suddenly buckled. He sat on the running board of the jeep. In the scorching sunset the colonel's face was ruddy. He searched Steve's face. "Can you keep it up?"

Steve thought of tomorrow and the next day and the next,

trapped in this capsule and the other trainers. He had a moment of despair, but he fought it off. "I don't see why not," he said.

Steve and the colonel dined in the officers' mess. It was a cool and lovely place; Steve had always enjoyed the food. But tonight he found himself so tired that he could hardly finish his steak. When they crossed to the BOQ in the desert night the stars had the pristine quality of bodies observed from orbital flight. They paused, staring up at them, and Steve felt for a moment the comradeship they had known before.

"Nice," he offered. Somehow it broke the fragile moment, for the colonel only nodded, stopped in the lobby to report their progress to Houston. Steve went alone to the room they would share. He sat on the bed, so tired he could hardly undress, until he decided that if the colonel found him sacked out in his clothes it would look as if he was cracking already. He was tugging at his sock when there was a light tap at the door.

"Gus!" Gus Scarbo shambled in. His cheeks were scribed with the trace of an oxygen mask worn too tightly, seamed with lines of fatigue as well. "What the hell are you doing here?"

"Rick flew me out."

"Why?"

"I want to save your frigging life."

"Not tonight," Steve said firmly. "I've got to get some sleep."

Gus ignored him completely. He sat on the typical BOQ rattan-and-plastic easy chair, lifted his feet to the chrome-and-plastic footstool, began to light his pipe. Steve looked at him curiously. Gus was overly calm; it meant that he was holding some explosive force within him.

"This Pilgrim thing," Gus began. "You ever read a novel called *Catch 22*?"

Steve had not had time for anything but technical publications for years. "No. I told you, Gus, there's no use going over it. I volunteered and that's it."

"*Catch 22* is a crazy book," Gus said imperturbably, "about a crazy war. By the time you're through with it you've got vertigo."

"Yes?"

"It's about the ETO, but it reminds you of the South Pacific—no, you weren't there. Of Korea. Bigger than life. Everything's jumbled. Everybody's nuts, because the whole idea of war is nuts to start with."

Steve had reasoned similarly and left the Navy. But Korea, at least, had been necessary and none of their own doing. Two of their shipmates had crashed in the Wonsan hills. And Skip Goldberg had died, tight-lipped, in Gus's sick bay. "I don't know what that has to do with this project," Steve observed tersely. "But do you really figure Catseye and Muller were sacrificed for the fun of it? Or Skip?"

Gus Scarbo flinched. Steve had mentioned Skip Goldberg once before to him and seen the same flash of agony cross his face. "To the sacrificees," Gus pointed out, not nearly as calmly, "it doesn't matter, does it? Heroics stop at the grave."

"You're a Navy doctor. If you feel this way why aren't you practicing in Louisiana or doing cancer research or something?"

Gus tamped down the tobacco in his pipe. His hand was shaking. "Because," he said slowly, "man is going into space. I have as much regard for the health of a Naval aviator or an astronaut as for a New Orleans prostitute or a bus driver. A life is a life. Each one is equally and supremely important to the one doing the living."

Steve regarded him. He was perhaps his best and oldest friend; he had never seen him so moved. "That's not the whole story, though, Gus. Is it?"

"I didn't boondoggle this trip to discuss my motivations,"

he said. "I'm interested in stopping this thing, period. And I will."

"Gus," Steve said, "I'm going to do it. I said I would. It's too late to scrub myself now."

"You're only one day into it! If you guys, all of you, stood together and refused to consider this thing—"

"It's underway, Gus! There is no way out! Can't you get that straight?"

"What about Mickey?"

Across the desert the engine caught and roared. From somewhere in the BOQ sounded a raucous laugh, then the clicking of high heels. Someone had captured an Air Force wife or a Lockheed secretary, Steve reflected. Once BOQ life had been normal to him. Now when he found himself in its crazy clutches he had a feeling of unreality. "Mickey," Steve said tersely, "helped me decide."

Gus Scarbo inspected the glowing bowl of his pipe. His high cheekbones, black eyes, and tanned skin gave him the look of an Indian chieftain trying diplomacy before some last, fanatic attack. "It wasn't far from here."

Steve knew that he meant the accident, suddenly saw the tiny desert operating room to which they had wheeled Mickey after the X rays. He remembered Gus staring in horror at a dried-up desert doctor while the old man described what he intended to do.

"No, Doctor," Gus had exploded in front of nurses, patient, and Steve. "Not on your frigging life. Try *that* on the next one they bring in." And he had commandeered the ambulance, and two hours later Mickey was under a skilled knife in a Los Angeles operating room.

"You told me that night," Gus said now, "that if she lived you'd never let her out of your sight again."

"That was a different Mickey," Steve grated. "Now, forget it! She's solid as a rock."

"You are her rock, you stupid bastard," Gus said. "When you don't come back—"

"You don't know as much about this as *she* does," Steve snarled, his fatigue dissolving in a wave of anger. "I *am* coming back."

Gus Scarbo smiled sardonically and hiked his chair closer. "Let me tell you something, my friend. Not about the hardware. About *you*. Let me tell you the facts of life."

6.

Somewhere during Gus Scarbo's low-voiced, drumming lecture the colonel and Rick Lincoln came to the room. The colonel lay on his bed impassively. Rick, in fine detachment, sat leafing through a battered paperback he found on the desk. Gus poked holes in Pilgrim while Steve, listless with fatigue, tried to plug them. "Look, Gus, we're starting again tomorrow at damn near dawn, and—"

Gus Scarbo held his eyes. "Do you owe me a listen or not? As I say, you're sucking off a one-gas system. You've been weightless en route for three days, breathing pure oxygen before you enter the lunar braking phase. Suddenly you're pulling g's. You know what that can do."

"I know what it's supposed to do," Steve admitted. "But pure oxygen has never affected *my* g tolerance. And I've had two missions in Apollo."

"You can move around in Apollo. That helps. You're tied to a cross in Mercury."

"It didn't hurt Gordo Cooper," Steve protested irritably. "He only went thirty-six hours."

Steve had once pulled 18 g's on the "wheel," the giant 50-foot centrifuge in the Flight-Acceleration Facility at Houston. He reminded Gus, who shook his head.

"Your tolerance can vary. It can fail you. Look, there are three men in Apollo. Even when it goes for the moon, it doesn't matter if one of them blacks out a little. Even when it kicks LEM loose, there are two of them aboard to land it. But you—" Gus pointed his pipestem like a gun—"you're supposed to land alone!"

Steve looked vainly toward the colonel for help, protested weakly; "Nobody's proved pure oxygen or weightlessness lowers g tolerance."

"Nobody's proved a year of pure oxygen won't give you pneumonia, either," Gus said. "But lots of us think it might."

"Gus, those are calculated, considered risks."

"Calculated risks," Gus Scarbo smiled. "Considered risks . . . You know, it always amazed me in the Pacific how people who considered risks never seemed to be around to consider the remains of the people who took them." He drew a paper from the knee pocket of his old-fashioned Navy flight suit. "On the way out here *I* did a little risk considering. Would you like to hear some of the 'risks' I considered?"

Not one of Gus's arguments had been dishonest. Three days ago Steve would have been on his side. But now that he was committed he could show no sign of weakness, especially before the colonel. The shadowy NASA experts who had briefed him before he left Washington were no match for Gus's fervor, but the time for talking was past. "Gus," said Steve, "I'm pooped. Can it keep until breakfast?"

"Unless I convince you," Gus said, "I will be far, far from here by breakfast. It's now or never."

"Never's OK, Gus," Steve murmured. "My mind's made up."

Gus stared into the bowl of his pipe. Finally he looked up. "Even if I think these are not risks?" he begged. "If I think they're close to certainties?"

Rick put down his paperback. Even the colonel glanced at the doctor. Steve swallowed. "Shoot."

"All right. You're walking around in 200-degree sunlight and minus 200-degree shade. Suppose the air conditioning in your biopak fails?"

"Suppose it fails for the first guy that steps out of LEM? Are you against Apollo too?"

"Of course not. But if *he* starts to roast or if *he* starts to freeze, there's somebody sitting in the lander to go help him. If the visual contrast screws up his depth perception and he falls flat on his face, his partner can haul him back to the capsule. You, my friend, are a quarter of a million miles and a year from help!"

"My biopak's no more likely to fail there than next week in the chamber. And I don't believe this crap about contrast and depth perception. I'll adapt."

"I'm glad." Gus relit his pipe. "OK. Let's discuss micrometeorite penetration . . ." He had done homework. Steve could expect a micrometeorite to penetrate his pressure suit once every twenty-five days he remained outside the shelter.

"I expect to be in the shelter within eight hours, though!" It was a fallacious, stupid comment, but he excused it by his fatigue. God, if Gus would just let him go to bed.

"Steve," Gus chided him. "You know the Game theory better than that. This can happen the first minute you get out of the Mercury, or while you're looking for the shelter, or some time you're out gazing at the view. You don't have to wait twenty-five days for it."

Steve pointed out that, conversely, he might not be hit in fifty days, or the whole year. He reminded Gus that, at any rate, the sealant in the suit was supposed to plug the hole until he could reach his shelter.

"That's an interesting theory," Gus said. "I wonder how it feels to be hit by a dust-sized particle that's traveling 7,000 miles an hour?"

"It probably stings," Steve said briefly. "But that's life."

"I wonder what the complications are," Rick broke in, "assuming the pressure suit *does* seal up and you're happily on your way back to the shelter if, say, this speck of dust is lodged in your left testicle?"

"Thank you, Rick," Steve grunted. "You're a sweet guy. I'll try to stay out of the rain."

"In the shelter?" Rick prodded.

"In the shelter."

"That's interesting, too," Rick observed. "You know statistically how long you can expect a shelter that size to sit on the moon before a meteorite big enough to penetrate it hits it? And lets out all your air—whoosh?"

Steve shook his head.

"About nine months," Rick smiled. "Just about nine months."

"If it's hit it'll hold pressure until I repair it," Steve said. "It's got an emergency pressure valve that pops and—"

"Sure," said Rick. "There you are, playing grab-ass with moon fairies in your shirt-sleeve environment and a pebble going a couple of thousand knots bounces off your head. Then you repair the shelter? Or is *this* a calculated risk?"

"You guys are forgetting," Steve pointed out. "I'm burying the shelter."

Gus Scarbo nodded. "In six feet of 'lunar rubble,' right? In the trench it scoops out hovering with its own rockets?"

"That's right."

"Thus," Gus said sweetly, "affording you protection from radiation as well. Right?"

"Affirm," Steve sighed. He trapped a yawn in his throat.

"I wonder," Gus speculated evilly, "what the actual consistency of 'lunar rubble' is? I've heard everything from cotton candy to volcanic rock."

"Keep up," Steve suggested. "It's dust over basaltic rock, from the Surveyor data. And it's six times as easy to lift as it would be on earth."

"We *think!* We *think*," Gus's voice rose. "But suppose the dust never settles, because there's no atmosphere to slow it down?"

"It'll settle eventually," Steve said. "You've been reading the wrong books."

"Have I?" Gus was on his feet. "Or have these bastards in Washington—the calculators of risks? Have they calculated what happens when a solar flare hits while you're burying this capsule and gives you a real quick dose of radiation? Around 4,000 rem, for instance?"

For the first time the colonel stirred. He stretched with feline grace. Across the desert the jet started again, warbled, and cut out sharply. The chase down the hall was terminating next door in earnest male entreaty and reluctant female assent. "He stands there and cooks," the colonel said mildly. "That's what happens, Gus. He cooks."

"Yes," Gus agreed. His eyes were distant. "His life is actually more important to him than the moon, the sun, and the universe, but we have decided to let him stand there and cook."

The colonel shrugged. "If *he* hadn't volunteered, I'd have made them let me go. And you wouldn't be able to talk me out of it either."

"You have a very well-developed death wish," Gus remarked. "I don't think Steve has."

"According to Freud, everybody has," the colonel said.

Gus looked at him coolly. "Maybe. Sometimes, when pain's unbearable, you're sure everybody does, because—more often than the layman thinks—the patient begs for death." Gus began to tap out his pipe. "But there was a boy once . . . Well, a risk was calculated for him and 80 percent of his body was burned because he was forced to attack a fortified valley in a tired F-4U and they knocked out his supercharger. And when he got back to the carrier . . .''

Goldberg, Steve knew suddenly—Skip Goldberg, with his giant frame, gold front tooth, vibrant, unrestrained laughter or rage; his hellish liberties in Pearl or Yokosuka or Tokyo. ''Skippy-san'' to the laughing geishas. And behind it all, a brilliant, probing mind, and a joyous love of life.

''This kid—Steve knew him—was entitled to use his death wish, if he had one. He was certainly in agony. He was certainly going to die anyway. But he hung on and on and on. Until—'' Gus dropped his pipe. He leaned over to pick it up. ''Well, anyway, as far as I know, it's the only life he ever had. So, when I find a healthy death wish in a healthy individual, I wonder.''

The colonel's eyes were chilling. But he said softly enough: ''Death wish or not, Doctor, I want to go. I'd give my right arm to go. I guess I would give my life to go.''

Gus Scarbo stood up. He glanced at his watch. Then he smiled into the colonel's grey eyes—a smile of lonely, bitter anguish. ''Don't sweat it, Colonel.'' He followed Rick to the door, paused. ''If they *never* let you go, you've still got your needle.''

There was dead silence. The colonel was a frozen statue. When he spoke it was so quietly that Steve could hardly make out the words. ''Get out of this, Gus,'' he said. ''Stay out.''

Gus regarded him impassively. He turned to Steve. ''I'm going back to Clear Lake.''

Steve's heart began to thump. ''Yes?''

''I'm going to talk to Mickey.''

Steve found himself on his feet. ''So help me, Gus, if you do, I'll break your neck!''

''She's as much my patient as you are.''

Steve swallowed. ''I'll break your goddamned neck!''

"All right," said Gus, "but she's an alcoholic. She needs your help, and you're not going to break her heart."

The door closed quietly behind him. Steve stepped toward it, changed his mind. Wearily he moved back to the bed, began to take off his shoes.

The colonel was staring after Gus. "Is she?" he murmured. "Mickey? I don't believe it."

"No," said Steve softly. "No. She is not."

7.

Sy Larson felt a hand on his shoulder. He had been sitting at Archy's console in the Integrated Mission Control Center since noon. He was checking communications for Archy as the giant tracking network, so recently involved in Apollo Three, flexed its muscles for Pilgrim.

Sy hated the console. He was a lawyer by training and had been an FBI agent. Although he had learned a great deal about circuitry and communications during a two-year Air Force sentence as a navigator, he despised the endless checks of flight testing. Well, he had only to maintain his cover as a working engineer for the next fifteen days—no, fourteen—until the shelter capsule was launched and the story broke. And there was a certain idle satisfaction in knowing that he had the brains to help the program in this small technical way.

He turned, took the message, and handed his earphones to

Archy Gorman, deep in a call to Australia. He moved to a phone in a booth set between two giant bays of clicking relays at the back of the amphitheater.

The voice on the other end was a lighthearted CIA agent well thought of in Washington. "This is Clem Cummings, Sy."

"Yes?"

"I found Scarbo. You know where he'd been?"

Sy hated rhetorical questions. They had been looking for Scarbo for twenty-four hours. Mrs. Scarbo herself hadn't known, or wouldn't say, where he was; how would he know where he had been? But Cummings was well-connected and Sy hid his irritation. "Where, Clem?" he asked, politely enough.

"Edwards. He boondoggled a hop with one of the astronauts."

"Where is he now?"

"At the Lawrence place, with Mrs. Lawrence. You suppose when these guys are in orbit old sawbones gets a little of that stuff?"

"I don't know, Clem. You might ask."

He hung up and returned to the hated console. Now that Gus Scarbo was safely pinpointed, he felt better.

Gus Scarbo sat on a beach towel with Mickey Lawrence on the lawn sloping to Steve's pier. Stevie wallowed in lake mud as he began another frantic three-minute attempt to bail out the sunken rowboat.

"So," Mickey went on, "if Steve buys the program, it's because he decided that he'll come back. He promised me. So it doesn't bother me any more than the F-106 did, or Apollo. Besides, if *you* hadn't thought I was strong enough for this sort of thing, we wouldn't be here."

She was right. Steve would never have been selected as an astronaut if the board had known of Mickey's history; wives were screened as carefully as the candidates. He himself had steered the board away from the truth because he knew how much selection meant to Steve. But he had never guessed that a sober, conservative program like Apollo could lead to a suicidal fiasco that was bound to kill her husband and shatter her to bits. She was on her back in a bathing suit, her eyes hidden behind large, dark glasses. He wished that he could see them.

"It *doesn't* bother you, Mickey?" he asked carefully. "I see . . ." He must find the courage to tell her what he thought. But the words must be right. He would have to use a scalpel, not a butcher knife, for she must be very precariously balanced behind the healthy housewife-at-the supermarket façade. He wondered if she was a cured alcoholic? No such thing, he had always said. He could not tell if she was looking at him from behind her sunglasses. He glanced at the abdominal scar just showing above her trunks. It was white against the tan of her skin. If there were adhesions, they did not show. If there were psychic adhesions, they did not show either.

"Pretty good result?" she smiled.

Gus blushed and nodded. "Very good."

"A small price to pay," she murmured, "for a cure. One small red sports car, fully covered; one medical bill, likewise covered by the Convair family plan; one three-inch scar."

"Uncovered," observed Gus.

"To remind me I can't ever drink again," she told him. Suddenly she removed her glasses and at last he was looking into the dark green eyes. "Why'd you go to Edwards?" she demanded. "To see Steve?"

All he had to do now was to tell her the risks, the real risks, and even if she were as strong as the colonel's wife, she would fold. And Steve would drop from the hysterical plan. His tongue felt thick. He could not lie, so he nodded.

"Why, Gus? To try to talk him out of this?"

Across the lake they heard an outboard whine. He wondered if it belonged to one of the astronauts, marveled that any of them could play at a time like this. "We discussed it," he admitted.

She sat up, looking out at the lake. "And . . . ?"

Gus shrugged. "He wants to go."

"Is it safe, Gus? As safe as he thinks?"

He listened for the tiniest rise in tone, the faintest constriction of voice muscles that would mean hidden, restrained hysteria. He could hear none. The voice was calm and quiet, just as it had been before. He could not bring himself to test it and he could not pass on to her the problem of stopping Steve. There were other roads to take, more perilous, but just as sure. He arose. His knees creaked. He was forty-four. All week long he had felt sixty. "As safe as he thinks?" he shrugged. "Well, I knew a New Orleans banker who wouldn't ride in a taxi. A produce truck killed him crossing Bourbon Street. He wasn't as safe as he thought."

She looked up at him unsmilingly. "That's a pretty crummy answer, Gus."

He nodded. "It's a pretty crummy question."

He rumpled her hair and went home. Crossing his lawn he glanced at a man reading his electric meter, who smiled cheerfully. "Been cutting down on your air conditioning?"

"Not deliberately."

"Reading's lower . . ."

Twenty minutes later Sy Larson learned that Gus had called Eastern Airlines for an evening reservation to Washington, that the agent with Cummings had had to compromise himself but that Cummings would take up the actual surveillance. Sy blessed modern electronics and Clem Cummings, and effectively blotted Gus Scarbo from an inevitably growing list of security problems.

8.

The NASA car stopped outside the enormous Space Environmental Building at Clear Lake. Steve, in the back seat, studied Mickey.

He had phoned her from Edwards. When the colonel had touched down at the long, single airstrip at the Manned Spacecraft Center she had been there to meet him. With some anxiety he learned that she had seen Gus, but the doctor, thank God, had apparently lost courage, for she seemed as steady as when he had left for Edwards. He tried to bolster her further by telling her of the landings he had made, of how well the tiny capsule had responded: "No brain of its own, Mickey, but it's very literal; it does exactly what you tell it. And it's built like a Swiss watch!"

Instead of relief he caught fear on her face. "You've changed about it. You're getting more like the colonel was."

"No!" he protested. "The colonel would go for broke, no matter what. If things looked bad, I'd back away."

"OK," she said softly. "OK, Steve . . ."

He watched, vaguely worried about her, as the driver pulled away from the curb. Then he entered the cavernous building. He looked up at the monolithic stainless-steel test tube that contained his tiny lunar world. It was a domed cylinder, high as a ten-story building, with a circular hatch 40 feet in diameter. The outside of the chamber was studded with glass ports like crystals set in the walls of a mosque. Giant carbon arcs were being swung into place outside them, arcs which would simulate on him and his shelter the glare and radiant heat of the sun through an airless void. A year ago they had hoisted a lunar lander inside, and he and the colonel had spent twenty-four hours entombed with it.

He glanced at his watch. It was ten minutes before the chamber would be sealed and the pumps would begin to gulp up the air inside. He climbed a hundred feet up a steel stairway and entered the chamber through an open air lock. He stepped to an observation balcony set halfway up the black walls, walls nitrogen-cooled to simulate the infinite capacity of outer space to absorb warmth and light. Far below, dwarfed by the chamber itself, stood his shelter. It looked like a beer can. It stood erect. His first task would be to check his ability in a pressure suit to lower it to the prone position in which he would live in it. Technicians were swarming over it; a bulldozer was crawling across the chamber floor, spreading black, volcanic rock around it. The voices of the workers echoed eerily through the vault.

Steve looked away from the tiny shelter. Across the chamber the slim, greying Environmental Facility Director leaned on the balcony rail. When he saw Steve he smiled wryly, waved, and shook his head. *Not me*, his expression read. *Not on your life*. The environment below, in half an hour, would be as dangerous as the moon's. There was a team of medics standing by, there was an emergency repressurization system, there was every safety device that could be designed. But it would all be too late and everyone knew it. If his suit burst or his shelter failed, he would be as dead here in seconds as he would be in the lunar void.

The director's head-shaking irritated him, but he forced a greeting. It echoed falsely across the chamber. The director glanced at his watch and picked up a microphone. "All personnel evacuate Chamber A. Seal main and auxiliary hatches and air locks. Energize main pumps." Red lights began to flash and a muted bell began to gong.

Steve turned and descended to don his pressure suit.

He sat in his pressure suit on a bench in the dark green air lock outside the chamber. When the gauge he was watching matched the almost perfect vacuum within the chamber, he got up clumsily. He knew that when he opened the inside hatch the glare of the solar arcs would blind him if he did not protect his eyes. He reached up to drop the dark filter over his face plate, but found himself suddenly reluctant to cut himself off. Last year the colonel had been with him; now he was alone. He tipped his head solemnly to the thick glass port through which the colonel and the Facility Director peered. On the real lunar surface there was a predictable danger that he might be out of radio contact even when he reached his shelter capsule, so they had decided to stage the same isolation here. He would be watched continuously for the next seventy-two hours, but, barring emergency, would have no communication with the world outside his hostile vault. He moved his shoulders under his biopak, pulled down the dark filter, spun the wheel on the air-lock hatch, and stepped onto the moon.

The chamber was 65 feet across. In the middle his shelter squatted over a hole in the rubble like the depression that its braking rockets would make on the lunar surface. His spirits dropped; the shelter looked as small here as it had from the balcony. It stood vertically on its landing tripod now, but it was still a cylinder only 12 feet long from the base to the beacon flashing on top. It seemed completely unlivable; he was sure that when he had it prone it would look no better. Between him and the shelter lay the worst terrain that the basaltic regions of northern Oregon could provide. He knew that the rocks were deceptive, had been laboriously drilled out to make them lighter, but the task of burying the tank nevertheless seemed almost too much to contemplate.

From a traveling crane high in the chamber structure dangled a sling supported by two huge springs. He reached up, drew it down, and snapped it to rings which had been added temporarily to his suit. Now five-sixths of his weight was supported by the line—a rough approximation of the result of lunar gravity. He found that already his breath was coming hard. He had a panicky moment of vertigo under the partial support of the line. Then he oriented himself in the glaring, black-and-white chamber and began to shuffle toward the dazzling cylinder, fighting for traction under the annoying sling.

When he got to the shelter he pressed a red panel on the stainless-steel bottom. A lightweight entrenching tool, very strong and wide, dropped out. It was made of magnesium alloy. He soon found that it had the best features of a shovel, a hoe, and a pick. He began to scrabble in the rubble. In an hour he had lengthened the hole under the shelter to a trench 15 feet long and 4 feet deep.

He rested for a moment, then, suddenly conscious that the colonel was watching, passed on to the next step. He reached up to the shelter and swung down a supporting leg hinged to the top of the capsule. He screwed it out clumsily to its full length, glad to see that his pressure-suit gloves were capable of it. He anchored the foot of the leg under the shell of an Oregon boulder. Then he piled other boulders on top to wedge the leg more firmly and began to ease the capsule down to a horizontal position. Five-sixths of its weight was supported by a chain from high in the chamber. Padding back and forth for an hour, he leveled it gradually by shortening the support leg and adjusting two of the landing legs. When finally he had it prone, he spent another half-hour lowering it into the trench.

He stepped back for a moment, regarding his work. The shelter lay invitingly before him, snug in its bed. The beacon had turned itself out as the capsule reached the level position —a precaution against a light on the real mission beckoning him to a wrecked capsule. Tomorrow he would start to pile rocks on the shelter until he had a 6-foot blanket of lunar earth to protect himself against radiation and meteorites. If he made it in the three days it would be a boost to his own morale. And to Mickey's, he thought, leaning tiredly against the cylinder wall.

But now he must enter the shelter. He ran over in his mind the procedure. "Dust off . . ." He pressed a green panel by the shelter hatch, drew from a shallow cavity a long nylon brush, and began to sweep down his suit from top to bottom. On the moon, lunar dust might clog the air-conditioning system. Here in the chamber dust fell downward, but under lunar gravity it would deposit on him nearly as easily as on the ground he disturbed. He spent five minutes dusting himself for practice, replaced the brush, and took a deep breath.

He began to spin the wheel on the entrance. It was an oval hatch 5-feet high, at the base of the prone cylinder. It opened easily, too easily, he felt. He detached himself from his lunar-gravity sling, let it spring upward. Then he stooped and crowded into the shelter's cramped air lock. He felt along the bulkhead "eight inches from hatchway," found a switch. He flicked it and a dim light glowed.

He closed the exterior hatch and turned a master valve to pressurize the air lock. He would leave his pressure suit on like a raincoat in a vestibule on a wet day, as further insurance against introducing dust to the living compartment. He waited for the air-lock pressure to build. It did not, so he checked the hatch gasket. It hung limply, leaking like the rubber padding of an old refrigerator door.

He fought down his panic and ran over in his mind the

air-lock stowage for emergency gaskets. He found the locker; in twenty minutes he had installed a new gasket and the air lock was properly pressurizing. Suddenly he noticed a note on the hatch. "Gasket jarred loose in landing, Steve boy. Next time, check before you waste your oxygen." It was signed by the colonel. Steve crumpled the note, stiff with anger. When the air lock had pressurized he cautiously eased off his helmet. The dry, rubbery smell of oxygen reassured him. In five minutes he was out of his suit. He uncranked the inner hatch, stepped into his living quarters, dogged down the air-lock door behind him, and looked around.

The wooden mock-up he had inspected had not prepared him for the feeling of being caged in steel. A bunk lay along one side of the cylinder, a bare table along the other. The tank walls were green, his bed was green, the valves and pipes were green. Communications equipment jammed the front bulkhead; the gauges of his Environmental Control System brushed his head when he stood erect. A chemical toilet nestled under food supplies. The covers of a few novels among the technical manuals above the desk gave the only color to the green dimness of the tube.

Intellectually he had realized how tiny his womb would be, studying it in wood and on charts. In three metallic dimensions it was horrifying. He thought of the instant death lying just beyond an inch of steel, of his pressure suit beyond reach in the shelter's air lock.

A windowless pipe, he thought, the forward torpedo-room of a miniature sub, a storm-drain . . .

Beneath the stilts on which his childhood home had clung to the Berkeley hillside had lain a 12-inch storm-drain. One foggy, boring day when he was ten the skinny boy next door had challenged his courage, his strength, and his girth, then snaked through like an eel. Steve could still remember the moist, fetid smell inside, the scraping rusty sides, the panicky certainty that he was stuck fast and would die entombed under his own home. From somewhere, since he was doomed anyway, he had found calm and begun to inch forward an arm, a foot, a shoulder, one member at a time until at last he had squirmed to the blessed smell of fog and the light of day.

He very nearly panicked now. He grabbed a copy of his schedule from the rack above the desk, leafed through it in search of a task to divert himself, as a religious man might fumble in fright through a Bible. The schedule called for sleep, food, a systems check, and, tomorrow, more digging. He lay down on his bunk. In a few minutes his fear, his anger at the colonel, his claustrophobia had eased.

Only a great and secret apprehension stayed with him, but it was not enough to keep him awake and soon he slept.

9.

Gus Scarbo faced the two NASA aeromedical men in the Washington office of the senior flight surgeon, who was an Air Force colonel. Both were furious, but the Air Force man spoke with steely control.

"What you don't seem to understand, Gus," he said tensely, "is that you're out of this. You've told us how you feel. OK. It's not your problem."

"Those kids are my problem, goddamn it, no matter how you try to stuff me in a corner! And you're going to find it out!"

He slammed the door behind him and started down the hall. Through the open door of the headquarters Public Affairs' office he glimpsed Joe Garcia, Astronaut Public Relations officer from Houston, leaning angrily on the desk of a NASA administrator. Joe was staying at his hotel. Gus would see him this evening anyway and learn without embellish-

ment of whatever had triggered him off, for Joe was painfully
honest. But it was so comforting after his own abrasive
morning to see someone else beating his head against an
official wall that he stopped outside to light his pipe.

"It's a panel show," Joe was explaining. "A month ago
we promised the network the whole crew! Rick Lincoln and I
couldn't carry it alone if he was Bob Hope and I was Bing
Crosby! This organization is in no shape to piss off the
National Broadcasting Company, whether you guys know it
or not! I need Steve Lawrence and the colonel, and I need
them fast!"

The administrator simply spread his hands, shrugged, and
moved to his coffee maker. Joe Garcia stormed out, face
flaming. "Will you tell me," he demanded, "what the hell is
going on around here?"

"As a matter of fact," Gus said softly, "No."

Joe Garcia looked him in the eyes for a moment. "I didn't
think you would," he said finally. He turned on his heel and
headed toward the plush carpets of Holy Land, where the
Chief Administrator reigned. Gus watched him sadly for a
moment, then turned away. He had his own problems today.

Senator Ralph Fellows had not made a single move behind
his cluttered desk as Gus Scarbo talked. Now that Gus was
through he had a momentary notion that the Senator might be
half-deaf or senile and might not have been listening to the
medical data at all. But then he saw that there was nothing
senile about the bright, hard eyes. The Senator pulled at his
nose for a moment, asked suddenly: "How long have you
been in the Navy, Doctor?"

"Twenty-three years, sir."

The Senator nodded. "Did you assume I knew about
this?"

Gus was suddenly alert to danger, but he could not twist
the truth. "No, I assumed that part of the reason for secrecy
was to keep your party out of it as long as possible."

"I see."

Gus moved uncomfortably. He had anticipated indignation at the Administration, delight at a new weapon to use against the President. Politically he did not care; he was only interested in the results. But he had expected shock at least.

"I assumed, Senator, that if you'd known about this, you'd have reacted. Publicly."

" 'Reacted,' " the Senator smiled thoughtfully. "That's interesting. You expected me to react like . . . what's his name? Pavlov's dog? Or a rattler when you step on him?"

"I expected you," Gus said carefully, "to react like the ordinary human being who sees a fire. I expected you to spread the alarm."

The keen eyes studied him. "Maybe you did expect that." Senator Fellows got up suddenly, stepped to a jumbled bookcase lining a wall, extracted a volume. He returned to his desk, tossed it across the table. "You're a naval officer, Doctor. Did you ever hear of the Espionage Act? Or the Universal Code of Military Justice?"

Gus tensed. "Yes, sir."

"Or this in here? 18 U.S. Code 798? Read this, Doctor, sometime! You tell me this Pilgrim Project is top secret, and yet you come here and spill it to me without so much as a check with the Secretary of the Navy or Sec Def or the CIA. What the hell kind of a naval officer are you?"

"I'm a doctor first."

"Yes?"

"When I see a human life in danger, I react," Gus said thickly. "Like Pavlov's dog."

The Senator didn't answer. He nodded at the book. "Regardless of what the Navy can do to you, regardless of how many years a general court-martial might 'award,' you know what a federal court would do?"

"For what?" Gus Scarbo felt his anger rising. "You're not a Russian attaché! You're not the man on the street! You're a United States Senator, and if an officer can't come to you with a pseudo-military secret, we're in pretty damn bad shape!''

The Senator sat down. His eyes glinted. ''Don't yell at me, young man. I know I'm a United States Senator. I also know I'm no exception to the Espionage Act, which happens to be the law of this land.'' He slammed his palm on the desk. ''Ten years, Doctor. Ten goddamned years, making little ones out of big ones! Does that give you pause?''

Gus Scarbo looked into the cold eyes. ''Of course it does.''

The Senator seemed to relax. ''Then you should have thought of that before you leaked this.''

Gus hated the term. ''Leaked? I've never 'leaked' anything in my life!''

''Leaked! I don't know what I'll do about this.''

''About Pilgrim?'' Gus asked. ''Or me?''

''I will not make one move about Pilgrim until I determine that the move would be in the national interest. No. About you.''

''I see.''

''In the meantime, let me warn you. If you put your head further on the block, *no* one in my party will stay the axe. Do you understand?''

Gus Scarbo nodded. ''Yes, sir.''

When he stumbled on the steps of the Senate Office Building a guard looked at him curiously, as if he were drunk. It might not be a bad idea at that. He caught a cab and returned to his hotel.

Senator Fellows turned back to his desk. The light on his phone was blinking.

''I have the Assistant Director of the Central Intelligence Agency, Senator,'' his secretary said in her mining-town twang.

The Senator had not changed his mind in recent memory, but now he rubbed his eyes tiredly. ''Hold it, Myrna. Let me think . . ." In a city where sincerity was a cloak to be donned or ripped off he had just been talking to an honest man. Maybe he had frightened him into silence. That was really all that even the head Boy Scout in the White House could expect him to do. Hanging him was not his job. "I don't want him, after all. Get me the Old Man in San Francisco."

He swiveled his chair and looked at the framed front pages of a yellowed newspaper hanging next to the window. *FEL-LOWS DEFIES UNION*, the headline complained, probably set on the clanking press by the Old Man himself. *BIDS FOR CONGRESS*. The date was 1920. The paper was defunct, the Marysville, California, *Nugget*. The Old Man, as a young mining-town radical, had been its editor. He had opposed the Senator, which was one reason that the paper had died even before the town. Now the Senator thought of the Old Man in San Francisco as an editor tamed by his publisher. Fire still crackled in his clear, precise prose, but the Senator was sure that his owner supplied the match.

He and the Old Man were friends now. And surrender had not dulled the reporter's perception. In an hour sipping Chianti or strolling Chinatown's markets he could feel the city more delicately than his publisher or the Senator could in a week at the Bohemian Club or Pacific Union.

"He's on, Senator," his secretary called. Ralph Fellows picked up the phone, listened with delight to the harsh, bitter voice. "What's it to be today, Ralph? Cross section of your whorehouse vote? Or an opinion as to whether you can get away with a federal poll tax on the Nisei?"

"Neither one, you Wobbly relic." He hesitated; the Old Man could smell a beat across 3,000 miles. Unless he wanted to be responsible for leaking the Pilgrim story himself he had to be very careful. "Southern California's loaded with space contracts," he began. "So's the peninsula. But how would the city itself feel if I took a stronger stand on NASA extravagance?"

"This Sodom," the Old Man said sourly, "thinks

NASA's an Egyptian harem keeper and Apollo's a new hair tonic. Rant and rave in the chamber at will. Not that you wouldn't anyway.''

The Senator thanked him and hung up before the Old Man's suspicions became aroused. He called his secretary. ''Bring me my speech.'' The reckless Navy doctor had interrupted him dictating the speech with which he would in a few days open his remarks to the Senate on next year's NASA appropriations. The speech would cut NASA dry. Without funds the man could not be brought back and, so, would never be sent.

On the day that a public announcement was made he would jam the wheels of Pilgrim as effectively as if the program had never been conceived.

''Where were we?'' he asked the grey-haired secretary.

'' 'Not the least is the unknown radiation hazard . . .' '' she quoted.

'' 'Not the least,' '' he corrected, '' 'is the possibility of a sudden lethal radiation dose of 4,000 rem.' ''

He sat back. He was glad he had decided not to crucify the doctor. It would have made him uncomfortable when he reached that line on the floor.

10.

Steven James Lawrence hung in the morning sun of southeast Texas like a dripping block of ice in tongs. He was suspended in his pressure suit from the jammed yoke of the Low-Gravity Operations Simulator towering over the center. He was high enough to see the distant buildings on Houston across the lowland plain, supported solely by the "iron jock," a steel girdle that passed around his middle and under his crotch. The girdle was spitted near the small of his back by a steel bar which led to the giant tongs. He was very uncomfortable and his own contribution to his plight had not pleased him or the people below.

Thirty feet beneath him, standing on imitation lunar soil under the huge bridge-like crane, a group of engineers and technicians tried to control their irritation. Every few minutes one of them would look up at him, smile thinly, and shake his head. He felt like an idiot. He began to sweat and reached too abruptly to the biopak on his shoulders to change his suit temperature. He was gimbaled like a ship's compass, free to move in any direction, and the motion swung him upside down.

Cautiously, with the blood pounding to his head, he began to right himself, using the swimming motion they had learned. When he was vertical again he sighed. It was the first kink in his schedule. Yesterday morning he had moved gratefully back to earth from the lunar environment of the chamber after seventy-two hours burying and living in his shelter. Yesterday afternoon he had finished his navigational phase. In four hours he had flown three speeded-up lunar missions in the Lunar Trajectory Simulatory—sitting confined in a 70-foot-diameter room and riding a ''crab'' slowly again and again from a 1-foot earth to a 6-inch moon, shooting Canopus, the sun, and the moon-earth system on the way. Last night he had spent a cramped hour in the Flight Trainer while the operators and the colonel at the console tried, often successfully, to trick him with every disaster that could befall him on the pad.

He had been looking forward all week to this morning's session. Last year all thirty astronauts had gamboled lightly around the Low-Gravity Trainer, one at a time, five-sixths of their weight suspended from its gimbals. Trying to outdo each other, they had performed prodigious high jumps, somersaults, ballet leaps, had horsed around with insane, 20-foot strides.

He had known that this morning must be different. Today he must master an odd shuffle, the only gait that would keep him from toppling like an inverted cone in an environment in which gravity was cut to almost nothing but in which the eternal laws of momentum remained the same. And he had mastered it, too, found it not really impossible.

Then, with five minutes to go, he had succumbed to a childish desire to leap high for a parting fling with the device, although they had warned him that the bearings had been jamming. And here he was, hanging like a damp union suit. Someone on the ground pointed up. Steve twisted, spotted a sling being lowered from the traveling platform 20 feet above him. He eased it around his arms like a helicopter pickup, reached back, and managed to unlock the iron jock. Ignominiously he was lowered to the earth. He popped his face plate, faced the colonel and the restrained engineers.

"I'm sorry, fellows. There was no excuse for it—I must have flipped."

The technicians smiled, forgiving him. Rick Lincoln, who had hardly melted since Steve had volunteered, said: "You should have stayed there. They'd have to feed you and they never could have launched you in the crane."

But the colonel had not softened at all. They were due at the Flight Trainer in ten minutes. "Let's go, Steve," he said coolly. "Do we need lunch?"

Steve was not sure that he could stand another four hours buttoned in the capsule; it was shrinking by the day. He needed no lunch; what he needed was the break.

But he plugged in his portable air conditioner, hefted it, and followed the colonel dutifully to the van.

Sy Larson sauntered into the Integrated Mission Control Center. He glanced next door into the Flight-Trainer room. A cluster of men around the Mercury training capsule meant that they were inserting Lawrence for another hop.

Today the world-wide tracking network was manned with the personnel who would actually handle the flight, their voices brought to the training capsule from Bermuda and Hawaii and Australia. The astronauts who would act as Capsule Communicators had fanned out; they were spotted from Zanzibar to the Sea of Japan. The simulation would be a dress rehearsal of the first phase—the "parking" orbit around the earth from which Pilgrim would be flung toward the moon.

Someone had phoned Sy from Washington; he had time to

return the call before the operation started. He dialed the operator, soon heard Clem Cummings' voice on the line and learned that Gus Scarbo had been seen entering Senator Ralph Fellows' office. "But the Senator never squeaked a word?"

"Not to us. And he hasn't made a move publicly. I think Scarbo's given up. He has a reservation home."

Sy Larson tugged at his ear doubtfully. "I just wish we had some leverage. In case he *hasn't* given up. Maybe we could kind of help him along."

"Sy!" The Washington man seemed shocked. "Didn't anybody ever warn you about entrapment?"

Sy moved impatiently. Clem could be noble because his only responsibility was to gumshoe around. Sy's was the security of the whole Pilgrim Program. "Just to shut him up if he gets nasty again?"

The voice on the other end was quiet for a moment. Sy wondered if he had gone too far. "I'll beat him to the airport tonight," Clem Cummings said finally, "and fly back with him. If I can sit next to him, maybe we can find out just how selective he is."

For the second time in the week Sy felt a warm glow toward the Washington agent, toward his own supervisor, toward the CIA. The pay was small and the strains great, but when they sent help they sent the best. It was not yet the FBI. But it was becoming a great team.

Steve Lawrence lay on his back in the crammed Mercury training capsule and blinked his burning eyes. On the panel 2 feet from his nose the readings blurred. He reached to the console light and turned up the ruddy glow. It didn't help. He looked out the window. The dark earth spun ponderously outside, just as he had seen it from real orbit on his Apollo flights. The long hours of cockpit simulation had broken down his sense of reality.

All at once he was not looking at a projected image 20 feet

outside his window. He was in earth orbit, approaching the point at which he would be hurled irrevocably toward the moon. In minutes he and the men who tracked him must decide whether to risk the three-day journey or whether he should re-enter the atmosphere and land. Intellect fought instinct. Consciously he knew that the "out-the-window" displays, however clever and elaborate, were movies, that his capsule was made of plywood, that he was anchored to the soil of Texas. But it did no good to know it when all of his senses screamed otherwise.

He moved his stick gently to break the spell. It only enhanced it; as he raised his nose the moonlit horizon dipped in his window. He could actually feel the motion: he was as surely in orbit as if 1,500,000 pounds of thrust had hurled him there.

How had it happened? And what had he forgotten? He had a great and empty remorse at the things he was going to do and had not done; letters he was going to write in case he did not return. To Stevie, to Gus Scarbo. And Mickey—my God, had he said goodbye to Mickey?

"Pilgrim One from Houston Cap Com," the colonel's voice crackled. "Stand by for time to injection."

"Roger," he said automatically. His eyes began to sweep the jumbled panel. Where was his back-up stopwatch? In his ditty bag? He was behind schedule—the capsule was controlling him, not he the capsule. He glanced out at the earth. It had disappeared and only a black, star-filled void remained. He had drifted from his correct injection altitude. He fumbled with the stick.

The colonel's voice seemed to hint of alarm. "Pilgrim One, this is Cap Com! What is your attitude?" Lousy, he almost screamed. I want to abort. Instead he began to adjust his nose position, trying to fly the capsule with one eye on the "eight-ball" and one eye open for the moonlit coast of Africa below. At last he had leveled himself, but by that time the colonel was counting.

"Stand by for countdown to injection minus thirty: ten, nine, eight, seven . . ."

He dropped the ditty bag and got ready to punch his panel clock. Suddenly he realized that he was burning with heat. He glanced at the cabin temperature gauge in the corner of his panel. It was set on its side so that normally its arrow would match the others in its group; now, unsure of the blurred printing on it, he had to tip his head to read it: 120 degrees and climbing!

He wanted to break in on the colonel, to report his problem; he could not, so he grabbed quickly at the rosette-shaped heat-control handle and turned it full counterclockwise. The heat dropped, and he went back to his ditty bag. Then the colonel's chant broke through.

". . . Four, three, two, one, mark! Thirty seconds to injection!"

He jabbed at his clock, missed, hit it again and started it. A full second late. Maybe two. Would his mid-course correction make up for the error? Or would he swing helplessly past the moon? He tried to remember. Suddenly he was freezing. "Clock is running," he reported. "Cabin thermostat is out."

"Roger, Pilgrim One," the colonel said.

In the next thirty—no, twenty-five—seconds he must decide whether to go or not. He was shivering with cold; he twisted the cabin heat back and in seconds he was burning again. He stared at the panel. His cabin pressure was dropping. All at once from the left side a red light blinked. *Landing Bag Deployed* read the printing over the light. He glanced at his clock. Eighteen seconds to injection, seventeen, sixteen . . .

"Cap Com, Cap Com," he called, trying to keep his voice calm, "I show landing bag deployed, cabin pressure dropping, cabin temperature fluctuating! Do not inject me! Intend to abort on the next orbit. Do not inject!" There was a deathly silence. "Acknowledge, Cap Com," he demanded. He glanced out the window. The first light of dawn was tingeing the African coastline. He shifted to his emergency frequency, hand shaking. "Acknowledge, damn it! I intend to abort."

To his right a hinge squeaked and daylight poured into his capsule. He stared, tense with shock. The colonel was looking down at him. "Roger," he said. There was not the vestige of a smile in his eyes. "Relax, Steve boy. You just aborted."

Steve found that his hands were clenched tightly. Waves of nausea washed over him. "OK," he said thickly. "Then let me out of this goddamned thing!"

"Don't up-chuck," said the colonel. "It wouldn't look good."

As Steve stripped down outside the trainer, Rick Lincoln strolled in. He ignored the colonel, who was writing up the hop, and winked at Steve.

"You done nobly, Buddy."

Steve looked at him quickly. For the first time there was no irony in his eyes. I'll be damned, he thought. "Frankly, Rick, I panicked. Maybe I shouldn't even have aborted."

"You're supposed to do in the trainer what you'd do in the air. I'd have aborted."

The colonel looked up. "We didn't throw him anything that he couldn't have worked out in the trans-lunar phase."

"You always were a hero," Rick said. "I'm with him."

Rick left and Steve and the colonel were alone. Outside, in the Integrated Mission Control Center, Archy's voice droned sonorously as he conducted his critique. The electric clock above the trainer read 1:00 P.M. There was time to get home to help Mickey pack for the Cape; he was to follow tomorrow.

The colonel finished his write-up. "Steve?"

Steve was pulling on his shirt. He stopped, a clammy knot settling in his stomach. "Yes?"

"Get Rick to fly you to the Cape."

Steve swallowed. "Where will you be?"

"I'm going to Washington. I'm going to advise the President not to send you."

Steve found that his throat was too tight to answer.

"You may not believe me," the colonel said, "but it is not because I personally want to be the first. It's more than that, now."

"Why is it?" Steve asked thickly. "I'd like to know."

The colonel faced him. "It's because I'm afraid you'll panic and kill yourself. Because I'm afraid you'll abort unnecessarily. Because I'm the only one who wants us there badly enough to make it all the way."

11.

Gus Scarbo tossed in his sleep on a Washington hotel bed, but he was 8,000 miles west and eighteen years back. He stood in a carrier sick bay, looking down on a scorched and blackened face, smelling the ether and alcohol and burned flesh and listening to a chant of pain.

"Holy . . . jumping . . . Jesus Christ, Gus! Jesus . . . Mary . . . and Joseph!" A bright gold tooth gleamed as the massive Jewish features roiled again into the caricature of a smile. "Hey, you'd think with all . . . with all those frigging relatives . . . a guy'd have it easier than this!"

Gus swallowed. "You'd think so." The charred hand grabbed his convulsively; powerful muscles contracted. Skip Goldberg, apparently, had enough nerve ends remaining to suffer the tortures of hell. Gus was sure that if he didn't somehow free his fingers he would never operate again, but he bore it as if by doing so he could draw some of the agony from the ruined body on the bunk.

Forward of the sick-bay compartment the starboard catapult began to work again, hurling in ponderous rhythm the tense, terrified young automatons and their aircraft toward the Korean peninsula and the next strike.

Shh—boom. A rattle as it retracted. Shh—boom, rattle. It was joined by the port catapult. Shh—boom, rattle, Shh—boom, rattle. Shh—boom, rattle.

In the wardroom they had sung a song in time to its beat:

"Sh—boom . . . rattle.

Round and round went that great bloody wheel . . .

In and out went that great prick of steel . . .

Stay, oh stay, the maiden cried . . .

Stay, oh stay, I'm sa-it-is-fied . . ."

Skip Goldberg's spasm passed. "Where'd he go?" he grunted.

"Father? The chaplain?"

The seared head nodded imperceptibly. The skin was unscorched past the helmet line but the hair had burned anyway.

"To get the Protestant, I guess."

"No I bet he . . ." Another wave of anguish passed. "I bet he's going to ask them to fly that rabbi over from the flag!"

Gus nodded. "He might at that."

From the depths of his pain, at a moment when he seemed to be unconscious and the corpsmen were sure that he had died, Skip had startled them by opening his eyes and demanding the last rites. The ship had no rabbi, so the Catholic chaplain had stumbled down the ladder, complete with altar box and Torah. Skip had subjected him to a searching interrogation on Judaism and flunked him. The studious young priest had missed the gleam in the reddened eyes and fled topside.

"Gus!" Skip demanded now. "You ask them! Ask for the rabbi!"

Gus looked at the young man sharply. The gold tooth

gleamed. Gus himself smiled for the first time in hours. "In the middle of the strike-of-the-year? Skip, they'll make me pour salt on your wounds!"

"Go ahead, Gus! I heard . . . I heard he was scared shitless of choppers. Go on!"

Gus hesitated. He hated to leave Skip's side, would never forgive himself if the boy died while he was gone. On the other hand, if he could promise Skip the rabbi to bait from the brink of eternity the humor of it might keep him going for hours.

But for what?

He glanced at the wreck on the bunk. He had first seen Skip flashing down the ice in college hockey; he had been an overpowering fullback at Columbia and a skier as well. And tomorrow the great heart and lungs and legs and brains would slide to the bottom of the sea. It was cruel to prolong his agony, even for Skip's last joke. Yet, if that was the way he wanted it . . .

Gus looked for a corpsman to stand by in his absence, girding himself for the battle he knew awaited him topside when he demanded a helicopter. But Skip's hand tightened again. "Never mind, Gus," he decided. "Why scare the poor bastard?"

His breath was becoming labored. Suddenly he yelled in pure, animal anguish. The shout squeezed Gus's soul; a corpsman with a hypo tray put it on a stainless-steel table and lurched whitely from the compartment. Very, very slowly the tense body relaxed. "Son . . . of . . . a . . . bitch," Skip murmured.

"Yell," Gus swallowed. "If you feel like it, yell!"

"Key of G?" Skip Goldberg murmured. "Gus, give me another shot?" It was far too early; he had given him a half-grain of morphine less than an hour before. But Gus nodded and moved to the tray. He picked up the syringe. He heard the bunk springs creak and looked up. Somehow Skip had found the courage to bear the pain of raising his head.

Red eyes peered from the coal-black skin like embers in a fireplace. "Gus?"

Gus found that his mouth was dry. Don't, he pleaded across the aisle. Don't, for Christ's sake, ask me. His hand was shaking so badly that he could hardly hold the vial. He wiped its top, plunged the needle through. When he looked up Skip had collapsed again back on the bunk. His lips moved. "No, Gus, you'd never forget it. Stay loose. I'll sweat it."

For an eternity Gus stared at the vial. When he drew out the syringe there were 20 ccs in the needle. Gently, quickly, before his tears blinded him, he found the vein.

Oh Merciful Father . . .

Shh—boom, rattle. Shh—boom, rattle.

The phone rang and Gus Scarbo was wide awake. He fought out of his twisted sheets, felt blindly on the bedside table. It was the hotel desk, waking him for the evening flight. He put the receiver back.

Shh—boom, rattle. Shh—boom, rattle. He stumbled to the window, looked out at the grey Washington sky. Across the street a pile driver pounded at the foundations of a new government building. *Shh—boom, rattle. Shh—boom, rattle.*

God, if he didn't get out back to Marion he would go mad. He lurched to the wallet lying on his bureau, checking to see that he had his ticket. He was putting it down when he glimpsed a familiar picture. He pulled out an accordion of photos: Marion in a bathing suit, himself with Al Shepard in his outboard, Stevie Lawrence cutting his third birthday cake. At the end of the chain was a yellowed, scuffed shot someone had taken in a geisha house high on the hills over Sasebo. Sitting cross-legged at a Japanese table, one huge arm about each of two giggling geishas, grinned Skip Goldberg, tooth and all. Steve Lawrence regarded the lens through drunken, half-lowered eyes. Gus himself sat glowering in massive dignity at the camera.

Shh—boom, rattle. Shh—boom, rattle. Gus Scarbo found himself tense with anger. He slammed his palm on the bureau top. "No!"

He phoned the airline and canceled his reservation. He had dined with Joe Garcia the night before and Joe knew nothing of Pilgrim or his own revulsion at it. He called Joe's room. "That 'Meet the Press' thing tonight, Joe, or whatever? You want *me* on it?"

"You?" Garcia hardly hesitated. "I think you'd be interesting as hell!"

"I'll be," Gus Scarbo promised quietly, "as interesting as I can."

12.

Sy Larson, feet on his desk in Archy Gorman's deeply carpeted office, leafed through the security manual on Pilgrim. In less than a week pressure on him would be off; public announcement of the program would be made the moment that the shelter capsule landed successfully.

He dropped his feet and straightened. He was satisfied so far, despite what may have been a tiny leak, now plugged, at Goldstone, California. He had worked hard. Tonight he would drive in to Houston for dinner and a movie. He suddenly remembered a secretary in Life Support Systems he suspected of nymphomania. The phone rang while he was reaching to call her. It was Clem Cummings, the Washington agent. There was nothing lighthearted in his voice now. He had lost Scarbo.

"I waited at the passenger ramp. Then I checked at the counter. He'd canceled his reservation."

Sy was unable to hide his irritation. "Did you check his hotel?"

"He's still registered."

Gus Scarbo floating around Washington in a mood of righteous anger was enough to give you ulcers. "Clem," Sy pleaded, "will you for Christ's sake find him?"

Cummings' voice rose a half note. "A brilliant suggestion, Sy! Just brilliant!"

The phone clicked. Sy Larson decided not to drive into downtown Houston. He would wait here for word.

The colonel waited miserably in the White House's oval study wishing that the Vice-President would calm himself. It was hard enough to sit in this room and wonder whether your own motivation was selfless or selfish without watching your ally cracking before your eyes. The President was breaking loose from a dinner in the State Dining Room below to see them. The Vice-President had shown less nervousness at the top of a Colorado ski lift last winter; the strain on the youthful face was agonizing to observe. He is as obsessed with winning this race as I am, thought the colonel, but stewing because he has to watch it from the sidelines.

"Now, damn it," the Vice-President warned, "be careful how you put it. He's been shaken up enough since he read Garrow's column. Telling him he picked the wrong man isn't going to help."

The colonel felt a spark of anger at Phil Garrow, the columnist he had speared so neatly at the press conference: "We were running out of oxygen, Mr. Garrow. Not space." He picked up the open paper on the coffee table.

The Apollo program is an inhuman risk of human life . . . The colonel could imagine what he would print in a week when he found out about Pilgrim. He went on. *This hot-and-cold running war will be won in the jungles and on the seas and in the air, and, if not there, in the cities. It won't be won on the moon.* If he had not impaled Garrow on a shaft of wit based, after all, on a lie, perhaps the column would not have been written. "They always get the last word don't they—the press?"

The Vice-President shrugged. "Sometimes I think we pamper them too much. We feed the papers and the networks so much information they get spoiled." He glanced at the clock, moved to a TV set in a walnut cabinet near the President's desk. "We give them Rick Lincoln for a panel show tonight; they scream because they don't get you and Lawrence." He flicked through the channels, found the one he was looking for, turned away. "Does anybody else down there think he's turned yellow?"

"Yellow?" The colonel stared at him. The Vice-President was one of his closest friends; he thought of him as potentially great, but unless he learned to see greys among the blacks and whites he could be more of a threat to the country than an asset. "Jesus, I never said he was yellow! This isn't a prep-school football team! It's just that I have a higher threshold of panic than he does. Something's bound to go wrong some-where—"

"It's not supposed to."

"Hell, it's going to. Serious or not. You know that."

"If it did, *you'd* go on," the Vice-President murmured. "But don't play that up tonight."

"I won't. But Lawrence is no coward. Maybe he figures he's got more family obligations. His wife . . ."

"What about her?"

The colonel felt his face stiffen. "Forget it. Anyway, the guy in that capsule has to be looking for an excuse to land instead of an excuse to abort. Or we might as well scrub it now."

"Tonight, if you sound like a *kamikaze*," the Vice-President warned, "you may scrub it all by yourself."

The colonel shifted irritably. "Don't you think I know it?"

He looked away quickly. It was a poor way to talk to the

Vice-President of the United States, no matter how close they were, but nobody had to tell him when the project teetered; he had helped to balance it for a year.

Steve deposited his son in the upper bunk. It was the last bedtime before his launch. Mickey would go down to the Cape, but unless the colonel somehow convinced them in Washington that he was unfit for Pilgrim, he would not see Stevie again for a year. Or ever again? He stared at the glowing face, cherry red from a tussle in the living room, at the pink ears beneath the brush cut, at the nose, like Mickey's, broad and blunt. He has my eyes, he thought, looking into their blueness; if anything happens, I am leaving that. He had been avoiding the thought all evening.

He tried to think of something to leave him with, but the secrecy of the program restricted him. He would deposit a letter for later, but what did you say to a six-year-old anyway? What did a soldier say the night before he left, or an Arctic explorer? Stiff upper lip, old chap? Take care of your mother? Don't forget to keep the woodbox filled? He decided to save the goodbye until after breakfast.

Stevie was batting a rubber mouse hung from the night lamp above his bunk. Steve inspected it. "Who's your friend?"

"Space mouse," explained Stevie.

Steve suddenly wanted it very badly. "Could I have it, Tiger?" Stevie's face crinkled in such agony that Steve laughed and rumpled his hair. "I was kidding," he said. "See you at breakfast."

"TV," Stevie demanded. "Until Mom comes in."

Steve kissed him, flicked on the battered TV set on his bureau, clicked off the light. At the door, he turned. His son was already staring at the set, lost in a program that he could no more comprehend than an encyclopedia. Steve watched him for a few seconds. Then he left the room.

Mickey was washing dishes. In their first Navy years at

Patuxent River, quartered in a steaming Quonset hut, he had helped her every night. "Save a few for me," he said suddenly.

"You haven't wiped dishes in years," she murmured. "Why tonight?" He could not answer, because he didn't know.

"I just want to. That's all." He started across the lawn to say goodbye to Marion Scarbo.

The President leaned back in his chair behind the desk. The Vice-President had held the floor for ten minutes, telling him of Pilgrim's accelerating momentum. But the President sensed that he was road-grading for what the colonel had to say, because he was sure that the colonel had not flown all the way from Houston to join in a happy duet.

He must hurry them to the point; he had a late meeting with two young Russian diplomats now sipping brandy below. When he had left them at the table they had been grinning like cats and he suspected that the autobahn was about to open again—only to shut, probably, in another week or month when the Kremlin felt the need to test his stance again.

"So much for the hardware," he said, cutting off the Vice-President. "Colonel, how's your protégé?"

The colonel's tanned face was drawn and taut. He licked his lips, seemed to feel a need to move, got up from the couch behind the coffee table. "Well, sir," he said, "that's why I'm here."

"I assumed so," the President said.

The colonel groped for words. He rubbed his temples, looked past the desk. As he did, he seemed to become fascinated with something across the room. He swallowed and a frown flashed across his balding forehead. The President spun his chair. The TV set in the walnut cabinet was on, murmuring softly. The colonel moved to it, turning up the volume. The President peered at the panel program on the screen.

Rick Lincoln he recognized immediately, sitting before a fieldstone fireplace with the moderator. The astronaut Public Affairs officer he knew too, a Joe Garcia. The other face he had to grope for. He had seen him somewhere in Houston during a tour of the center—a medical man, the astronaut flight surgeon. Scarbo was the name, he remembered suddenly, a Navy doctor.

"What's wrong?" the President asked sharply.

"Maybe it's all right," mused the colonel, his eyes still on the screen. "He's not an idiot, I guess, but I wouldn't have put him on the air . . ."

He seemed reluctant to leave the set. The moderator thanked Rick Lincoln for a description of the Apollo athletic program, then turned to the doctor.

"Now Dr. Scarbo, we all know that the physical and mental stamina required of these Apollo candidates is a very high one. Ice-cold foot baths, running on treadmills, the idiot box with the flashing lights. I wonder if you'd tell us what particular test you consider the most important of them all?"

Scarbo stared at his hands for so long that the President began to wonder whether he had heard the question. Then he looked up. His eyes were bloodshot and there were dark circles beneath them.

"No, sir," he said in a soft Louisiana drawl. "I'm not going to discuss trainee selection. I'm going to discuss a secret project—a project to beat the Russians to the moon. A suicidal project."

The Vice-President gasped as if he had been hit. The colonel swung from the set. "Call them," he ordered the President. "Get him off the air!" Automatically the President's hand moved for the phone. He had it out of its cradle before he realized that it was too late. He put it back, and watched with fascination as the man on the screen continued.

"It's called," the voice went on inexorably, "Project Pilgrim."

"No, damn it!" yelled the Vice-President. The President

had a crazy impulse to turn off the set. On the screen the moderator was regarding the flight surgeon with an amused, half-credulous expression. Rick Lincoln leaned forward in his seat. He spoke bitterly, not to the moderator or to the camera but to Scarbo; the President had an odd feeling that he had anticipated him and was as angry with himself for ignoring his premonitions as with the doctor. His voice was very smooth, but his smile was no smile at all.

"I think," he said coolly, "the doctor is discussing some of the earlier studies that were made regarding feasibility of—"

Joe Garcia was on his feet on the screen. "This whole discussion," he said brutally, "is ridiculous. I will stake my personal reputation on that! I don't know why you'd want to mislead the public, Gus, but neither NASA nor I will have any part of it!"

The Public Affairs officer was so convincing that for a wild instant the President had a surge of hope. If Scarbo shut up now, if he said not one more word, the incident could be carried off as a misunderstanding, an unfortunate choice of words, the rambling of a medical man who knew nothing of the real facts.

The doctor was regarding Garcia almost sadly. "No, Joe. This is real. This is firm. This is now." He turned toward the camera. "Within ten days NASA intends to launch a man to the moon in a Mercury capsule, modified but designed originally, as everyone knows, for earth orbit."

The Vice-President lunged toward the desk. "Phone them," he demanded. "Phone them, damn it. Or I will!"

The President looked at him for an instant. The Vice-President groaned and returned to his seat. "You're right. It's too late. It's just too goddamned late!"

The drawl beat on incessantly: ". . . to launch him on a sixty-six-hour trajectory. No provision is made for his return for at least a year. He'll be subject to unacceptable risk of meteorites, intense heat and cold, solar radiation. The man who was chosen is a civilian, a Korean veteran, of proven courage in test work. He is not a foolish man, but in this instance he's been very poorly advised. The American public can save his life by concerted effort, telegrams—"

The moderator came suddenly to life. "If this is secret, Doctor, this network can't permit—"

"I'm almost through," the doctor said mildly.

"You're through all right," grated the Vice-President. "You're through!"

"Turn it off," the President said wearily. A light on his telephone was flickering. He ignored it. "Turn it off, Colonel."

Steven James Lawrence stared at the television in the Scarbo living room. On the screen a nightmare had been played and now with Marion Scarbo crying across the couch it was turning into delirium. An adolescent with a cretinous forehead and a large mouth was displaying his teeth to an ecstatic family; he recited carefully that he had 25 percent fewer cavities, then faded into a crazy montage of crashing guns, rumbling tanks, and diving planes.

"I knew it," Steve swallowed. "The second I saw him!"

With a stab of panic he thought of Mickey. She had been doing dishes, thank God, not watching TV. He must tell her of this, before Stevie did, or before the phone rang and reporters began to plague her, or before some incredulous neighbor called; he must somehow smooth over the terrors Gus had predicted. And yet, with Marion crying, he could not simply dash out. It suddenly occurred to him that if he had not demanded that Gus be cut in, it would never have happened. Oh, God! Why hadn't he taken Archy's advice? Why had he insisted?

Marion stopped crying. She was looking at him strangely. "Steve, have you said you'd do this?"

"Yes."

"I'm going to Washington," she decided suddenly. "I want you to come with me."

"Marion, I can't. The schedule's too tight."

"The *schedule's* too tight? Then quit!"

"No."

She peered into his face. "Why not? He's your best friend. He's in trouble for you. Show him that it wasn't for nothing. Show him you believe in him. Show everybody!"

"I'll do what I can," Steve promised, "but this comes first."

"This comes first?" she cried. "What came first in the desert that night? If Mickey had died on the way to L.A. he'd have been through then! What came first tonight?"

His eyes burned. She was right, but he could not quit; he had no answer; he could only shake his head.

" 'This comes first,' " she said again bitterly, moving across the room. Shakily she lit a cigarette. She was a quiet woman; in fifteen years Steve had never seen her angry. Now she swung to him, eyes blazing. "That's why he's so much better than you, all of you! Somewhere, somehow, he even lost his religion for one of you! I know; I can tell! But for you people, you golden boys, something else always comes first. The strike or the ship, or the plane or the goddamned mission!"

"Or in this case," exploded Steve, "the country! Did you ever think of that?"

He passed the carnage on the TV set. Then he was striding home across the lawn.

In the oval room the colonel turned from the lifeless TV, trying to dampen his anger at Scarbo. The President was tapping a pen thoughtfully on his bronze desk calendar, his face lined with disappointment, his mouth sagging.

"Well, gentlemen," he said. "This may well dispose of Pilgrim."

The Vice-President spoke too swiftly: "It doesn't change

the physical facts! Just the political ones. It really doesn't change a thing!''

"Not even the Russian schedule?'' the President said.

"We can't quit because they're liable to beat us by a couple of days,'' the Vice-President protested. "We have a dream, damn it, to live up to! We've made a promise!''

"That the moon,'' murmured the President, "won't be 'governed by the hostile flag of conflict'? Yes. Well, we won't risk our Administration for a dream.''

"We said once,'' the Vice-President reminded him, "that if we're not first on the moon we will not be first in space and one day soon we will not be first on earth. Does that fact change because some psycho doctor spills his guts on a television show?''

"No,'' the President admitted, "it doesn't.''

"That's the real risk, damn it! It transcends the political risk!''

"You make it sound so simple,'' the President said. "It's a failing of youth. You might try to overcome it. We will not risk our Administration to send a man to the moon, as we would not risk the life of the man! Is that clear?''

The Vice-President nodded, but the colonel saw a tiny muscle working in his cheek and knew from experience that he was not through yet. The President laid down his pencil and leaned back. More softly, he said: "This is my dream, too. I want us there first. If we are not, my grandchildren and yours will suffer for our sloth. On the other hand, I think they would suffer also if my party was drummed out of power for trying to win this race. We'll see what the reaction is.'' He looked at the colonel. "Now, you had a report for me on Lawrence's training?''

The colonel had rehearsed what he would say on the flight from Houston; he had been steeling himself for this moment for the past twelve hours. He had catalogued his points. Lawrence was unquestionably the only civilian who could have been chosen, but they had simply overloaded a human brain as one might overload an electric circuit; the Mercury capsule was too complex to learn in three weeks, or six. No question of courage, no question of motivation. Purely an elementary problem in human engineering: demand too much too quickly from the pilot and he will crack like a mouse in a maze.

The words were on his lips when he had a sudden vision of the President arising, shrugging, canceling the mission because the obstacles had simply piled too high. He heard tires crunching on the driveway three floors below. There was a polite murmur from the portico; the dinner must be dissolving. From the tone of the voices the colonel doubted that anyone there had yet heard the news. He took a deep breath. "On schedule," he said.

The President nodded, and his eyes never left the colonel's face. "Any recommendations?"

A second phone on the desk began to flash. The colonel heard a cricket chirping on the lawn. "No recommendations, Mr. President. No recommendations at all."

Steve Lawrence entered his living room through the French doors from the lawn. In the kitchen he could hear Mickey at the sink. Thank God for that. Quickly he took the phone off the hook. He hesitated at the door between dinette and kitchen. Stevie had been watching TV. He moved to his son's room.

He knew immediately that Stevie at least had seen Gus. Cross-legged on his bunk, he was wide awake, orbiting a Mercury model that Deke Slayton had given him. Steve hesitated. He had tried for days to visualize the moment when someone must tell Stevie about the flight; there had been no way to predict his reaction.

"You saw Uncle Gus?" he asked carefully, touching his cheek. It was hot.

"Yes." Stevie would not meet his eyes. "He said somebody was going to the moon."

Steve braced himself. "It's me, Stevie. I'm the one that's going."

The face turned blank, the eyes vacant. "He said so, but he was fibbing, though."

"No, Stevie."

"Mom said."

Steve tensed. "What?"

"She said you couldn't."

Steve swallowed. He rubbed the stubbled head. "If I do, Stevie," he said, "you're going to have to take care of her until I get back. OK?"

"OK," Stevie agreed cheerfully. "I'll bail out the boat."

"You do that," Steve said. He kissed the chapped lips; now Stevie smelled of milk and potato chips. He pulled on the mouse and turned out the light. He started for the front of the house, dreading what he must face. There was a faint crash from the kitchen and he was sprinting down the hall.

Mickey stood stiffly at the sink. She looked down at the shattered bourbon bottle in panic as she heard Steve's footsteps in the hall. She had taken the bottle from the shelf, moving like an automaton, when Gus went off the air; she had poured herself a drink and stared at it for a crazy instant. An involved butterfly experiment of Stevie's on the window sill had caught her eye; she had tossed the drink down the drain and in a fit of anger smashed the bottle. She heard Steve pause at the kitchen door, grunt as the odor hit him. He turned her around and studied her face.

"You dropped it," he said, with the old bitterness. "Well, there's Scotch in the living-room cabinet." He whirled and slammed through the kitchen door.

She stiffened in shock, began automatically to clean the sink. Her mind was blank; she would not let herself think. Through the kitchen window she could see him in the moonlight, leaning on the rail of the battered pier. On the worst night of his life she was failing him. Suddenly she was racing down the lawn.

"I didn't drop it, Steve," she whispered. "I smashed it."

He studied her for a moment. "Because it was a temptation? Well, I'm proud of you." He took a deep breath. "But you were tempted. You haven't licked it. How in hell can I leave you and Stevie? What'll I do, Mickey?"

She looked at the moon, hardly paying attention. It was a copper scimitar above Clear Lake. It would rise and fall and rise and fall, and she knew that each night the dawn line would creep further to the east until on the eleventh night from now it would no longer be a sword but almost a sphere and he must be on his way to meet it. If he had the courage to cross the silent void she must have the courage to let him.

"Steve?"

"Yes?"

"If I told you I wasn't tempted, that I was just trying to scare you into quitting, would you believe me?"

"Jesus Christ, Mickey! Let's not play games!"

"You married a child," she blurted. "Gus scared me. But I wasn't tempted in the least."

He wanted to believe her and he did; she could tell from the grasp of his hand on her own. Together, before they went in, they watched a cloud pass the face of the moon. So far, she thought, so damn far. "Will you see the earth?" she asked. "When there are clouds."

"Clouds pass," he said huskily.

She thought of the game she played when he was gone, pretending that he watched her through the day; she wondered if she would be able to evoke his presence in the dark of the moon or when clouds covered the sky.

PART THREE

The Third Week

1.

It was 5:20 A.M. by the electric clock on his desk when the President entered his study. His Press Secretary was due at 5:30. He poured himself a cup of coffee from a Silex gurgling on a sideboy and moved to the windows. Wisps of pink tinged the southwest sky. Today would be a hot one, he decided, in more ways than one. When he had awakened he had gone to the Rose Guest Room for a look at Pennsylvania Avenue, half expecting to find pickets. There had been no pickets yet, but he had a feeling that the avenue would not sleep for long.

Ned Mooney knocked on the study door and entered from the Treaty Room, moving like one of the enormous cranes at the Cape. The dull eyes glowed more redly than ever from his pallid face.

"Morning, Ned," the President said. "Cup of coffee?"

"Good morning, Mr. President," Mooney murmured, in

his beautiful low voice. He sat in his favorite leather chair, teetered the cup of coffee in his huge hand. "I'll start," he began, "with the wire services. They're playing it straight. They've determined that Scarbo is a Navy commander with twenty-three years in, a wife and no children, born in Louisiana. UPI got a man over to interview him after the show last night and got no comment. Then the FBI got there."

The President remembered that he had left no instructions for Scarbo's treatment. The doctor had acted traitorously, but certainly from deep conviction; besides, his case would be a political time bomb to be handled with the greatest care. "Where is he?" the President asked, suddenly worried.

"Naval Hospital, Bethesda. Confined."

"Who put him there instead of the brig at the Naval Gun Factory?"

"Well, me. I called the ONI and told them you'd want it that way."

"Good," sighed the President gratefully. "Go on."

The Press Secretary continued, inflecting his voice in unconscious imitation of the newscasters he had spent half the night listening to. He had total recall; he never consulted the notes on his clipboard. "In general," he concluded, "nobody editorialized. The reason is that they hadn't decided whether there really was a Pilgrim Project. Scarbo could have been drunk or nuts."

"What about today?" the President wanted to know.

Mooney shrugged. "Today they'll know. The radio commentators will be the worst. Lowell Thomas and Fulton Lewis will bleed all over. On TV the networks will probably play it straight. Chet Huntley'll try to do something in depth on it tonight and never quite do it. Some of the local stations may nibble at the moral implications. They'll all reflect the papers, though."

The President braced himself. "OK, let's get at that."

Ned Mooney put down his coffee cup and began to tick the

papers off on his fingers, occasionally glancing at a list he had compiled. "We'll follow the sun from east to west. In New York the *Herald Tribune* will do anything editorially with it that'll sell papers. Probably moralize. You'll get your most enlightened editorials out of *The New York Times*, of course. They may even go along."

"You think so?" the President asked hopefully.

Mooney nodded and continued across the country from east to west. The evaluation was in accord with the Mooney theory: "Editors like to think they mold opinion. It molds them. They write what will please it. They seduce the public and the public seduces them and the offspring is an idiot, an inbred misconception that the parents will protect till their dying day."

"The *Seattle Times*," Ned Mooney concluded, "will want to withdraw our tracking stations to our own borders and the hell with the moon. *L'Humanité* in Paris, the London *Observer, Der Sturm*—they'll variously deride us. And now, thanks to Doctor Scarbo, *Time* and *Life* will have time to do cover stories on Lawrence; *Newsweek*, too."

The President stared. "My God, Ned, *Time* and *Life* supported the space program. They can't turn on it now!"

"Can't they?" Ned Mooney had worked for *Time*. "How's this? *The woman and the little boy will wait for the news in the little house by Clear Lake. If Lawrence dies they will doubtless move out. In the big house on Pennsylvania Avenue, they will be waiting too. If he dies or even fails, they may be moving, too.*"

The President crossed the room, poured another cup of coffee. His hand trembled. "If *Time* wrote that," he asked, trying to keep his voice light, "would they be talking about an election defeat?"

"If he's sent against the will of the country? And gets killed?"

"Yes."

Ned Mooney pulled at his lower lip. "At *least* an election defeat."

It was very quiet in the room. The clock on the desk droned softly. "And at most?" the President asked.

Ned Mooney swirled his coffee. Finally he looked up. "Impeachment?" he suggested. "Maybe impeachment."

The President moved to the window. Ruddy streaks of sunlight lay in strata across the sky. Early morning traffic was beginning to move. "I doubt," he said, "that anybody's mentioned that word in this room since Andrew Johnson."

Ned Mooney nodded ponderously. "Who," he reminded him, "only risked impeachment when he bucked public opinion. Don't ever underestimate the power of the public on the press and the press on the public."

"What'll I do?" he asked Mooney.

"Go on the air. Tell the story. Straight."

"When?"

"Tonight. Tomorrow at the latest."

The President nodded. "Tomorrow."

"Thank you, Mr. President," Ned Mooney said. He glanced at his watch. "The *Post* and the *Star* must have hit the street. I'll go down to the mail room."

The President went back to his quarters. He awakened his wife for breakfast. Leaving her room he paused at the window. Three solitary pickets marched in a silent circle on Pennsylvania Avenue. Two were women, a fat one and a skinny one, and both wore shapeless dresses and carried roughly painted signs. He could not read the printing across the wide driveway and lawn, but the women had the look of those one saw outside revival tents.

He decided to eat breakfast in his study while he worked on his speech.

The Old Man in San Francisco was not really so old; just sixty-five. But for half an hour in his cubicle outside the city room he had felt somewhat over eighty, staring at the face of the new electric typewriter they had forced on him. As editor he had been able to resist it for years. But the pressure had grown too great. The whole building had shifted. Accounting needed his old one. Would he just try one on for size?

And so he had gone all the way, had demanded the newest of the new. There were no flashing keys, even, to give the illusion of physical labor. Just a space-age silver sphere that bounded merrily along to his machine-gun pounding, giving everything serious which he wrote an air of irreverence. Follow the bouncing ball, they used to say in the movie houses. He tapped out a headling: *PATRIOT OR SUICIDE?*

Ike Eisenhower had once said: "Anybody who'd spend forty billion dollars in a race for the moon for reasons of national prestige is nuts." The Administration had not only been extravagant to conceive Pilgrim—it must have been financially insane. The quote was as good a lead as any other, he guessed. Although it would please his publisher, he found that he could not use it. A stupid, senile statement, he knew suddenly, not worthy of Ike. He ripped the paper from the new typewriter and let it slide to the floor.

Maybe the *kamikaze* angle was a better lead. And yet . . . Once he had met Lindbergh and ever afterward carried an image of a tall, quiet young man with a soft, shy smile. For a flight perhaps equally suicidal, the country had applauded; in thirty hours America had been the symbol of a new and shining age.

Of course, Lindbergh had conceived his own mission. Lawrence was being thrown to the lions by grey figures in Washington for political gain. The trouble was that he was not honestly sure that the President was this Machiavellian.

For a lead, then, what about the secrecy? The Administration had not only controlled the news, but throttled it. That was an issue that could still, after forty years of tightening chains, kindle his rage. And yet there was an excuse for that, too. From what he had heard the project *depended* on secrecy or the Russians would sprint to win.

He had a sudden flash of regret. Ralph Fellows had known

of Pilgrim when he had phoned with the ridiculous question of reaction to NASA expenditures! If he had only run down the lead, sniffed around more! Angrily, he stood up. The hell with the editorial. He had hours to write it; that was the advantage of an evening paper. He'd take a stroll down Market and around Union Square and see what the masses had to say. At the door he heard his typewriter moaning. He had forgotten to turn it off again. He glared at it and left as the phone began to ring.

In the old Senate Office Building Senator Ralph Fellows regarded his work while he waited for his San Francisco call: *Remarks on How We of the Senate Can Prevent the Disbursement of Further Funds for a One-Man Lunar Landing Attempt . . .*

He glanced at his watch. It was almost four; if he was going to circulate it on the floor before his speech he would have to move quickly. But he had an odd reluctance to make a move until he had talked to San Francisco. He called through his open door. "Any luck?"

"No, Senator," his secretary answered. "He went out for a walk."

The Senator decided to work on his speech later. He would be able to present it in the chamber ten days earlier than he would have had it not been for the misguided Navy doctor, but perhaps he would let the President have his say first, so that he could have the last word. Anyway, he had to face a TV interview on the Senate Office Building steps at 5:00.

"Bring me that breakdown on NASA's budget," he called to his secretary. "And phone the Navy Department. Find out something about Lawrence's war record."

He despised bathos, demagoguery, and sentimentality. He intended to keep the interview strictly at pocketbook level. But the doctor had said Lawrence was a Korean veteran. It would do no harm to have the facts.

2.

Steve Lawrence, flying from the rear seat, waltzed the jet trainer through the Florida sky in time to western music pouring through his headset from Orlando, a hundred miles ahead. On the way up the Texas coast Rick Lincoln and he had done nothing more serious or space-like than to fly a parabolic trajectory; a dive to mach .8, a gut-cramming climb, then over the top and down for the few seconds of weightlessness that Rick could squeeze from the creaking plane.

Then Rick had for some reason lapsed into sullen lethargy and Steve had taken over from the rear seat and danced through slow rolls, loops, Immelmanns, and lazy eights as his nerves relaxed and the blue Gulf twinkled beneath. The familiar green of the Mississippi, Alabama, and northwest Florida coast unrolled below, lush and restful from 20,000 feet as the fairway of a good golf club. Just past Pensacola

Beach he dropped to wave-top level, flashing along the dazzling sand, skimming the surf, rocking his wings madly at every group of sunbathers that flicked into sight.

Now the Patrick Air Force Base omni-beacon began to sing its initials into his headset. They were at the Cape. "You got it," he told Rick reluctantly, shaking the stick. Rick flung a wing viciously at the morning sun and swung into the Patrick traffic pattern. The engine sighed as if sorry the fun was over.

Bursting his bonds for an hour had raised Steve's spirits. But they dropped again as Rick rolled back the canopy and the heavy Florida air poured into the rear cockpit. A thousand feet below them the narrow strip of sand leading to the Cape slid by—the motels, restaurants, gas stations, and used-car lots that the road from Melbourne had spawned.

He disliked the whole area. It was Las Vegas and Los Angeles and Coney Island strung together like a mismatched necklace of cheap beads. Altitude ordinarily softened highway communities, blending harsh colors and hiding the billboards, but it took more than altitude to melt the hurried tracts and garish motels of Indialantic, Canova Beach, and Cocoa. Standing balanced atop it all to the north was the desolate Cape itself. From the air, to Steve, it was a grotesque, big-headed dwarf with tiny feet and a prominent rear pointed perkily to the Atlantic.

The old launching sites from which Al Shepard had first rocketed down-range were very near the tail end of the dwarf. But the sites had marched north up his body for years, across the sand and scrub. The Mercury-Atlas pads were at the small of his back and the first Saturn launching complex lay at the shoulders. The two pads of Complex 37 were well up the skinny neck. From one the Chuck Wagon shelter would be launched. He tensed as the incredible position he was in struck him with full force. In a week, if Gus or the colonel had not wrecked the schedule, he would follow from the other.

He glanced further north. Almost finished, at the head of the dwarf, were the tallest buildings in Florida, the vertical assembly skyscrapers of the advanced Saturn boosters. Next to them was the launching complex from which the Apollo shot would go to pick him up. He yawned nervously, popping his ears.

Rick Lincoln called Patrick tower for landing, clutched at the thickening air with his dive brakes, and all at once Steve was floating through the moist heat toward whatever Gus Scarbo's two minutes on TV had scared up below.

An hour later he sat in air-conditioned darkness in the astronaut quarters on the upper story of Hangar S, listening to Rick Lincoln lecture on lunar terrain.

The Presidential Press Secretary had sent instructions that he was not to be seen by newsmen for as much as a moment; the press had been evaded at Patrick Air Force Base and barred from the Cape. He had been spirited into his pre-flight quarters with no more strain than if he had been an anonymous engineer reporting for work. Now he sank back in his deep leather chair, almost ashamed because he was enjoying Rick's lecture while the world outside exploded in a burst of recriminations, charges, accusations, and admissions.

It was cool and comfortable in the living quarters. In the hangar bay below white-smocked technicians were weighing the Mercury capsule with scales delicate enough to notice changes in its center of gravity caused by the Florida tides. Steve would live here and eat in the dining room in the block-long dining trailer below until six hours before his launch.

There was something of the what-will-you-have-for-your-last-meal psychology in the svelte furniture of the quarters, the striped cushions, the reclining chair in which he now sat, the quilted spread in the bedroom next door. Last-supper décor or not, Steve reflected, it was a wonderful citadel when the press howled for interviews.

"OK, Buster," Rick said now. "Orient yourself. You've seen this one before."

The black-and-white face of the moon leaped into stark relief on the silver screen. The picture had been shot through the giant reflector at the Pic du Midi Observatory in the French Pyrenees. On the image were superimposed the grid lines of the familiar forty-four lunar areas of the International Astronautical Union. The slide projector buzzed and a new plate appeared. It was another excellent one, sharp and clear.

For some reason Rick had been the first to see that the study of lunar geography could make the difference between life and death for the first fifty men to land on the moon. Someday navigational aids would stud the peaks and craters; someday roving vehicles, abandoned outposts, and emergency shelters would make a mistaken landmark no more serious than one on earth. But until that time came only knowledge would prevent the first men from becoming hopelessly lost.

And so Rick had studied the face of the moon as thoroughly as the navigation that might get them there. His desk was full of sketches, translating the vertical photos into landscapes. Some of the astronauts had been amused at first. "Laugh, you bastards," Rick had said. "I can always sell them to the science-fiction magazines. But someday you'll be standing there with egg on your face, arguing with your partner whether that crater's 10 miles this side of the mountain or 50 miles the other side of it. And neither one of you'll remember how high they are. And there won't be haze to help you."

The closer Apollo had come to the big day, the less grinning there had been. Now Rick was an acknowledged expert. "OK, Steve boy," he said. "This is a new one to you." The projector buzzed and a large and brilliant photo slipped onto the screen. Steve frowned at it, trying to recognize the terrain features before Rick pointed them out.

"The Struve Area?" he guessed.

"That's right. I'll start with Schröter's Valley . . ."

It was far north of the locale in which he must land, far from the Surveyor beacon and the intended point of impact of his shelter. But it was a measure of Rick's thoroughness to show it and a measure of something else as well, some extra care for his well-being.

"Rick?" Steve interrupted.

"Yeah?"

"How do you feel about this now?"

"Lousy."

"Because of the risk?"

"Yes . . ."

"There's something else, isn't there?"

For a long moment Rick stood silhouetted in the darkened room, his face in shadow. Finally he said, very bitterly, "I feel lousy because I discovered something."

"What?"

"That I couldn't have done it, goddamn it! Even if I had been ordered."

Steve felt closer to him than he had ever felt before. "I think you could have."

"Bullshit! I could not play Russian roulette; I could not climb into that capsule." He looked down at Steve in the shadow. "You know what that means? It means I look at a stewardess on a plane and wonder if she can see it, and I want to pick her up and find out. It means I wonder if the colonel's got me figured. It means when I lay my wife I wonder if she knows, too!"

"I'm not in that capsule yet myself," Steve observed. "I have my own doubts."

"You are losing them by the hour." Rick shrugged. "Well, there's one thing I can do."

"Yes?"

"I may not be heroic enough to try to get there first, but I know every cow-turd crater on the face of the moon. If you listen to me you just may not get lost."

Steve let him continue, watching the beam from his flashlight leap across ridges and clefts to rest like a tired firefly on a valley at the northern end of the Sea of Storms. Steve knew the area almost as well as Rick. Months ago, on a scheduled trip to Lowell Observatory in Arizona, the moon had begun to exert a tidal fascination for him, too. He found that he wanted to learn its face not only for the first Apollo flight, but for the ones that would follow. Someday, after all, he and other men would fan out to explore Schröter's and Schiaparelli, and all the other mountains and valleys and craters and faults; would map the moon from the 30,000-foot Liebnitz Range to the depths of the Newton Crater. And follow the sun around its sphere to know the hidden side as well . . .

From the night at Lowell Steve, aroused from his preoccupation with engineering systems, had become captivated by the landscape he began to imagine. He had sketches in his own desk now. And sometimes he had lain awake, stiff with fear that their own crew would not be among the first, that too many others ahead of him would know the stark beauty of lunar mountains and jagged rills. He tensed with excitement. Of all the Russians and Americans who stood at the threshold, the door to this bleak, mysterious land might after all be opening first for him. Alone . . .

"Schröter's Valley itself," Rick droned on, "curves like a dry riverbed. Think of it as a snake crawling toward Herodotus Crater. Surveyor Four pictures indicate a length of about 50 miles and mean width of 3, wall-to-wall. You can see the steepness of the sides. The mean slope is—"

Someone had entered the room. Rick stopped. They had left word that they were not to be disturbed; this was the last lunar session. The light flicked on. It was the colonel, face stubbled, as if he had not had time to shave. He nodded at Steve. "How's it feel to be a celebrity?"

Steve's heart began to pound. "Did you see the President?"

The colonel moved to the huge lunar atlas on the coffee

table, flipped the pages idly. "I saw him."

"Did you . . ." The words almost stuck. "Did you get me scrubbed?"

The colonel looked up. "You're very concerned. Why?"

Steve moved to the atlas. It was opened to the Grimaldi Area on the edge of the Ocean of Storms. He pointed between Flamsteed and Hansteen craters. All at once he knew the truth. His finger trembled. "Because, damn it, I want to go!"

The colonel nodded. "You're going. I can't foul things up. Not now." He spoke hoarsely. "If anybody goes, it'll be you."

Steve discovered that he was weak with relief.

The colonel studied him. Then, for the first time in a week, he smiled. "You know," he said softly, "I think you're catching it. I do indeed . . ."

"We're at Schröter's Gulch, heading south," Rick interrupted. "Unless you want to come, maybe we'd better get on with it."

The colonel shook his head and went to superintend the capsule check. Steve settled in the darkness, thinking. "Catching it." He was no fanatic. He would not let himself become one. He had promised Mickey, but he wondered if the colonel was right.

3.

Senator Ralph Fellows watched from the worn leather chair in his brownstone Washington flat as Charlie Choy, his ancient Chinese houseboy, fiddled with the dials. The President's face came alight on the TV screen. Choy stepped back, parchment face beautiful in wonderment as always when the miracle was accomplished and a picture actually appeared on the tube.

The Senator sipped his ginless tonic. He had cut off alcohol two years ago because he found himself awaiting his evening cocktail with too much anticipation. Tonight he considered relaxing the rule. For some reason the President's predicament did not amuse him. In fact, the thought of his plight had all day made him obscurely jumpy and irritable. A drink might calm him, but even to Choy he hated to show weakness. He put aside the impulse.

The President smiled shyly and Choy grunted in disgust.

He had never voted; for forty years Ralph Fellows had been sure that somewhere in his history lurked the threat of the Immigration Service. But the old Chinaman had strong political convictions. Ralph Fellows should be President and the incumbents could try to sway him as they pleased. So someone, at least, was impervious to the earthly Presidential charm.

The President, when he was trapped, was a truly effective speaker and this was one of his better nights. He was weaving a web already, speaking straight to the screen with the deliberate, solid air of candor that seemed lately to hypnotize the voter.

". . . Our project was undertaken eighteen months ago. The Soviets had promised co-operation in a joint moon venture. But when the Soviet space platform was launched, it was launched in secret. This despite Soviet assurances once that they actually had no lunar ambitions; this despite their signature on a U.N. prohibition of military weapons in outer space.

"Project Pilgrim had already been conceived and rejected. It was launched again the next *day* on the drawing boards of our own engineers. The Soviets had breached the faith, so plans for Pilgrim were also launched in secret. We were *not* asleep . . ."

The Senator shook off the homey spell. Don't mention, he thought sardonically, the day after the Russian launch, with NASA hysterical and the White House a madhouse. Pilgrim was the convulsive gesture of a man caught with his pants down. You *were* asleep, you and your young men. Tell them so.

"The project," the President continued, "was authorized by me on April 18 . . ."

"But not by Congress," Ralph Fellows murmured. "Tell them."

". . . Authorized, of course, only after conferences with scientists in the fields of propulsion, space biology, and astrophysics . . .'' But the astrophysicist who gave it birth renounced it, the Senator reminded him. Tell them that! ''Project Mercury astronauts were consulted,'' the President continued. ''They agreed that the element of risk appeared to be high . . .''

Senator Fellows raised his eyebrows. A tactical mistake to admit it? Or a wise move to painlessly mention the risk in case Project Pilgrim was launched and unsuccessful? But it would *not* be launched!

The President went on: ''The first two Project Mercury astronauts who were asked were among the most experienced Americans in space. They did not find the risks unacceptable. Both volunteered for Pilgrim.'' But they were military men. Mention that! Risks for your country are part of a military career. What about the next one asked? What about the civilian? ''When, to make sure that our desire to internationalize the moon was not misunderstood, a civilian astronaut was consulted, he also volunteered . . .''

The Senator moved uncomfortably. He had been wondering for days exactly why Lawrence had agreed to go. Pressured, probably, or somehow bribed, or simply too inexperienced to know what he was doing. Or were the risks perhaps not as great as the press was painting them? It didn't matter. The President's next year's budget, thank God, was before the Senate; tomorrow the President would find Apollo grounded, broke, insolvent. Without Apollo to rescue the astronaut next year, there could be no Pilgrim launch now.

''At the same time that we started Pilgrim,'' the President continued, ''this country introduced in the U.N. resolutions which, if accepted, would have made Pilgrim unnecessary. These motions sought to put teeth into the 1961 resolution of the General Assembly that celestial bodies were international territory, not subject to domain of any of the powers.''

The Senator grunted. The President was skirting an area

that made him uneasy. Why *had* the Russians been so reluctant to allow teeth in the resolution? Why were they changing their tack, if the moon was of no use? Why had they gone ahead alone? Prestige?

The President lately gave the illusion on TV of looking the viewer individually in the eye. The Senator shifted in his seat.

"No one in the free world knows today," the President finished, "if our daughter, our ward, on the endless journey through space could be turned against an individual nation or group of nations on earth." He seemed tired. He paused and went on. "But our strength requires that if there is even *risk* to our own country, we act. Our convictions require that if there is risk to free men anywhere, or their children's children, we act." The President's face filled the screen. Close up, his image was that of a very weary man. "It has become my sorrowful judgment that there is such a risk. I have acted. I ask for support." He paused. "I ask for *your* support." He nodded unsmilingly and he was gone, and on the screen loomed the Great Seal of the United States.

Choy turned off the set. On his way to the dining room to lay out the Senator's solitary dinner, he paused. "Boss?"

"Yes?"

"Why you want to stop us going to the moon?"

The Senator gaped. "Don't tell me," he murmured, "you think we ought to go?"

Solemnly, Charlie Choy nodded. "I think."

"For Christ's sake, why?"

"I don't know, Boss." The bleary eyes seemed brighter. "I die pretty soon, maybe, and . . . Dinner two minutes."

The Senator watched him shuffle from the room. He had learned in the smoky mah-jongg parlors of Placer County and along the muddy Yuba not to waste time on Oriental thought processes; mining-town Chinese lived in a political vacuum, anyway. But to find the oldest Chinaman in captivity supporting a trip to the moon shook him to his roots.

Maybe the old boy had heard somewhere that the Chinese invented rockets. The Senator arose, shaking his head, and went in to eat.

4.

Sadly, because now he must go to face his typewriter, the Old
Man saw the President's image fade from the screen as the
young bartender turned off the set. He found himself listening for the rumble of the Powell and Jackson cable car
outside. When he heard it there would be plenty of time to
pay up, swing aboard, and ride to the office to do the
editorial. But then he remembered that the tracks had been
torn up years before. Silent electric buses climbed the hills
now. He could not hear their approach. So he must wait
outside in the fog. Progress . . .

He reached for his change. Now that the President had
spoken, there was no more excuse to delay. "Man," the
bartender nodded at the blank screen, "that bullshit artist can
make you think we *ought* to go to the moon!"

"Maybe we should," the Old Man said, to keep the ball
rolling, or to procrastinate further. A big blonde with a

martini complexion sighed from the end of the bar. She was one of hundreds, the Old Man reflected, who had been regulars here over the years. They seemed always propped on the same barstool: Cheri, Frankie, Ethyl, Sue, Maudie, Lydia, Frankie II. He was thinking in rhyme more and more. Senility, probably, puckishness, or maybe just boredom.

"Intercourse in outer space," the blonde remarked to no one in particular. "This chap, he came up to me . . ."

My God, thought the Old Man. "This chap . . ." Are they speaking British this year? The Old Man looked down the bar at the others and felt very old indeed. For years the place had been a businessman's hideaway. Montgomery Street bankers and Grant Avenue advertising men had haunted it with mousey, intellectual little secretaries. Now the cheap imitation leather was older and the prices had dropped, and beatniks and students had come.

A pasty-faced young man, a graduate student, perhaps, from UC Extension up the street, took up the challenge. "Why?" he asked the Old Man, looking through his beer bottle as if it were a telescope.

"Why what?"

"Why should this Lawrence idiot go to the moon?"

The Old Man shrugged. "Beat the Russians, I guess."

"Outer space," the blonde continued to the bartender. "Chap came up to me at the Yankee Doodle and started tapping me on the arm. I asked why. You know what he did?"

"*Why* beat the Russians to the moon?" the young man with the beer bottle demanded again.

One of his companions, hiding behind a beard, seemed deep in thought. He was a lean youth with pale blue eyes; the beard was an unfortunate affectation, for he had a firm jaw. During the President's speech, while the young man had watched the screen with a kind of amused disgust, the bearded youth had followed each word with increasing attention. "I'd go," he said, now, surprisingly. "I wish to hell it was me."

"Why, Hero?" asked the graduate student.

The bearded one thought it over. "I just think it's great, that's all."

The other snorted. He lived obviously in a world in which nothing was great.

All at once the Old Man was impelled to order the bearded youth another beer. I'm not a fag, either, he told him silently, when he hesitated. Just a worn-out editor: drink up. The boy decided suddenly and filled his glass.

"Why do you want to go to the moon?" the pale-faced lad insisted.

The bearded youth's voice was very quiet, as if he were talking to himself. "To see how it is."

"Lonely, man, at first," the other said. "And I'll tell you how it'll be later. You want to know?"

"Go on, Dad. You will anyway."

"Lock step! That's how it'll be." His face suddenly blazed. "And it won't matter who gets there first. Hot dogs and fill-in-the-forms, you Yuk, and I'm bringing the boss home for dinner and I wish they'd draft that kid of mine before he goes to Cuba! That's how it'll be!"

There was a moment of weighty silence. The bartender cleared his throat. The blonde ignored the outburst. "So the guy taps me on the arm," she told the Old Man, "and he hands me this." She passed down a business-sized card. "Can you imagine?"

He put on his glasses. The card was tattered. *I am a Martian. My sexual organs are in my fingers. You have just been screwed.*

The Old Man smiled faintly, passed the card to the bearded youth, who glanced at it and gave it to his pale-faced friend. "This Lawrence cat," the pasty-faced boy said bitterly. "He's who's getting screwed."

The bearded one seemed not to hear him. "God," he murmured. "I wish it was me."

The Old Man, warmed by an odd excitement, decided to feel the pulse of Market Street before he wrote his column.

At 10 P.M. Senator Ralph Fellows, cleaning his false teeth, heard the phone ring. Irritably he put the plate in a water glass, hurried to catch the bedside extension before Charlie Choy took the easy way out and told whoever it was that he was asleep. It was his secretary.

"The supply-capsule launch," she said, "is planned for ten A.M. tomorrow at Cape Kennedy. I knew you wanted to speak to the President before it was decided, so I thought—"

"Thank you, Myrna," the Senator said. He hung up, stared at the phone. He could probably get through to the White House. The President was not reckless. He had little doubt that when he told him what he was going to do he would cancel the supply launch. He wondered how much money it would save to stop the supply capsule now. Probably not much, if it was already on the pad.

He had no real obligation to scuttle it. If it was a failure, let the Administration stew in it. And if it was not, the Senate would after his speech tomorrow prevent the manned launch anyway. By election time all that anyone would remember was that the Administration had spent $50 million on a housing project on the moon that no one had ever used. The risk was all the President's. If your enemy insisted on backing to the edge of a mineshaft to fight, why try to restrain him?

He replaced the phone and crawled into bed. But it took two hours with Bender's *American Law of Mining* to put him to sleep.

5.

The President waited while TV technicians moved the last of the lights from his executive office in the West Wing. He was almost reluctant to see them go.

On a couch flanking the marble fireplace squirmed the Vice-President. He was as restless, the President thought, as a tomcat at midnight. Facing him on the matching couch sat Ned Mooney. Compared with the tense young politician the Press Secretary was a mountain of calm. The President sighed. When the last technician left, when Ned Mooney gave him his comments on the speech and followed, he would be alone with the Vice-President and there would be nothing to do but decide on Chuck Wagon.

"Ned, what did you think?"

Ned Mooney smiled noncommittally. "In general? Well, as a newspaperman I have to admit that in terms of logic and content your talk may have left something to be desired."

The Vice-President broke in angrily. "I think it was great!"

"Go on, Ned," the President murmured. He was suddenly depressed. He had written the speech himself, wanting to make sure that nobody got between him and the viewer. "Next time I'll call you in earlier."

Ned Mooney got up. The President had known him since he covered the Senate; he had never seen him enthusiastic. But now he was grinning like a college cheerleader. "Next time," he said softly, "do it the same way! It was sincere. It showed."

The President was moved. "Do you think I convinced anybody?"

"Believe me, Mr. President! The uncommitted—you convinced. Nobody ever convinces the others."

They watched him leave the room, his haunches swinging like a pachyderm's. "My feelings," the Vice-President said, "exactly."

"Thanks." He walked back to his desk. "We'll know tomorrow."

"They can't stop Chuck Wagon tomorrow," the Vice-President said significantly, "so it may not matter."

The President glanced at him speculatively, but said nothing. He thinks I am wavering, he thought, and is pushing me again. He moved to his desk, half-sat on its top, gaining strength from the solid oak. In his oval study upstairs, Lincoln's simple desk reminded him of the fitness of Presidential humility. But this ornate masterpiece seemed to pulse with the power of office. It had been hewn from timbers of an ice-locked British man-of-war freed by an American whaling skipper. Queen Victoria had presented it to Rutherford Hayes when the warship was broken up in the '70s. It was as eternal and doughty a piece of furniture as the old girl must have been herself.

The President picked up the Washington *Star*. An enormous wirephoto of the Saturn booster, stark against the

Florida sky, took up the second page. Perched atop its last stage was a slim Polaris braking rocket; capping it all was the ridiculous tin can in which a man was to live for a year. If he decided to launch it. If it landed safely on the moon. If he was allowed to launch the man. And if the man landed safely on the moon to find it. He folded the paper.

"I wonder," he mused, "if the Russians'd send it back?" The Vice-President looked at him blankly. The President smiled. "If something went wrong and it landed in Siberia, do you think they'd make a desk out of it and send it back?"

The young man knew exactly what he was talking about but did not consider it worthy of reply.

"You know," the President observed, "I haven't heard you laugh for a month?"

The Vice-President smiled thinly. "I haven't heard anything funny. OK, now there's a mechanical 'hold' right now, but the Chuck Wagon launch is scheduled at—"

"Can you stop Ralph Fellows on the floor?" the President cut in.

"No," the Vice-President said, startled. "Look, even if he's got the votes to cut NASA next year, it can't hurt Chuck Wagon tomorrow!"

"It's funny," the President mused, "I haven't heard from him tonight."

"Why should you?"

"Why isn't he trying to knock out the supply launch? With a threat? He would if he *didn't* have the votes."

The Vice-President's eyes narrowed. "That old bastard!" he grated. "He *wants* us to launch the shelter. He's trying to trap us!"

"I think," said the President, "you're a hundred percent correct."

The Vice-President began to pace the room. His color was mounting; he looked as if he would like to put his fist through the window to the Rose Garden. "OK," he spat finally, "let's trap *him*. Let's launch, anyway!"

The President regarded him grimly. It was time for a lesson in the complexities of the Presidency. If he could not drum them through now, the country might suffer for it later.

"Let me describe for you a potential situation," he said. "You can color it as you please. We launch Chuck Wagon tomorrow. Ralph Fellows bulldogs the Senate into cutting next year's Apollo budget. Chuck Wagon lands successfully, so we would like to launch Lawrence to inhabit it, but we know that Apollo cannot rescue him next year because it will slip from lack of funds. What do we do?"

"Launch him anyway," the Vice-President snapped, "and go for a supplemental! Congress isn't going to leave him there."

"That's true," the President said. "Then is that what you would do?"

The young man flushed more deeply, but nodded. "Absolutely."

"I see," the President sighed. He regarded the oaken desk, the American eagle bursting from the wood of its face, glaring over widespread wings as if searching for a target for arrow or olive branch. "Do you have any concept of what that might cause? You're a lawyer. This is a provable, malicious, arbitrary overriding of the fiscal desires of Congress by the executive branch, remember!"

The Vice-President for the first time seemed shaken. "Yes, but . . ."

"But, hell!" exploded the President. "Suppose I were impeached? Where would you end up?"

The young man shook his head doggedly. "This is more important than political ambitions."

"Because this is a dream! We have been swinging a club for civil rights! We've been sending troops into pestholes and civilians into the jungle, and we've hardly started yet! What happens to the rest of the dreams? Do we flush them down the drain to beat the Russians to the moon?"

For a long while the young man held his eyes. Then,

suddenly, incredibly, he shook his head. "I don't know," he mumbled.

"All right," said the President. "Do we launch that fifty-million-dollar shelter tomorrow and let Fellows point to it in November, empty, rusting in the middle of that goddamned plain?"

"Maybe," the Vice-President murmured, "we better wait."

The President felt better. "Do you really think," he asked softly, "if we don't launch the shelter tomorrow we'll ever launch the man?"

The Vice-President shook his head worriedly. "No. What the hell *will* we do?"

The President looked out the French doors. An evening thunderhead, glowing orange at its base from the lights of Arlington, had drifted over the Potomac. Lightning flashed suddenly, silhouetting the Washington Monument. For an instant the President saw in it the Saturn on the pad. They had gone too far to turn back.

"We'll launch the shelter capsule," he said slowly, "as we planned. We'll hope the Senate lets us launch the man."

The Vice-President looked into his face. Then he nodded. "Yes." He grinned, a little ruefully, and then the face turned wonderfully warm and radiant and the President felt a tug of nostalgia for a happier day. "Yes, sir."

"Good night," he grinned. "Sleep tight."

The young man nodded and left. To the President he seemed not to have shrunken, but to have grown. He liked him better that way.

6.

Steve Lawrence lay sleepless in bed at the Cape Carib Motel. Headlights from late Cocoa Beach traffic swept the drapes and vanished. Beside him Mickey sighed and burrowed deeper into her pillow like a small child hiding from school.

A girl giggled in the parking area outside. He wondered what time it was. Across the patio the steel-drum orchestra was throbbing still, so it could not be after midnight. He must sleep. Tomorrow would start at 6:30 when a Cape Kennedy security car would pick them up to breakfast at Hangar S, where no stray reporter could bother them.

"Ma—til—da! Ma—til—da!" chanted a local Belafonte, to the muffled Caribbean beat that had become Cape Kennedy's folk music. "Matilda take me money and run Venezuela . . ."

His mind raced over the things he must do. If he planned carefully he could keep Mickey near him for the next eighteen hours. They would be their last hours together. Tomorrow he would see his shelter launched from the blockhouse; Mickey could watch it there, too, on internal television or through the periscope assigned him. He was suddenly wide awake, wondering what was happening on the pad. T-minus-zero for the shelter launch was 8:34 A.M. But just before they had slipped off to sleep after the President's talk, there had been a "hold" for a frozen valve. He was reaching for the phone when Mickey stirred. No, he thought, stopping short. If the valve was still frozen there was nothing he could do about it. To keep up with him tomorrow she would need all the sleep she could get.

Assuming the launch was successful, the press was scheduled for a crack at him afterward. He wondered if he really wanted her there to see him sweating under the barrage. "What odds do you give yourself, Mr. Lawrence? When do you think Apollo and the LEM will be able to rescue you? Do you feel you've learned the Mercury capsule well enough?" He had replied to these mentally, though, already, and the trivial ones too: "Yes, ma'am, there was a Bible in that shelter capsule. I'll be busy, but I'll probably read it."

About the Big Question he wasn't sure. He wasn't sure of the answer and he wasn't sure that he wanted Mickey to know he wasn't. "What *is* your motivation, Mr. Lawrence? *Why* have you volunteered?" Did he reply with the stiff pride of the patriot, or an explorer's far-off gaze, or smile a Lindbergh smile and keep his peace?

He put the dismal choices from his mind and searched for a chink in the rest of the day's schedule. If he could find a free hour there was an intruder-proof beach near Complex 37 for a swim with Mickey. Perhaps after the astronaut meeting . . .

When the press was through with him he was scheduled for a last conference with the astronauts as a group, those not already at Zanzibar, Canton Island, or Woomera as Capsule Communicators for his own launch. They would finish the plans for next year's rendezvous on the lunar surface, would estimate how much help Steve could give his rescuers in the Lunar Excursion Module. To that meeting he should take Mickey, too. No matter how technical the language became, it would strengthen her faith to hear them discussing his rescue.

Rescue? Without warning he began to shake. The Pilgrim Project was impossible, a nightmare. He was a simple test pilot, assigned to Apollo. When he awakened from the dream all would go as they had planned for years.

He was clammy and cold. He fought a crazy impulse to crush Mickey into his arms, to cling to her, to face the world with her tomorrow and tell it he would stay. He saw himself striking a pose: "I regret that I have only one life to give to my country. I'm sure you'll understand that on further thought I've decided to save it for my wife and me."

His face was damp. Cautiously, so that she would not awaken, he groped for his handkerchief on the bedside table. He must be careful all day tomorrow. He must show no weakness. After tomorrow, in the preparation for his launch, she would practically disappear. So the last four days would pose no problem.

But tomorrow when they were alone together, he must be careful.

She awakened him at dawn, her hand toying with his hair. One moment he was asleep and the next he was looking into the pixie eyes as she lay on her side, twirling a strand.

"Time to get up?" he asked huskily.

She shook her head. "Only five . . ."

For a long while they lay looking into each other's faces. How little and how much you know, he thought, about the woman you love.

"Did you sleep?" she asked.

"Yes," he lied. "You?"

She nodded. "And then," she murmured, "I had a dream. Kind of a dream anyway . . ."

She sat up, her eyes distant. The dim morning light, through yellow drapes, tinged her skin with gold. He traced the curve of her leg beneath the sheet, feeling a great warmth rising but letting it rise before taking her into his arms.

"I dreamed," she remembered, "or thought, anyway . . . remember Stevie and the pier?"

He nodded. He and Stevie had been shoving off from their creaking dock to go fishing in the Scarbo outboard. Stevie had spotted a forgotten bait can on the pier. At the last and worst possible moment he had jumped from the stern, missed, and landed in the rusting, splintering piles. For a frozen instant Steve had seen him mangled in the propeller, spitted on a piling, ripped open on a spike. Then Stevie had bobbed to the surface, laughing and thrashing.

"I remember," Steve said.

Mickey's face was tight. "Only . . . when he came up he was all cut and he was bleeding. And somehow it wasn't him. Steve, it was you!"

A departing guest slammed a car trunk outside, called to someone to hurry. Steve looked into the oval tanned face. "A child who saw something he wanted," he explained softly.

She smiled a little. "I see . . ."

"If it is dangerous to jump for the pier," he promised slowly, "I will stay in the boat. I've told you that. Children act on impulse. I'm not a child."

She studied him for a long moment. "Have you an impulse?" she asked.

"An adult impulse," he murmured.

"I would like," she said, "for you to give in to it."

After breakfast Steve had an idea calculated to show Mickey how solid a prospect was his rescue. He told the NASA driver to swing north to the nearly completed pads and towers of Complex 39 so that Mickey could see at close range the Advanced Saturn Vertical Assembly Building. Its enormous doors gaped as if waiting for the boosters that would

next year fling the Apollo lunar mission to his aid. But the
building, the steel tracks leading from it to half-finished
pedestals, the canal down which the giant boosters would be
floated, had an air of abandonment. Too late he realized why.
The workers were gathered somewhere to watch the supply
launch. He told her why the complex was deserted and she
pretended to accept it, but the effect was deadly; it was
impossible to visualize a successful firing from so desolate a
spot. So he told the driver to go on.

At the guard post half a mile from his own familiar Complex 37 he heard Mickey suck in her breath. Across the flat
scrub two Saturn I boosters spired, brilliant white in the early
Florida sun. They were twins. But men were swarming over
the umbilical structure of the right-hand one; it was sucking
liquid oxygen and its skin was thick with frost; on its top
perched the minuscule shelter.

The other, a thousand feet away, was deserted, and nothing rode its nose. Steve's tiny Mercury cabin would not be
hoisted to its top for another two days. By that time, if all
went well, the shelter would be resting on the moon. But
Mickey's eyes were on the empty booster, not the active one.
He sighed and squeezed her hand.

As they approached the blockhouse the behemoth launch
service structure left the Chuck Wagon rocket and began to
crawl along tracks to a central position. It was a ponderous,
prehistoric beast, high as a twenty-story building. Sometime
in the last week it had squatted over each launch pad, plucked
up the components of the million-pound vehicles, and raised
them unit by unit beside their umbilical towers. Now it would
hold its distance as the first of its creations burst its shackles
in a cascade of flame.

The blockhouse was a beehive structure equidistant from
the two launch pads, seemingly much too close to the flame
deflectors beneath the rockets. Mickey had never been in the
Launch Control Center during a firing. As a pot-bellied guard

looked at her pass, Steve saw her glance at the steel entrance door. It weighed 23 tons and looked it.

"Claustrophobia?" he smiled.

"A vault," she murmured.

"You'll be glad for all that steel, Mrs. Lawrence," said the guard, "if that baby blows up on the pad."

Steve stared at him. "That's an interesting speculation for her," he said tightly. "Since if the next one goes I'll be in it." The guard flushed and Steve followed her down the passageway.

Steve, sitting in the front row of the glassed-in observation balcony between Mickey and a Florida Senator, looked down at the control room. No one was wandering anymore; everyone was intent on his panel or console. "T minus 50 seconds," said the voice on the intercom.

The Test Supervisor at the rear of the amphitheater stood suddenly, stretched, and sat down again, as if the strain had become too great to bear quietly. "T minus 40 seconds, counting," his assistant said into a microphone. He was a bald young man with thick glasses and thick lips; he sat sidewise, casually, at his panel next to the Range Safety Officer. He seemed determined to earn a reputation today as a calm voice in a storm of emotion.

"Lox tanks pressurized," another voice cracked, taut with excitement. The reports picked up in frequency. "Countdown time synchronized with vehicle operations, " said the Test Supervisor. "All oscillographs on," a woman's voice reported.

The Senator from Florida was using the huge lens of the periscope. When he saw Steve craning he very quickly swung it back and Steve turned it so that Mickey could see, too.

The frosty, sweating vehicle filled the lens. A puff of vapor shot yards to the side, then dissipated. An umbilical line swung free, dangled for a moment like an elephant's trunk, disappeared into the tower. Some internal tremor dislodged a chunk of frost from high on the third stage; it spun lazily in the bright sunlight and crashed on the flame deflector.

"T minus 30 seconds . . ."

"Lox bubbling 'off' . . ."

"Range safe . . ."

Steve smelled cigarette smoke and the stale ozone of too many electrical circuits, found that he was gripping Mickey's hand too tightly. He licked his lips. The maddening chant went on: "T minus 25 seconds. A hold for any reason after this point will necessitate a scrub . . ." Please, God, no holds. No holds . . .

"T minus five seconds . . ."

"Retract swing arm . . ."

A long arm from the umbilical tower swung back, hesitated as if reluctant to trust the balance of a pile of blocks, then continued and vanished into the tower.

"Fluid pad!" A half-million gallons of water per minute poured over the flame deflectors in a minor Niagara. Dazzling rainbows wreathed the pad. He heard Mickey draw her breath.

"Four, three, two, one . . . zero!"

Two rock-hard columns of white-hot flame appeared instantly. The blockhouse was deathly still. A barely discernible vibration began to build.

"Ignition, engines five and seven!" Two more columns of flame joined the first. Still the vehicle stood immovable.

"Ignition, engines six and eight . . ." Two more engines caught and flame was cascading from the deflectors in a golden torrent, turning the water into billows of steam. Now the rumble in the blockhouse could be felt from toe to head. The vehicle stood clamped but the capsule on its nose swayed visibly as the rockets strained to be free.

The bird shuddered in frustration. Ice showered from the

upper stages, spun into the caldron below. The 14-foot concrete shell of the blockhouse pulsed with life. Time stopped; for a moment Steve was sure that the hold-down clamps had jammed and the rocket would burn itself on the pad to a pool of molten liquid.

"Hold-downs released!" The yellow steel shackles sprang aside.

"First motion!"

"Lift off!"

The motion was so minute at first that Mickey missed it. "It isn't going," she breathed. There was an odd catch in her voice. He glanced at her quickly. Her face shone with hope. Sick for her, he touched her hand.

For now the ball of flame turned pear-shaped. The vehicle inched from the pad; it was feet from the pedestal, then yards. Then Steve saw the top of the umbilical tower whisk past the engine nozzles and the Saturn was up, up, up, accelerating endlessly into the Florida sky. The hard lance of flame on which it rode turned suddenly from gold to red. Almost unnoticeably the trajectory began to arch. For what seemed like hours the periscope followed it until its flame was a memory in the sapphire blue. Sweet and true, he knew, and running hot . . .

The intercom crackled into life. In its background someone cut loose with a Rebel yell. He looked down. The engineers and technicians were exuberant. Even the bald young man with glasses allowed himself a smile. "T plus 30 seconds," he said. "Disarm water system . . ."

Steve stood up. He felt drained and weak. The Senator arose. "I may have to fight for your launch on the floor of the Senate tonight," he said. "Any second thoughts?"

Steve shook his head. "No, sir."

"So far so good?"

He glanced at Mickey. She was smiling stiffly.

"So far," he said softly, "so good."

7.

Senator Ralph Fellows climbed aboard the rubber-tired, blue-grey subway car in the basement of the Old Senate Office Building. He indicated the seat next to him for the red-headed Senator from Georgia. The little train started its one-minute trip to the Capitol.

"Goddard Center," the red-headed Senator remarked, "says the shelter's running right on the nose."

Ralph Fellows peered at him sharply. He had had a restless night. "Look, Red, nobody says you have to support me. If you think these eggheads ought to go ahead, say so."

"I *didn't* say so," the Georgian remarked mildly. "And I don't intend to abandon our position. I simply observed—"

"Sorry, Red," Ralph Fellows said. "You want to see this?"

He handed him a copy of his remarks on next year's appropriation bill, then opened the *Los Angeles Times*. He read swiftly, scanning the reaction to last night's Presidential address with growing curiosity. He looked at a man-on-the-street column, uneasily aware that it had been slanted so that the majority of those interviewed approved the project.

"I'll be damned," he said aloud. Quickly he tore open the San Francisco paper. He had tried without success to reach the Old Man this morning. He glanced at the headlines: *SHELTER SHOT GOING.* Then he turned swiftly to the editorial page, smoothed the paper back:

RUB TWO BOY SCOUTS TOGETHER

Anti-Administration forces, among them this paper occasionally, call the young men around the White House Boy Scouts and the President the scoutmaster when they are displeased with him, which is usually.

Presumably Astronaut Steve Lawrence is a member of the troop. Trustworthy, loyal, helpful. . . . The rest of the oath escapes us.

It doesn't matter. Oath and scouts have become a symbol of fun, anyway.

How do you start a fire? Rub two Boy Scouts together. Laughter.

The Senator stiffened, sensing danger.

A Boy Scout seems to have been rubbed. And fire has kindled in certain youth of the North Beach coffee houses and the tourists' Barbary Coast, where there were no fires before and certainly no Boy Scouts.

Sparks glow when you talk to boozy young sailors along Market Street: "We'll beat 'em, Buster. I knew it all the time."

In his Chinatown pad a young artist in a beret doesn't laugh, but says: "The greatest!"

And he doesn't even say "man."

It is doubtless time for cold-eyed politicians to throw water on the fire.

But it has been nice to see it glow for Lawrence as it did for Lindbergh in the eyes of the American youth.

The subway had stopped and the Georgian was waiting politely for him to leave the car. He had an impulse to crumple the paper and hurl it away. Instead he handed it to the other Senator. "Read this, Red. We're 'cold-eyed politicians.' "

Walking up the ramp, the other man glanced through the editorial, then at the masthead. "Jesus, Ralph, I thought you and the publisher slept together!"

"Apparently," Ralph Fellows said, "he owns the paper, not the editor." He should be angry and should be hurt. He should hope the Old Man would get drunk to celebrate his mutiny and break his neck. And yet, for some odd reason the Old Man's rebellion made him feel younger than he had in years.

The Senate chaplain droned the invocation. Senator Ralph Fellows studied the crystal bottle on his mahogany desk. Under the bottle lay his remarks. Like most Senators, he used the flask as a paperweight. Once the bottles had held sand to dry Senatorial ink. And it was said that some of them had held good Kentucky bourbon, too, to stiffen the nerve when tempers were short and a cloakroom caning or a duel in the Virginia dawn were hazards of national politics.

Stephen Douglas had once sat at this desk. Ralph Fellows picked up the bottle. It was smooth in his hand, of a glossiness one never found today; its angles and facets were sharp and uncompromising. He wondered if Douglas had kept it filled with sand or liquor.

Black was black and white was white in the day of the Little Giant. For weeks he had stood at bay in this chamber, Lincoln's chamber, lion mane flowing and massive shoulders squared, and shouted them all down. In his brilliance he was blind, but he saw Lincoln as evil; he would topple him if he brought the country crashing with him. And yet . . . when the guns rumbled he had looked into the eyes of his tall, gaunt enemy. Then he had nodded and ridden to the border states to plead Abe Lincoln's cause.

"And Heavenly Father," chanted the chaplain, "let us not fail in our efforts. We reach for the stars and the planets so that Your Word shall rule them and free men shall tread them unafraid."

The Senator sat bolt upright. He stared at the chaplain's bowed head. Only with an effort did he keep from rising in protest. He sank back, cold with anger, and drew his remarks from under the bottle. He was the first out of his seat when the clerk completed his quorum call. He looked into the eyes of the young man in the chair. In them he saw for the first time uncertainty.

"Mr. President?" he called briskly.

"The Senator from California," sighed the Vice-President. Briskly, and without using the notes, Ralph Fellows began.

Steve Lawrence emerged dripping in swimming trunks from the warm Atlantic water. He sat in the late afternoon sun of Cape Kennedy and watched Mickey padding barefoot along the orange sand. She was looking for doubloons. The colonel had told her when he jeeped them here of a treasure armada driven on the Florida beaches in 1733.

"I'll find some," she promised. "The law of averages." Because in all her life she had never found a doubloon.

It had been a glorious day, despite the rush. The launch had been flawless, its course was still arrow-true, the press conference had been easy—it was as if secretly even the journalists were wishing Pilgrim well. And in the living room of his quarters atop Hangar S, the final plans for his rescue had gone so smoothly that even Mickey must have been cheered.

And still, on the way to the hidden beach, when the colonel had glanced at his watch and said that they ought to be burning candles because Senator Fellows was starting in Washington now, Mickey had looked away, as if ashamed of her own thoughts.

Now she raced toward him along the wet beach, her feet exploding golden bursts of sand. She dropped to her knees, grinning evilly. "You look like Apol—" she began. The smile faded. "You look like a sun god."

He knew that she was fighting to keep the very thought of space from between them for the rest of the day. He kissed her lightly. "You look like . . . who? A water nymph? Lorelei?"

But the fun was gone. She gazed out at the brassy chop of the mild Atlantic. "Hans Christian Andersen's mermaid?" she suggested.

He knew the story but he tried to divert her. "Entice me, Lorelei. Tempt me onto rocks . . ."

"I saw her, you know."

"Hmm?"

"When Daddy was attaché in Copenhagen. The Little Mermaid's statue, on a rock in the water. Off Langelinie Park. Waiting all alone, looking out to sea, and everybody would come to see her and she never moved even when they took her picture . . ."

Her eyes were wet. He moved his lips along the back of her hand. "She was a mermaid," he reminded her. "So the prince *couldn't* come back. You're no mermaid and I will."

"Tonight?" she asked softly. He had to shake his head. He had a last pressure-suit fitting. It might take until midnight. And he needed his sleep.

"When?" she wanted to know.

Tomorrow his isolation was supposed to begin. The medics were afraid that if he left the shelter of Hangar S he might be exposed to mumps or a virus or a head cold; even his food from now on would be under microscopic analysis. He was not supposed to leave the Cape. The hell with it. He'd talk them into it; otherwise he'd go over the wall like a West

Point cadet. They would have one more hour alone. "Sometime before Saturday."

He heard the jeep engine and sat up. The colonel squeaked to a stop on a dune and got out. He looked down at them, his face sick. "The Senate!" Steve guessed. "He killed it in the Senate!"

The colonel shook his head. "The Russians, Steve. They launched. Half an hour ago."

Steve scrambled to his feet, breathing heavily. It would be almost a week before dawn would come to the Sea of Storms. "It's too early!"

"You can blame your boy Scarbo for that!"

Steve found himself shaking with anger, as if the Russians had cheated in a game. To land by radar or earth shine was too awful to contemplate. "He'll kill himself! It isn't worth the risk!"

"To a Russian," the colonel said, "maybe it is."

Senator Ralph Fellows had concluded his introductory remarks; now he summarized them. "I have been assured, gentlemen, that the radiation dose is there. I have been assured that when the man has been there for a week he will have absorbed it . . ."

He knew himself to be a more effective speaker in the Senate than in public. His peers he could address, sometimes even sway, with solid, undramatic fact; he was completely at home on the floor. "Meteorites and micrometeorites will rain on the moon, as they have for millenniums. When the man has been there a month, he will have been hit . . ."

He saw the Administration's trained poodle from Ohio make a note and start to jiggle impatiently. The young Senator had been briefing himself, he knew; he would tear into that statement when he had the floor. Steal his thunder, then: "To be sure," he continued, "those who would toss the man to the moon have assured us that he will be protected if he can bury his shelter. I am no astronaut, Mr. President.

But I have been a hard-rock miner. I can assure even the young gentleman from Ohio that what works in the laboratory does not always work in the shaft.''

He paused, looking into familiar faces on both sides of the chamber. They trusted him, to right and left. He sensed that the authority with which he spoke was solidifying their convictions. He had given even doubtful Senators the material to justify to their constituents a vote for a NASA cut. By the time he finished, he knew elatedly, he would have won. He had a few more coffin nails to pound into Pilgrim, though.

There was not a man in the chamber who would not by tomorrow have felt from his mail the odd, youthful groundswell for Pilgrim. Well, he would dampen that, too. Not like a ''cold-eyed politician,'' tightening the purse strings, but on grounds of humanity. ''This young American civilian has proved his courage in war. Do we have a right to ask him to prove it in this senseless race?''

He leaned on his desk. It was time for a passing glance at the dollar. ''For, gentlemen, it *is* senseless. Senseless and very, very expensive. The Russians may well have trapped us. For what this has and will cost . . .''

He heard the Vice-President's phone buzz softly. He looked up, saw the Senator from Ohio move quickly to the Chair, confer with it, and return to his seat. Ralph Fellows pointed to the Ohio Senator. ''Let me ask the gentleman from Ohio, now that he has apparently settled down, if he knows how many Strategic Air Command wings we might buy when this mission is prohibited?''

The young man looked up quickly. ''Is the Senator from California yielding?''

A tingle of alarm disturbed him. The junior Senator was too eager for battle. ''No.''

''Is it the Senator from California's opinion that there is more military value in the bomber-wings than in the moon?''

''There is no military value in the moon.'' He felt all at

once that he was losing control, that he had handed the offensive to the opposition.

"Sir," the young man asked innocently, playing with a fountain pen, "is this opinion based on the fact that the Russians are apparently allowing us to land first?"

Alarm bells were ringing wildly now. Something was happening. To give himself time, he looked up at the Vice-President. "I have *not* yielded," he said ominously.

The Vice-President cautioned his cohort, rubbed his eyes for a moment. Then he called Fellows to the Chair. "Senator," he said softly, flicking off his microphone and handing him a slip of paper. "I'm announcing this when you're through. I guess I have to show it to you before you get too far out on a limb."

He read the paper. The Vice-President's clean, rounded handwriting seemed almost alive. The Senator's hand began to tremble.

Large Russian vehicle departed space station 3:17 EST today on lunar trajectory. No Russ announcement. Goddard communications intercepts indicate at least one occupant. Deep Space Network now tracking.

With a great effort Ralph Fellows kept his face impassive. "Thanks," he said gruffly. "But I can take care of myself. If this is true—"

"It's true."

Ralph Fellows found his mouth dry. He glanced at the decanter of water on the Chair's desk. The Vice-President poured him a glass. He drank deeply. "Then why *launch* Pilgrim? Why back a losing horse?"

The Vice-President seemed to have aged in the last two weeks. His voice was tired. "Is that going to be your argument, Senator?"

"Argument? Hell, it's a fact! If a Russian's on his way, it's too late! Isn't it?"

"There's a difference between landing late and—"

"And what?"

"And never being allowed to land at all!"

"That's *your* argument," Ralph Fellows said, hiding his uncertainty. "Now can I continue?"

"Of course," the Vice-President nodded wearily. He glanced at the young Senator from Ohio. "He doesn't know it yet, but you have them. Don't you?"

"Yes," Ralph Fellows smiled grimly. "In the palm of my hand." He regarded his beaten enemy and found himself reluctant to leave the platform. "*Is* there a military reason?" he asked.

He had asked the President once, and he knew the answer, but he found that he must hear it again. "We don't really know."

Ralph Fellows shrugged and began to move down the steps. "Senator?"

He turned.

"The Russians seem to think so," the Vice-President said quietly. "Don't they?"

Ralph Fellows moved slowly back to his seat. Angrily he tried to throw off the feeling of discomfort, the twinge of doubt.

This was his Senate; he had served in it for almost thirty years. He had seldom stood in this room and vacillated. The way had always been straight, no matter now hard, once he had made up his mind. Then why this uneasiness today?

He stood by his desk, ready to continue, but the words would not come. He looked around at the cream-and-red marble, the solid leather chairs, the busts of Vice-Presidents high in the gold silk walls. He glanced at his notes. Next to them lay the Old Man's paper, front page up. The lead item dealt with the probable lifting of the Russian blockade on the autobahn; after twenty-four hours a U.S. convoy was apparently to be allowed to move. He felt a familiar surge of anger at the indignity. Someone coughed in the gallery. Ralph

Fellows' hand roamed the warm mahogany desk top, found the cut-glass sand-bottle. He gripped it tightly. There was utter silence. He looked up at the Chair.

"I yield," he murmured hoarsely, "to the gentleman from Ohio."

The Vice-President, his conscience writhing, listened to the young Ohioan with half an ear. The Senator was invoking the spirit and example of departed heroes from Lewis and Clark to Admiral Peary. He was overdramatic after Fellows, but somehow effective, boring in with desperate intensity. He had felt the flame of an enthusiasm that the President had sworn this morning was sweeping the nation. He was fanning it for the press gallery, but it was not all demagoguery. He was prepared, as well.

"My distinguished colleague from California complains of expense! We are the richest country on earth! We spend forty billion a year on conventional defense! He balks at five billion to reconnoiter a field that might make all our defenses obsolete! We spend as much on amusements as on space, three billion more each year on tobacco and liquor, *twice* as much on advertising . . ."

The Vice-President knew that he should be happy; when Fellows had succumbed, they had won. Nothing political could now prevent the launch. When the young man was through, he would announce the Russian firing from the Chair and the Senate, stung, would end up secretly cheering Pilgrim.

The Vice-President shifted guiltily. He wished he could have told Ralph Fellows of the other phone call, the one that had plagued him since before the roll call. But damn it, he could not. No one was sure, yet, and deliberately to rock the boat now would be fatal. He glanced at the data he had jotted down:

Noon position Chuck Wagon. Excellent trajectory at

30,000 miles. But then: *Possible problem: Shelter capsule radar beacon failing intermittently—strength fading.*

That was for neither him nor Fellows to worry about, was it? That was for the scientists to solve! Angrily, he crumpled the scratch paper and threw it in o the wastebasket.

8.

Doctor Franz Ludwig leaned back in the leather chair that had been placed in a position of honor befitting his age and astronautical standing. The Central Monitor Room at Goddard Space Flight Center near Washington seemed to be heading toward panic. Next to him Max Steiger, his full face glinting with sweat, fidgeted angrily. Franz Ludwig made no effort to hide his elation. Pilgrim was in trouble before it had even launched the man. On the shelter capsule was a radar beacon, like the one now faithfully beeping on Surveyor Six. But the shelter's beacon was fading.

The giant radar dishes around the world, the computers at JPL in Pasadena and the men next door, could track the shelter without its own help almost to the point of its contact with the surface. But without the radar beacon they would never pinpoint it on the moon. Without pinpointing it, they could not send the man. No matter how close to the old

Surveyor beacon they thought the shelter landed, they could simply not launch him to the surface of the moon and tell him to start looking.

Max Steiger flicked a switch on the intercom before him. "This is Central Monitor. Beacon strength?"

"Wait!" The voice on the other end crackled with irritation. In the last hour, as the Chuck Wagon shelter approached the point of no return, his son-in-law had been heckling the anonymous trackers in the computer room like a minor Hitler at a V-2 rocket site.

Well, Franz Ludwig thought grimly, you asked for it, *mein Sohn*. Suppose it was the *manned* capsule we were going to lose track of? Would you fall to the floor and chew the rug? After Peenemünde, in he U.S. Army processing camps in Germany and Texas, Franz Ludwig had heard an expression he liked. He hid a smile.

"What the hell's so funny?" Max Steiger flared.

" 'When in trouble, when in doubt, run in circles, scream, and shout.' " Franz Ludwig patted his arm. "Max! Take it easy."

"Yeah," Max Steiger said bitterly. "Take it easy . . ."

Well, Max's whole professional future rode with the shelter: the nice office at NASA and the home in Chevy Chase and the new car every two years. Franz Ludwig sighed, but understood.

He studied the technicians and engineers watching the last moments of the shelter's flight. He thought of the Integrated Mission Control Cen er in Houston with its whirring computers and tentacles to Goldstone, to Woomera, to Johannesburg, to here. And of the longer, more fragile thread to the tiny shelter hurtling toward the instant of retro fire. Tens of millions of dollars, hundreds of thousands of man-hours, stretched out along the delicate web; minute bits of information returned to jog electronic memories and trigger the synapses in the next room.

But when it had all been done, when every relay and circuit

and microswitch had been checked a score of times, the system was still man-made and was failing. He was no engineer. He dealt in simplicities of trajectory and clean compulsions of gravity and the sweep of celestial lines of force. But he could see in the lonely capsule a quarter of a million miles away a mischievous speck of dust, perhaps, that had escaped the gowned and masked surgeons of the clean rooms, or a minute droplet of water. And the minuscule piece of matter had interposed itself between the shelter's feeble voice and the men who waited to hear it, and a man's life might well be saved because of it.

Max Steiger glanced at him. "You're *praying* it craps out! Aren't you?"

"Yes," Franz Ludwig admitted. "If it's the only way to stop this, I am."

Steiger got up suddenly and moved closer to the tracking board, as if to cow it into submission. The "scoreboard," as the Goddard people called their transparent tracking display, was enormous. It stretched along the whole front wall of the room. It was made of plexiglass; projectors behind it could etch on it the planets in their paths, or the mountains of the earth, or the topography of Mars.

On it now was displayed a map of the lunar landing site. The dawn line was approaching it from the right, still several days away. In the semi-darkness the faithful beacon on Surveyor Six was represented by a pulsing red light in the shadowy Sea of Storms. Toward Surveyor, fifty miles above the moon's surface, crawled a tiny orange rectangle, urged by the computers next door. It denoted the shelter capsule. As long as the hundred-foot dish antennas at Goldstone and Johannesburg could distinguish its faint radar pulse, its position would be known. But when the beacon finally failed and the giant ears of radar lost it in the jumble of other echoes from the rocks and boulders of the moon's terrain, the rectangle would change to a circle. A question mark would have been more appropriate, the doctor thought. Now the orange rectangle passed across the dawn line into the darkness in which it would land. The lighted capsule was a minute ghost following the real one as it passed from shining daylight into night.

Dark or light did not matter to the shelter. Its responses were triggered by its altimeter; it could land as well in lunar night as day. A manned landing was another matter. For a sickening instant the doctor thought of the Russian. His Vostok was not represented on the screen, for he was only halfway to the moon by now. Tomorrow, when probably he must commit himself to land, he would peer through the same darkness. For the Russians to ask a man to trust to an automatic landing, or even the feeble half-light of earth shine, was barbaric.

Perhaps when the world learned today that the beacon on the U.S. shelter had failed, that Pilgrim was scrubbed, that the panicky race was over, the Russian cosmonaut could swing past the moon and return. The Russians could, after all, try again in a month.

Max Steiger returned, flopped to his seat, stared bitterly at the tracking board. "So beautiful a launch, so nice a trajectory . . . and so goddamned dumb a payload!"

He was right. There was no reason to think that the shelter would not retro fire perfectly, brake to a hover, and land somewhere near Surveyor Six with scarcely a jolt. Its searchlight, triggered on landing, would start to rotate patiently. It would become a solitary lighthouse waiting for its keeper, and its keeper would never come, because its voice had failed. Or almost failed . . .

"Signal," snapped the intercom. "Strength one . . . fading, fading . . . Gone."

Max Steiger slammed his hand on the arm of his chair. "Damn, damn, damn . . . !"

The doctor glanced at the pulsing figures below the scoreboard. One minute to retro fire—no, fifty seconds, forty-nine, forty-eight . . . The room tensed. There was no responsibility here; the flight had been controlled, as the manned launch would have been, from Houston. Here at Goddard they had had only to watch and answer questions. But the tautness of the engineers was a physical force.

"Four, three, two, one, fire!" Max Steiger counted under his breath. The orange rectangle continued, then almost imperceptibly began to slow its pace.

"Retro fire OK," the intercom said. "Deceleration four g's." The rectangle was still a rectangle; incredibly the enormous radar dish at Goldstone was clinging to its target, picking its shape from the pocked maria and surrounding craters and rills of Oceanus Procellarum. It seemed impossible that, without help from the shelter, radar could hang on so long.

Below the display flashed the altitude above the moon. *One hundred thousand feet, ninety, eighty.* . . And still the little rectangle stayed a rectangle and not a circle. *Seventy, sixty, fifty thousand feet.* . .

All at once the rectangle was gone. Max Steiger groaned. A red circle was growing by the second like a cancer on the screen. Its area showed the scope of possible shelter-landing sites. It grew swiftly because when you lost a moving target its possible strayings became larger the longer it strayed. The altitude reached a thousand feet and the circle was far too big already. The predicted time to touch-down showed now on the board. "Eight seconds, seven, six . . ."

It was a shame. Regardless of how one felt about the risk, it was shattering to see so much human effort almost succeed and fall so short.

"Zero," Max Steiger muttered. "Impact."

"We think," Franz Ludwig corrected.

The circle had stopped growing at touch-down. But it was almost 20 miles in diameter. The doctor calculated swiftly. Over 300 square miles in which the capsule could be. He got up and stretched. Someday men would find the shelter. Someday a lunar explorer would crest a crater or peer across the Sea of Storms at a blinking light, and then, when no one really cared, they would learn how accurate the launch had been. So . . .

He started to turn away from the panel when a word came over the intercom: "Contact!"

Max Steiger jumped to his feet. "Where?"

"Gone," the voice said sadly. "One last pulse. And gone . . ."

"Where, though, goddamn it! Where?"

"Somewhere north of Surveyor Six," the disembodied voice said. "I couldn't get a fix. Just a quick pip. And it was gone."

Max Steiger faced the doctor. "It survived," he whispered. "It's there."

"But where?" smiled Franz Ludwig.

"Do you suppose," Steiger asked softly, "the signal's just attenuated? Too weak?"

"Maybe," Franz Ludwig said, puzzled. "Why?"

Max Steiger's eyes narrowed. There was something feral, dangerous in the beefy face. The doctor had seen the expression the night that Max had shouldered himself into the car near Peenemünde, with the Russian artillery blasting to the north. He had a premonition of evil.

"What are you trying to say?" he whispered. "What the hell are you trying to say?"

"Maybe closer, maybe approaching the moon, he might pick it up."

Franz Ludwig stared at him. His heart was pounding. He grabbed the young man's lapels. "You'd ask him to go *blind*? And hope . . . just hope?"

Max Steiger removed his hands quite gently. He was far away. He seemed not to have heard him.

"Where," he murmured, "is my slide rule?"

9.

Doctor Franz Ludwig finished his plea in the green-plush Treaty Room off the President's study. The scientists around the massive table were silent. He regarded the faces, the blank ones, the faces frozen into pained dissent or deceitful respect. He had known most of them for years. They had been quiet academicians, modest and incorruptible men, utterly objective. But somewhere during the race they had been tainted and now they would not even listen.

A star chamber, he thought, and the Vice-President was the robed and hooded judge. He wondered if the last three weeks had been a nightmare or if he had died in his sleep and been plunged into hell. On the opposite side of the table were the NASA administrators; they had grouped around Max Steiger. Ranged along the walls behind them sat a few astronomers and microwave men from Harvard and M.I.T., like witnesses at a trial.

The young astronaut they were sentencing to death was not even here. Franz Ludwig knew that he was making a poor advocate. He had stumbled over phrases as he spoke. He was tired. When he was tired he thought often in German. And tonight was not the evening for faltering words.

"Thank you, Doctor Ludwig," the Vice-President said. He had been following him carefully and he seemed very worried. "Was there anything else?"

Franz Ludwig glanced toward the empty green velvet chair at the head of the table, wishing it were occupied. Three weeks ago he had sat waiting in this room to present his case to the President. He had lost. But even losing, he had felt empathy; he had sensed that the President trusted him. The President was supposed to be here tonight. Where was he? No affair of state could be more important than this. He cast about for another argument, any argument, to keep the floor until he arrived.

"To summarize," he began, "to search by eye a 300-square-mile area on the surface of the moon is not even as simple as on earth. The horizon there is much closer, *ja?*"

Ja? Damn . . . He must not sound like a comic professor, but like a competent scientist. Pleading for help, he caught the eye of a Princeton astrophysicist he had always respected. The man was on a NASA grant; he nodded but looked away guiltily.

"And," Franz Ludwig finished lamely, forgetting the last plaintive signal the shelter had sent after landing, "we do not even know that the capsule stands erect. Perhaps it crashed!"

He regretted the slip immediately. Max Steiger addressed the Vice-President. "That's not quite possible, sir. As you know, there was a post-landing signal. It definitely proved that the landing was successful. Furthermore, its approximate bearing was caught. This narrows the search area considerably . . ."

"I know," the Vice-President said. He smiled gently at the doctor, and Franz Ludwig felt that the young man sympathized with him but thought of him as a child to be permitted a slip now and then. "Was there anything else, Doctor?"

"Nothing else," Franz Ludwig said bitterly.

"Then," said the Vice-President, "we are agreed that—"

The President entered and when Franz Ludwig stood with the rest he was so tired that the room spun crazily. Frozen faces, massive chandelier, Vice-President, and a stately golden mirror over the fireplace orbited majestically. He grasped the table, got his balance, and resumed his seat with the crowd.

The President did not bother to sit down. He moved to the fireplace, whisked a piece of lint from the mantel. He turned to the Vice-President. "Briefly, what's been the general direction of this discussion?"

Franz Ludwig groaned inwardly. For the last hour NASA had presented its case. The flawless trajectory of the shelter capsule proved that the manned flight itself was feasible; there was an excellent probability that the capsule's beacon was not dead, but only sick; closer to the moon it might come in strong and clear. And if it did not? That was no problem either, apparently. A U.S. Weather Bureau scientist and a NASA optical expert testified that Gordon Cooper, a hundred miles high in Mercury, had spotted huts in Tibet and a vehicle in Arizona. It seemed that to see the shelter from an altitude of a hundred miles with the naked eye was almost a certainty, now that it was a primary need.

The President had a question. If the radar beacon was not merely faint but gone; if the 12-foot-high shelter in the glaring waste could *not* be seen from orbit, what then?

"Doctor Ludwig," the Vice-President admitted quite fairly, "is afraid that if the shelter isn't spotted from the air the astronaut might land too far from it to find it on the ground."

"That is true," Franz Ludwig broke in. "The odds are very poor."

The President moved opposite him. He leaned on the table, looked into his eyes. He seemed more rested, younger than he had been three weeks ago. My God, thought Franz Ludwig, something has brainwashed him!

"Suppose," the President murmured, "he doesn't see it from the air—"

"He will not!"

"Suppose he doesn't see it?" the President repeated, scanning the faces. "There's no question of his being able to abort?"

"Of course not," Max Steiger exclaimed. "Without a move on his part, he swings past the moon and returns to earth!"

The telephone on the receptionist's desk by the door buzzed softly. Someone somewhere answered it. Franz Ludwig felt a marrow-deep weariness. You have had children, he wanted to tell the President. If Lawrence were your son, would you send him? Can't you understand? He wiped his mouth. "To toss him up there for nothing but a look, Mr. President? And hope he comes back? No! It is even worse!"

"Not *hope* for his return," the President said. "He *would* return. Wouldn't he?"

Franz Ludwig licked his lips. He had built his life on the certainties of celestial mechanics; facts were facts and the astronaut would indeed return if left in the charge of the great, immutable laws of force. But he would be riding a man-made device and man was not God; if he had to return, they were forgetting the fiery beast of re-entry, waiting for a slip. He shook his head stubbornly. "It is not right!"

"But Doctor, you drew the trajectory." The President's eyes were thoughtful. "You see, Doctor, the country needs this now. The country wants it. I think we must give it every opportunity to succeed."

"*Wanting* it does not change the odds!"

"You said once that good intentions didn't change them either," the President remembered. "And maybe you're right. But . . ." He straightened and moved to the front of the table. "Gentlemen, thank you. I'm going to call Mr. Lawrence at Cape Kennedy. If he still wants to go, I intend to let him."

There was deep silence around the table. Then the President nodded goodnight and left the room. For a long while Franz Ludwig sat at his place while the others filed out. He was pretending to be fumbling with his papers but was really gathering strength to face his daughter knowing that he had failed. He sensed someone behind him.

"Franz?" Max Steiger mumbled.

"Yes?"

"I'm sorry. From the beginning, there was no chance. I tried to tell you." Franz Ludwig turned to the soft, anxious face that could grow hard so easily. He was very, very tired, but he knew suddenly what he must do. If no one else would listen, he must see the man himself.

"Now," Max said, "let's go home. Liz has a roast, and—"

"Just to pick up my things." He got slowly to his feet. "And then, to the airport?"

Max's eyes widened. "Are you going back to Huntsville?"

"Why? You will miss me here?"

"Franz!" Max Steiger pleaded. "You're going to help me monitor the launch! At Goddard?"

"If there *is* a launch . . ."

He felt an odd shiver. He stuffed his papers unsteadily into the battered briefcase. His weariness was almost too great to support.

"There *will* be a launch," Max Steiger reminded him gently, taking the case from his hand. "You heard the President."

"If there is a launch," Franz Ludwig promised, "I will monitor it."

And then the massive blow crashed through his brain. He felt it first when he stepped away from the great table. He lurched back to grab its edge. There was dull throbbing at first, behind his right temple, and all at once his left leg, arm, foot were asleep and his face, too, as if someone had struck him in the cheek. He clung to the wood, swaying, while the crystal chandelier rocked above him. All at once he was lying at the carved foot of the table and Max's face, eyes bulging, floated like a minor moon between him and the light.

Someone was loosening his collar. He fumbled for words. He wanted Max to remind the young astronaut—for now he knew that he could not—of how careful the steps must be when you danced with the heavenly bodies and how frivolously he had written the music. And to tell the young man for his wife, perhaps, what it was to be alone when the one you loved was too soon gone, for he remembered the astronaut's eyes and there had been no cruelty in them. But the English would not come.

"*Ich kann nicht . . .*" he began. "*Ich . . .*"

"*Was ist los?*" sobbed Max Steiger. "*Franz, was ist los?*"

"Anna?" grunted Franz Ludwig, and then there was only dumb silence. He felt that it would cloak him until the day he died.

10.

Steve Lawrence, waiting on the phone in the motel room, watched Mickey leaf blindly through a woman's magazine. "I'm sorry," he murmured to her.

He should not have come. He and Mickey would have been more insulated at the astronaut quarters in Hangar S; at least someone could have buffered him from the telephone. He had jerked an hour from the last-minute rush and even the hour was turning into a fiasco. Only the medics and the colonel and Archy Gorman knew where he was. But the time was almost up and he had been on the phone almost continually.

Well, this call at least had to be taken. It was from the President of the United States. When the familiar quiet voice came on the line they spoke of the silent beacon on the shelter capsule. Steve glanced at Mickey, chose his words.

"I can't," he admitted, "evaluate it as well as NASA can.

The possibility of aborting has always been great . . ." He saw that Mickey had stopped turning the pages. She was tense. He took a deep breath and continued. "But, with them, I don't see that this changes the odds on survival, Mr. President. If I don't spot it on my screen or out the port, I abort. That's all . . ."

There was a heavy silence on the line. He found that he was quivering, hanging on the President's words. They could not stop him now; it was monstrous, unthinkable.

"All right, son," the President said.

Steve sagged with relief. As if she sensed the decision, Mickey began to turn the pages again, but now her hands were trembling. He talked to the President of launch weather, and the President spoke quite sincerely and without flag-waving of the contribution of the mission to the country's pride.

Steve shifted uncomfortably.

He grasped the moment to mention Gus Scarbo. The President hesitated. "It depends," he said, "on how much harm he really did. If the Russian actually lands—"

"Scarbo's intention," Steve cut in, "was to save my life."

"If he triggered the Russians early and they beat us," the President said firmly, "he's sabotaged our whole program." There was a pause. "Steve?"

It was the first time the President had used his first name. Steve swallowed. "Yes, sir?"

"Things come up I'd like to do for people. Every day. And sometimes I can't."

"Yes, sir."

"Abe Lincoln could have done it, maybe. Things are more . . . impersonal now. Do you understand?"

"Yes, sir."

"But," the President said suddenly, "I'll see. . . . Now, *I* have a request."

"Yes?"

"Come back. Right away if you have to or be there when they go to get you. Consider it an order or a request. But you come back!"

Steve smiled across the room at Mickey. "We kind of feel," he said, "the same way ourselves."

He hung up the phone, reached for it again, changed his mind. He felt Mickey standing over him. "Call him," she murmured.

"How'd you know?"

"Call him. They'll let you through."

He put in a call to Gus in the detention ward at Bethesda and they did let him through. For a moment they talked, feeling for the rapport they had known. It was gone, but Gus sounded relaxed to Steve. Relaxed, or resigned. Mickey talked to him for a moment and Steve wandered to the window. He found himself sneaking a look at his watch. He was due at the hangar in twenty minutes for the final biopak checkout. He saw Mickey regarding him with a faint smile across the room. She said goodbye to Gus and hung up.

"He said to tell you to stay loose."

Steve smiled and she touched his lips. "What?" she murmured at the smile.

He shrugged. " 'Stay loose.' A guy we knew in Korea. He was always saying that . . . real gung-ho."

"But," she said firmly, "my man is not gung-ho?"

"Your man," he said softly, "is a mass of alarums, feeling always with the toes before taking the next step."

" 'Staying loose,' " she prompted, "only to spring faster for the exit."

"An antelope with twitching nerves, taut and cocked to . . . to . . . ." He ran out of words.

"Leap for safety at the sound of the hunter?"

"To leap for safety at the *thought* of the hunter."

The smile faded from her face and her green eyes were wet. "And he promises me this?"

Promise her, he thought. He would see her for a few hectic

minutes at the door of the trailer when it delivered him to the pad tomorrow, suited-up and ready in the glare of the pre-dawn searchlights.

And then he would not see her again for . . . Six days, perhaps. A year, perhaps. Or . . . If all went wrong in a roar of flame or a whisper in the void, then when would he see her again? What of the ketch they were going to cruise? What of Stevie streaking for the goal? And the diving trip to Trinidad? Did the dreams live on when one dreamer was gone?

"He still promises me this?" she insisted.

"He promises," Steve Lawrence said, "with all his heart." He watched the shadow fade from her ocean-green eyes. Then he kissed her and left.

11.

The air-conditioned van rumbled along North Cape Road in the pre-dawn Florida darkness. Steve Lawrence, encased in his rubber-jointed pressure suit, flexed his curved gloves under the eye of a technician. In a moment the pressure-suit man was replaced by a meteorologist. The weatherman unrolled a map. "The North Atlantic high we saw yesterday has moved roughly northeast . . ."

With part of his mind Steve followed his briefing, anxious primarily for the launch weather, but reassured with every turn of the wheels. The nerve-tightening stratus clouds that seemed to haunt every manned launch at the Cape had been breaking up when he stepped from Hangar S to the van; he had seen a few stars through the chinks.

Incredibly, he was calm. He had slept for six hours after leaving the motel. Sitting with the colonel in the astronaut trailer he had eaten a low-residue midnight breakfast of strained orange juice, steak, and poached eggs. He had succeeded in a bowel movement before suiting up. His pressure suit handled feces, but the process was complicated and he hoped to minimize defecation until he reached his shelter on the moon.

They had been leaving the hangar when Archy Gorman caught them. He had lost weight in the last weeks. Goddard Center had called. They had tracked the Russian as carefully as his own shelter; followed it almost to impact. It had been decelerating normally and touch-down seemed to be in the general area of Surveyor Six, as anticipated. They were assuming a successful Russian landing, despite lunar darkness and official Russian silence.

For a crazy moment Steve envisioned a meeting on the moon. It was an interesting, science-fiction proposition. Would you stick out your hand in friendship, take cover and watch, or run like hell? But the odds were small. Whether the Russian was returning immediately or living in his Vostok awaiting rescue, they were no more likely to see each other than two prospectors in the Mojave. There were other things to worry about today.

"T minus 147 minutes," snapped the radio in the van, "and counting."

The colonel looked up from the countdown manual. "You through, Swami?"

The weatherman finished. "We're predicting less than 10 percent cloud cover at the pad by 9 A.M."

"Physical ed time," announced the colonel. Without moving from his seat, Steve clasped his hands and began to tug, straining his muscles until he could pull no harder. Immovable Charles Atlas exercises were the only ones you could perform in a space suit anyway. They were perfectly effective, because muscles had no brains and could be fooled. He worked down his body, tensing his abdomen, thighs, calves, and toes. When he was through he was breathing hard and sweating in the suit. Every four hours in flight he would repeat the drill. On the moon, in the shelter capsule, he could take up more conventional exercise.

The van slowed and Steve knew that they were at the guardhouse to Complex 37. He heard the door open. The guard stuck his head in; the one who had pulled the *faux pas* on Mickey's blockhouse visit. "You guys got passes?"

"We're thirty seconds late," the colonel announced coldly. "Do you really need to play games?"

The man retreated, and the van started up. Steve glanced at the colonel. "Relax, Skipper." He paused. "Stay loose . . ."

A shadow of anguish crossed the colonel's face.

"Next year?" Steve said softly.

"Next year?" shrugged the colonel. "A lot can go wrong with an old man in a year . . ."

The van stopped. Steve shivered. He knew what faced him outside, what faced him and Mickey, who was waiting here to watch the firing from the blockhouse. There would be one TV crew from the networks, one still photographer from the wire-service pool, an official NASA photo crew. Not many, but too many. He could not subject her to the glaring lenses without seeing her first.

"Call my wife in," he said suddenly.

The colonel nodded and opened the door. Then she was climbing the short stairs, moving down the length of the van. They stood for a moment, looking into each other's eyes.

"Last night," she murmured, "I was thinking . . ."

"Yes?"

"I've asked you to do all the promising," she said. "I haven't promised anything."

"That's all right." He forced a smile. "You're a big girl now."

"No," she said, "I'm not. But I'm promising now, no matter what, no matter how much I want to—"

"Mickey, I know."

"You can't know and it's bothered you." He had to nod.

She took both his hands. "I'll never give in. I promise, Steve."

There were no tears in her eyes. And she did not ask for his own word again, and he found that he could not give it.

"I love you," he said. "I love you more than ever."

He kissed her for Stevie. Then he waddled to the door, out into the glare of the pad. He helped her down the steps, swung to face the cameras with his arm around her. Someone asked them to kiss. He shook his head. He squeezed her hand through the clumsy rubber glove and let it go. Rick Lincoln, with unsuspected gallantry, offered her his arm and they moved away.

Steve had thought through this moment and promised that there would be not the slightest hint of the theatrical. But he could not help himself; the immensity of the vehicle simply overwhelmed him. Slowly his eyes rose along the boosters sparkling with ice in the arcs. He followed the stark lines to the tiny, almost invisible capsule at the top.

He raised his hand stiffly to the sleeping monument of metal and power. He began to walk to the tower.

"T minus one-one-seven minutes . . ."

He lay in his couch. Through his open hatch drifted the smell of RP-1 fuel, exactly like the odor around a jet. The tiny cabin had an airplane smell, too, of rubber and plastic and oxygen, like all things man-made that flew. Until the hatch was closed he had no more to do. He found himself strangely relaxed.

Inches from his chest, under the altimeter, a wooden ignition key protruded from the panel. Somehow in the last hectic moments Rick or one of the other astronauts must have found time to glue it there. Someone had dangled from it a surprise from Stevie: the rubber space mouse.

Half an hour ago, during a lull, they had put a call through to Houston from him. Lying in the swaying capsule, he had talked to Stevie for a few minutes at the Scarbo house. "It'll be the first mouse on the moon,'' he promised. The talk had degenerated into pauses, longer and longer ones. Then there was nothing left to say. Now Steve swung the mouse with his finger and waited for the colonel to finish checking the countdown manual.

A grey-haired scarecrow in McDonnell Aviation overalls stretched across his lap to test an ammeter, hesitated, looked up defiantly. ''My wife, you know—''

''Yes?''

He had a Yankee face and a Southern drawl, and it was a moment before the words came out. ''My wife, she said 'God be with you.' ''

Steve smiled. ''What do *you* say?''

The man's eyes clouded unexpectedly with tears. He shook his head, grinned lopsidedly, and squirmed back out the hatch.

The Florida dawn had come quickly. In its brassy light the colonel stood on the platform silhouetted against a puffy cloud. The sky was deep blue, the cloud was stark white; everything on this morning seemed to be in gaudy Kodachrome. He found himself staring at the colonel's sky-blue overalls, looking at a bright orange girder on the umbilical tower, peering through his periscope at the red hard hat of a foreman 200 feet below. He seemed to be etching hues on the pallet of his memory as if he would be color blind the rest of his life.

The colonel closed the manual and leaned in. ''A few days ago,'' he said softly, ''I noticed something they'd left out. Did you?''

''Contraceptives? In case that Russian's a girl?''

The colonel did not smile. He zipped down the diagonal fastener over his chest, pulled out a carefully folded flag, wrapped in plastic.

Steve winced. ''My God . . . !''

''Not surprising,'' said the colonel. ''We live in a hurried age.''

Steve took the flag wordlessly, crammed it in the emergency case strapped to his biopak.

"T minus niner-one minutes," the loudspeaker blared. "Commence bolting capsule hatch . . ."

"Well . . ." The colonel seemed reluctant to go. "Steve?"

Steve's throat was tense. "Yes?"

"If we . . . if you make it—"

" 'We,' " muttered Steve. "OK?"

The colonel shook his head. "If you make it, we've won. Even if they've beaten us by seventy-two hours it's close enough. To the guy in Tulsa or Walla Walla, we've won."

Steve nodded. The colonel went on: "But if you bust your ass . . ." The colonel seemed to be forcing out the words. "Anyway, you've been ordered not to land unless you spot the shelter. Be *damn* sure you don't."

"I'm not *crazy*," Steve gasped. "And you seem to have changed your attitude."

"Maybe," the colonel suggested, "because you've changed yours."

They shook hands. For a long moment the colonel held his eyes and suddenly he was gone, and the men outside were positioning the hatch and it slammed into place and the sapphire sky was gone as well. Then there was only the shine of the pumps and the groan of tank walls freezing and the hiss of Lox and fuel and a dull rumble as the blockhouse swiveled the giant nozzles in a final check 200 feet below. The last bolt on the hatch creaked home. Someone banged twice on the capsule to signal his departure in the elevator.

He was alone. For a wild second the cabin seemed to shrink. He gasped for air. He was sure that the oxygen pump had failed and that he would strangle in the capsule before they could get back to drag him out. He took a deep breath and turned the handle on the check-off scroll

"Communications?" he asked into his microphone.

Rick Lincoln's voice snapped back. "Communications, go."

"ASCS, go," someone said shrilly.

"Aeromed, go," chimed in a flight surgeon in the blockhouse. The chants went on for an hour.

"T minus thirty-five seconds," the countdown voice said finally.

"Astronaut?" the colonel asked briefly. He had replaced Rick Lincoln as Launch Control Communicator and would fly to Houston after the firing to take up his vigil there.

"Ready," Steve grunted. He heard the last umbilical cord pop from its seat, bang against the skin of the first-stage booster. The periscope retracted with a whine. His only link with the world outside came now from the tiny window a foot from his nose. Through it a wisp of departing cloud moved across the sky.

"T minus ten seconds," the colonel began. "Nine, eight, seven, six . . ."

Steve put his hand on the abort handle, breathed deeply, as he had practiced. Nothing could stop the flight of the capsule now; if the booster went up in a sheet of flame he would still be hurled thousands of feet skyward by his escape rockets, to parachute into the waters past the beach. And then it came with glacial inevitability: "Four, three, two, one . . . zero!"

There was a thump below and he knew that the first two engines had ignited. Another, another, and another, and a million and a half pounds of leashed thrust seeped up the boosters, through the braking rockets, into the cabin walls, crept to the deepest pit of his stomach. And still the clamps gripped, forcing the thrust to build and build and build.

"All engines!" the colonel called. "Ignition all engines!"

With a distant brutal clank the clamps flew aside. Gradually, smoothly, a giant hand pushed him back into his couch; the swaying became wider; he was an ant on a wind-blown stalk of wheat.

"Lift off!" the colonel's voice crackled.

Steve jabbed the clock on the panel. "Roger," he heard himself murmur in perfect coolness. "The clock has started."

The altimeter above the crazy ignition key began to move, faster and faster until it was spinning. In the depths of his body he felt the upward rush, but until he glimpsed a wispy cloud flick past the window he could not really believe it. He was the one. He was on his way.

He knew all at once that booster separation would go smoothly, that his insertion and mid-course correction would be good, that in three days he would see at close range the stark and impossible world that no free man had ever seen. And feel it? And walk on it? Of that he was not sure at all.

12.

He awakened hungry. Fascinated with the growing detail of lunar terrain, he had studied it through his window long past his sleeping time on the second night. His panel clock read T plus sixty-one hours. He had slept four. Despite his hunger, his first thought was to open the louvers to see how the moon had grown.

But there were things to do first. He had only five hours before the moment of truth. First he reset the gyros in his computer; then he began to cleanse his body of waste. It had been difficult to urinate on the previous day: weightlessness always fooled the bladder. Now he succeeded in voiding. He flushed out the relief tube in his suit with a flick of a switch.

"Pilgrim One to Pilgrim Control?" he called.

He waited. The lag in Houston's answers was growing by the day. On the moon there would be a three-second delay before the radio waves could complete a round trip. The thought of it brought back the sudden sense of loneliness.

The reply came faintly: "This is Pilgrim Control, good morning, Steve. Go ahead . . ."

It was the colonel. He must have moved a bunk to the console; for two days Steve had heard no other voice. They spoke of Steve's physical condition for a moment and Steve pulled a packet of food from his cabin stores. He mixed it with water and squeezed himself breakfast, then turned a valve to empty the urine into the Environmental Control System.

Urine was reconstituted and would return to his water supply. It would be chemically purer than the water his son was drinking at Clear Lake, but Steve found it psychologically impossible to drink for hours after he had voided. He stuffed his empty food container into the waste bag, rolled the check-off scroll to "T plus sixty-one hours."

"Conditioning exercises: neck, deltoids, biceps, triceps, abdomen, gluteus maximus, thighs, and calves . . ." He strained each muscle in turn, reported the item to Houston. "Final check, manual attitude-control system," read the scroll.

Final! Five hours to go! His heart began to thump. To save the hydrogen peroxide that fed the tiny attitude jets, he had simply drifted since his mid-course correction two days before. The control system had not been used. Now he must find out if a valve had jammed or a relay frozen. He tried the nozzles one by one, easing his stick through roll and pitch and yaw.

"Houston from Pilgrim One," he announced triumphantly. "Attitude jets A-OK! On the nose!" Now the delay in answering seemed interminable. When finally it came, the colonel's voice was very, very weak. He opened his louvers and gaped.

When he had closed them the night before he had been 40,000 miles from the moon. It had been glorious even then, a crystalline, virginal world half filling his window, with the dawn line etching the Riphaeus Range into the bare backbone of a dinosaur. Now the dawn had come to Flamsteed and Hansteen craters in the vast, grey Ocean of Storms; it touched the saw-toothed brink of Grimaldi at the moon's leading rim.

He felt an odd sensation, half-fear half-love, for a land he might be the first to see. Perhaps a Neanderthal man cresting a hill would have sensed the same proprietary pull from an untouched plain. It was too early by hours, he was still 15,000 miles out, but so stark and contrasty was the surface that he had the illusion that if he used his binoculars he might already sight his shelter.

Knowing that it was foolish, ashamed of his weakness, he raised his glasses and began to look.

Steve moved irritably; the colonel's voice was barely readable. "We have you at 500,000 feet lunar altitude. Do you have . . . sight . . . of the shelter yet?"

Long ago the moon had ceased to be a sphere. It dominated him as the earth dominated a jet no matter how high one flew. "Down" had become where the moon was, not the earth. The lunar vista stretched vastly ahead of him, and Houston and the colonel became annoying distractions.

He did not answer, but swung the capsule slightly, lifted his glasses for the tenth time in the last half-hour. He searched all the way from the slopes of Grimaldi to the edge of Copernicus. He deliberately avoided the crevice near Flamsteed, because he had strained so hard at it that he was afraid to turn the odd shape into an optical illusion. He flicked on his radar, glaring at the green scope on the panel. At each sweep the faithful blip from Surveyor Six flared and died; it was closer with every turn, but there was nothing from the shelter.

He must reply to Houston, but he found himself reluctant to admit failure. He gave in to the crevice and raised his glasses to the strange shape. It had grown larger, with the rest

of the shadows in the side of the crater. Man-made angulari-
ty? Or his imagination?

The shelter? Or nothing? He called Houston, described the
terrain as best he could, milking the flight.

"I estimate the several small craters north of Hansteen to
be one or two hundred feet in height. The general surface of
Oceanus Procellarum from this altitude appears smooth and a
landing would appear feasible . . ."

He stopped for a moment and the colonel came back.
"Chuck Wagon shelter! Do you . . . have it in sight?"

He rested his eyes for a moment on the curve of the eastern
horizon. In ten minutes he would pass beyond it if he did
nothing to break his speed. It seemed impossible over a body
so large that he could not be falling, that the vast mass of it
would not overcome his momentum and yank him from
orbit. And yet, if he did not spot the shelter in minutes—eight
minutes—then, without a move on his own part, he would
clear the dawn line, hurtle through the far-side night, and in
less than an hour be falling back to earth.

He reported "no joy" on the shelter, continued, as he
searched for it, to comment on terrain. But behind his profes-
sionalism he was fighting himself. The crevice, the crevice
—what was in the crevice? He swung his glasses to it again.
The shape seemed to jump out at him. Man-made! He looked
away, then back. No, maybe not . . .

He must not allow himself to be trapped by curiosity, or
stupidity, or his role. He must be sure, no matter whose
hopes rode with him or how many millions prayed for success. He had promised the woman he loved. Three
minutes. . . . Two minutes fifty seconds . . .

He swung his glasses back to the crevice. The shape had
not changed, but all at once he knew what he must do.

He must land. If it was not the shelter, then he would die,
but if he returned safe and someday men found that he had
missed his chance, he would face a death of the soul that he
could not stand. If he must land to find out, he would land.

"Pilgrim Control!" he called. "Pilgrim Control! Believe I have sighted the shelter. East side of Hansteen . . ."

He was already starting his retro-fire check-off list by the time the colonel's voice came back. "Understand. . . . Request you verify. . . . Certain of sighting? Not to land unless . . ."

But by that time he was yawing the capsule until he was riding backward, his eye dancing between radar altimeter, attitude gyro, and velocity gauge. The clock ticked toward retro fire; his computer under the panel clicked as Houston sent it a minor bit of information; the clock hesitated, continued. The moment of reality rushed toward him.

Hand off the red button, return to earth. Push it, and the moon . . . But he promised her . . .

Four, three, two, one . . .

"Zero," he grunted.

He jabbed the button, restablized instinctively as his escape gear jettisoned with a jolt. Heat shield, chute, and life raft spun into eternal orbit, and he could not return.

Then the mighty braking rockets were pressing him into his couch.

In the great green amphitheater in Houston the colonel sagged at his console under the glassed observation balcony. He had not left the room for almost three days. Theoretically Rick Lincoln, with his knowledge of lunar terrain, was supposed to have the capsule-communication watch during this final phase, but the colonel had no thought of relinquishing the microphone until he found out if Lawrence had sighted the shelter.

His eyes were on fire, he needed a shave; his nerves were so tight that a clacking relay behind him had sounded for hours like an approaching railroad car. And now, with Mickey Lawrence in the glassed balcony behind him, he could not even allow himself the relief of striding up and down behind the console. He straightened his shoulders for her benefit, glanced at Archy Gorman in perspiring consultation with Rick Lincoln. Sy Larson, sitting next to him, looked over blankly. He had been checking transmitter voltages.

"I don't know, Colonel. All the channels check out OK."

"Archie," the colonel said tightly, "get this amateur son-of-a-bitch off the console. Now!"

Sy Larson looked up, startled. He studied him for a moment, then nodded and made way for Rick Lincoln. Lincoln made a quick check and shook his head. "Low capsule voltages. When he lands and his batteries get a rest we might hear from him again."

The colonel accepted it and moved closer to the tracking display on the plastic screen stretching along half the circumference of the front of the room. The familiar Flamsteed-Hansteen area stood out in photographic relief. The orange triangle that was Pilgrim One was slowing visibly; the old Surveyor probe pulsed faithfully. Everything showed on the screen but the lost shelter capsule resting somewhere in the Ocean of Storms. The giant radar dish at Johannesburg was hanging on to the Mercury capsule nicely and it appeared that Lawrence would land within very few miles of Surveyor. The colonel stared at the display, willing a miracle, demanding that the silent radar beacon on the shelter come to life. He found that his fists were clenched, his arms shaking with the effort.

He wandered back to the console. Lawrence was committed, his decision was made; the laws of celestial mechanics and his own flying skill would determine his fate on landing, but someone must tell Mickey whether or not he had sighted the shelter capsule. "Believe I have sighted" was not enough. He picked up the microphone.

He called the capsule three times; the room fell into tomb-like silence except for the inane clatter of the relay. He squeezed his earphones to his head as if he could press

Lawrence's voice from it. It was no use. Across the endless void came nothing but a faint crackle of static.

And in that moment he knew, as surely as if Lawrence had confessed it, as surely as if he had been in the capsule himself, that the man was not sure that he had sighted the shelter. He was no suicide, but he could have been fooled.

If he had not sighted it, he would be better off if he crashed. Next year they would as surely find him in the twisted wreckage as in the whole capsule and the thought of a slow death as his oxygen ran out was almost too much to bear.

"Believe I have sighted" was a hope, not a fact. It was the claim of a fighter pilot prodded by his leader to shoot in the dark. It was the cry of a child trying to please his father.

He had to close his eyes suddenly against burning tears. Slowly, very slowly, so that the woman in the balcony behind him could not tell his thoughts, he sat down. He kept his shoulders stiff and square, for she must never know what he knew.

Oh, Christ, he thought. Good Christ, what have I done?

"Pilgrim Control, Pilgrim Control," Steve called once, just after the main braking stage had separated. "Solid separation was at 32,000 feet." Then he was slowly, inevitably tilting backward, backward, backward and the motion felt far too violent after the lazy drifting flight. Through his window he took a last look at the gentle plain of Procellarum, a final glance at the solid eastern horizon. The horizon and the crescent earth which hung above it had slid below the edge of his window and his frame of reference was lost save for a few crystal stars in a velvet sky. All at once he felt that he had rotated too far.

In Houston he had done it all before, over and over, and once he had suffered vertigo and panic. Now it came again, but this time with reason, and his intellect felt it as well. He shifted his view from the window to the enormous eye of the periscope between his knees. The eye was black and empty. His mouth went dry. He was blind; he was sure that the shock of solid-stage firing had somehow disarranged the optics. Now, he was certain, he must land as if it were darkness, trusting to a thousand synapses in his computer with his reflexes at the mercy of a hundred transistors and micro-switches that did not care or hope.

But then, moving up the lens before him, he saw the eastern horizon, glorious and sharp. The lunar dawn etched low-lying craters from Copernicus to the Sirsalis Cleft. He looked at Grimaldi Crater as if it was an old friend. The vertigo was gone; there was a north—an up, a down. Then, as the field of vision continued to drop, he caught another glimpse of the light-colored shape in the crevice far to the north. It was gone in an instant, but from 20,000 feet the instant was enough. The shape was a trick of the early dawn light or an oddly formed rock or a gash from a recent meteor.

Whatever it was, it was not the shelter.

13.

At 2,000 feet the capsule had righted itself like a buoy in calm water and the periscope craning past its base was gazing on terrain directly below, level and bleak and pock-marked by only a few tiny craters. Steve fought through a fog of despair and checked his drift on one of the craterlets. It was moving only minutely across his scope. More important, it was hardly growing in size. The altimeter passed through 800 feet, clung to 700, wavered and continued down.

With hardly a touch of his hand his automatic control system and its computer had cradled him to perfect hover. He checked his radar screen for a last position on Surveyor Six. It was 4 miles away, somewhere northwest across the plain. He called Pilgrim Control, but heard nothing. He inhaled deeply, switched to manual control, and tested with a squirt of fuel. The rockets beneath him pulsed and his descent stopped. He rocked the capsule cautiously. The tiny reaction jets responded.

He drifted a few hundred feet to the south to avoid a shallow depression. Then he began to ease toward the drab and endless plains.

It was very quiet. He lay on his back staring through the dusty window at an ebony sky and a few stars. A hard beam of sunlight slashed across his body and glared from the panel to his left: otherwise the capsule was quite dark.

He had touched down gently, as gently as he ever had at Edwards. Then he had tried unsuccessfully to report his landing to Houston. Now for an hour he had lain in the silence, waiting while the fuel-cell battery rested and the dust settled outside. Whether Houston answered next time or not, he supposed that in a few minutes he must tighten the straps on the biopak nested in the couch under him, de-pressurize the capsule, and leave. For where, he was not sure.

He felt no anger at himself or the silent shelter radar beacon or the devious shadow. If he had not been misled by that shape, he would have imagined another somewhere. He would have landed, because an hour ago he had been, for a few inexplicable moments, either very foolish or very brave. Or not brave enough to return.

Now he was no longer brave or foolish. He was emotionally drained, dead as the sea of dust outside. He hated the vacuum of feeling. Go out yelling, or waving a flag, or crying or laughing, but not with a sigh. A pump in his oxygen system cut in with a smooth, reliable murmur. He began to wonder if he could drive himself to leave the capsule. Nursing from his biopack, moving strenuously outside, he would not survive a day. Inside, with the capsule's oxygen, he could last three or four.

In three or four days he would perhaps be prepared to die. But a few hours from now? Wandering on the blazing lunar plain, to know that his heart pounded in vain, that the body would in a few hours be rotting in the suit, that the mind would be nothing?

Now he felt emotion. It was terror; he was shivering with the shock of it. Stay with the capsule, of course! Don't open the least chink in it! Stay in the womb! He let the panic wash away, keeping his mind blank. Then he checked his voltages, tried the radio again.

"Pilgrim Con rol, Pilgrim Control . . ."

The colonel came back faintly. Nothing in the cold impersonal tone that space lent to the human tongue could mute the excitement in his voice.

"I read you now, Pilgrim . . . I read you! Very weak, but I read you!"

Steve reported a safe landing, described the site as he had seen it. But when he paused for an answer, he knew that his fuel-cell batteries were through.

"Understand landing," the colonel was transmitting. "All else unreadable. . . . Essential . . . transmit coordinates of Chuck Wagon shelter when you arrive at it . . ." And then the voice faded and was lost.

They still thought, or hoped, that he had spotted the shelter. Good. When the three or four days were up, when lying flat on his back he had misered through inactivity the dregs of his capsule oxygen and that in his biopak, then he might squander the last hour of it moving toward the faithful Surveyor, so that when they discovered him they would think he had simply been unable to find a refuge he thought was near. Mickey would never know he had cheated.

He glanced about the tiny capsule. Much to be thankful for, he thought bitterly. A soft landing, food, water for four days, and the little patch of ebony sky. All sorts of excitement, too. In four days the beam of sunlight would perhaps have moved to his lap. He could time it for amusement. And Stevie's mouse still dangled from the ridiculous ignition key. He could play with that.

Anger made his cheeks tingle. "The hell with that," he said aloud. "The hell with it . . ."

He cinched the shoulder straps on his biopak, locked his face plate, and began to de-pressurize the cabin.

Doctor Franz Ludwig lay in his bed on a floor of the Bethesda Naval Hospital reserved for administration officials and wondered how long he would live as a vegetable. He had been trying to will his left hand into motion for half an hour, to raise it from the sheet; he had given up. Lisa and Max had been there, and he had looked into the agonized face of his daughter and tried to tell her with his eyes that he had had a good life, because he had had her, and Anna, and the thrill of seeing some of his dreams come true. But he could not even pronounce her name.

There was a sudden bustle at the door. A Marine in khakis glanced in furtively, motioned to a huge scarecrow of a man, vaguely familiar, in a drab hospital dressing gown.

Franz Ludwig wrestled with a jumble of impressions, but when you could not put your thoughts into even silent words, it was hard.

"My name's Scarbo," smiled the scarecrow. "I'm the doctor who spilled the beans. On Pilgrim."

Pilgrim . . . Pilgrim. Franz Ludwig tried to sort the word from a thousand others. A dark word, an evil word, like murder or hell. The exact meaning would not come. He could only stare at the tall man.

"I thought you should know," the scarecrow said, very slowly and distinctly, "that the first step is over. He has landed safely. Do you understand?

He did not understand, but it must be very important, for the Marine was nervous and guilty and the doctor was very intense. Pilgrim, Pilgrim? Landed? The brain was a complicated, pulsing muscle. If you tensed it too hard, sometimes it would cramp. He felt that his own was cramping; tried to relax it. Pilgrim—a flash of a young man with a chipped tooth and blue eyes.

"He doesn't get you, Doc," the Marine was saying. "Come on, sir. We have to—"

"Wait," the scarecrow said. He moved his lips very close to Franz Ludwig's ear. "He landed. Lawrence landed. *Er hat . . .*" ι e shook his head, forgetting the German. He made a motion with his hand, landing it lightly on the doctor's chest. "He landed on the moon!"

The doctor saw a graceful trajectory soaring toward a silver sphere, an immutable curve as clean and precise as any other in sidereal clockwork. He saw it bend gracefully in flight and impact the satellite, drop gently to its surface like a leaf on *Lindenstrasse*. And the word, whatever it was— Pilgrim—was no longer a black, evil one, but a clean and shining thing. Summoning all his will, he nodded. The tall doctor smiled, squeezed his lifeless hand, and left quickly.

Franz Ludwig watched him go in the mirror above the bureau. Then he closed his eyes to sleep. He would need all of his strength to work on the arm tomorrow.

He stood for a moment in the black shade of the capsule, looking at the crescent earth floating above his southeast horizon. It was dazzling with clouds; even the shadowed portion shone softly. On the sunlit rind North Africa anchored a blue strip of Atlantic, but above it Europe was covered with stratus. Reluctant to subject his suit to the ultimate test of heat, he looked around for a moment at the glaring wasteland before stepping into sunlight. He kept a hand on the capsule against the inertial forces of his own motion, squatted to scoop up a little of the grey-black lunar dust. He held it idly in the light, feeling the sun on his hand, let it sift to the surface.

Finally, he took a deep breath, arose easily against the moon's weak pull, and stepped from frigid shadow into blazing heat. He moved very slowly to cushion the shock on the system on his back. The suit, the biopak, his body, all took the change of temperature without flinching—he remembered the head suitman, half-dead with fatigue, snarling at his own assistant while he traced a sticking valve in Environmental Repair.

He began to shuffle through the sandy dust in the rolling gait he had mastered at Houston two weeks and an eternity ago. He moved northwest toward Surveyor, keeping the white-hot morning sun to his right. Once he looked back. He had traveled hardly more than two miles across the flat surface but already his capsule had fallen beneath his horizon. He had another moment of terror, an irresistible desire to retrace his steps.

He fought it down and did not stop again for two hours. He had passed two or three small, low-lipped craters. They were surrounded with jumbled black rocks. He skirted them widely because the walking was easier on the dust. But now he spotted a hummock with a plateau on top; doubtless an older craterlet eroded over the ages by millions of micrometeorite impacts. It was hardly 30 feet high, with a gradual slope, but when he reached its crest his body was running with sweat. He had an insane desire to rip off his pressure suit. To die instantly in an explosion of tortured flesh seemed less horrible than to cook inside.

He must not panic. He stepped down a few feet on the shady side of the rise. While the suit cooled he began to scan the northwest horizon for a glimpse of the rim of Flamsteed or one of the ranges ringing the Ocean of Storms. They were still beneath the curvature, though, so he dropped his gaze, watching for a sign of Surveyor on the plain beneath him. A thousand yards across the grey desert, near a crater perhaps a hundred feet high, he spotted a crevice. He stiffened. There was something familiar about it.

The angle was different, but it was the one that had tricked him. And something within it was tricking him again. He began to move down the slope, his breath coming faster. For a moment he forgot his shuffling, careful walk. He stumbled, almost pitched forward. He put a hand down, caught himself, forced restraint on his legs as he reached the plain and started across it.

The crevice was in the shade of the crater. Around the crater was scattered lunar rubble from the meteoric impact that had hammered it out—black, basaltic rocks, pebble to cobblestone-sized. He picked his way over them to the brink of the gulch, accustoming his eyes to the deep black shade. He peered down and froze.

The crevice was a huge, shallow grave, not more than 20 feet deep. Lying half in it and half out of it was the twisted framework of a white spacecraft, blackened by an explosion. He began to shake. It was the Vostok.

The braking stages were larger than his own by a half. They were crumpled and destroyed, but through a split-open bulkhead he caught a glimpse of a work table and a broken tank, obviously for oxygen. The Russians had incorporated shelter with spacecraft, as the colonel had once guessed that they would. For a wild instant Steve thought of trying to rummage in the wreckage for anything that would help him survive.

It was ridiculous; nothing but an operating airtight shelter could do the least good. And there was no airtight shelter in this twisted mess. He was as dead as whoever had piloted it. His eye followed the strewn wreckage up the side of the crevice, stopped at a seared capsule on top.

It had retained more of its integrity than any other part. He skirted the crevice carefully, inspecting it. Circling the depression, he had to watch his footing. When he looked up again he very nearly yelled. The hatch was open. Halfway out of it a pressure-suited figure leaned, arms spread as if in supplication, or as if to gather in the plaudits of a crowd or embrace the world he had discovered.

But of course it was only the oxygen trapped in the suit. For as Steve moved closer—and he could have reached up and touched the man—he could see staring brown eyes in a black-stubbled face. The eyes were lifeless. A dried stream of blood led from the corner of the mouth. In the glacial shadow, near absolute zero, there had been not the slightest deterioration of the skin. In a few days, though, the sun would touch the capsule . . .

Steve's first impulse was to try to bury the man, but he knew that he himself would run out of oxygen long before he finished scrabbling in the rubble with his fingers or a piece of the wreckage. His eye fell to a limp rag hanging on a twisted strut beneath the Russian. He looked at it curiously, inched down the incline to get it.

It was a red flag with a gold star on it, and a hammer-and-sickle emblem. Steve picked it from the strut, looked up at the staring face, marveling. Whoever he was, he had known that unless he succeeded his country would try to hide from the world the knowledge that he had even tried; and yet his first and last thought on landing had been to plant the flag. Slowly, Steve climbed back to the man's level. He stared across the abyss into the lifeless eyes.

Then he began to move up the slope of the crater behind them.

Rick Lincoln had driven her home. Now she passed through the darkened house by Clear Lake, pausing in the living room to turn on the light under which Steve had studied, moving irresolutely down the hall, tossing a forgotten T-shirt of Stevie's through the open door onto his bunk. Rick had asked to stay, or to send Cindy, but she wanted to be alone.

She had sickened of the chain-smoking statues behind the glass in Mission Control; she had known suddenly that she could not watch one more second appear on the window of the timekeeper under the hateful map, could not bear one more look at the blood-red circle where he was supposed to have landed. She could not stand one more instant of the colonel's torture, either, his losing fight, when he faced the platform, to keep hope on his face for her.

She was certain that when the last second clicked into place, when there could be no more oxygen in Steve's biopak and still they had not heard, she would dissolve before their eyes. And so she had come home; they would phone her at the slightest hint of news.

She moved out to the lawn. She could get Stevie from Marion Scarbo, late as it was, and tell him that Steve had landed safely, but then he probably knew that anyway from TV before he went to bed. He was asleep, for the light in the room in which the Scarbos kept him was out, but a faint blue glow in the Scarbo living room showed that Marion was still watching the news.

She found all at once that she could not go to get him. Much as she wanted him, he would know when he saw her face that his father was dead or dying, and you could not explain to a six-year-old that a man was a hero if he had died chasing a phantom, for a dream.

The moon was gibbous, almost full, low on the western horizon. It was golden with the haze of the Texas plain, but she could make out a faint outline of the Ocean of Storms on its convex edge. She clung to the sight, fighting tears. She took a deep breath and began to try her game. Watch me, my darling. See how I grasp the rail of the pier with a firm and steady hand, lean casually on it, full of hope. Now, tell me: in a few moments, when the strain of your landing doesn't show too much on my face, should I get our son, wake him at this unearthly hour, tell him that you are safe, that it is only the silent void that separates us?

She found herself smiling. When she tried, when the moon was there, she could imagine him moving toward his shelter, maybe already lowering it—perhaps already safe inside, punching the buttons and tuning the dials that would let him tell her so. When you're through, my darling, or tomorrow,

take the time to step outside and look this way, and maybe I'll
know that, too.

A wisp of cloud from across the Gulf flew toward the
golden disk. She tried to stay it with her will, but it reached
the face of the moon and then there was nothing.

She closed her eyes. I asked you, Steve, should I get him
or let him sleep? And if I tell him that you are safe, will it be
the start of a year-long lie? Or what? What shall I do?
Tomorrow, maybe, I'll know how to handle him. I'll take
him with me shopping first and scrub the kitchen floor while
he watches the Mouseketeers, but now? What shall I do now,
you in the dark of the moon?

The moon stayed covered; the clouds thickened, but she
found herself moving anyway toward the Scarbo house. I am
walking steadily, head held high, you see? And opening the
gate. And tonight he'll sleep in his own bed and tomorrow we
will know.

He had climbed in the shade; even so, he was very, very
hot. He rested for a moment before cresting the lip. The man
in the wreckage was a puppet on a stage a hundred feet
below. He glanced at the earth hanging above the black
horizon. North America dominated the lighted crescent now;
the southern portion was shrouded with clouds; perhaps even
Houston was hidden under the veil in the sliver of light.

But it did not matter. Mickey seemed closer every moment; when it happened she would know, and know that he
had gone thinking of her, whether the moon had set over
Clear Lake or not. He mounted the last few feet into sunlight,
began to build a pile of lunar rocks on the edge. When the pile
was three feet high he carefully lodged the Russian flag on
one side of it, then reached into his pack and drew out the
colonel's.

It was smaller and had no staff, but he wedged it carefully
between two rocks and spread it out. Unless men disturbed it
when they came, it would stay forever just as he had placed

it, through the windless blazing days and the silent frigid nights.

He moved a few feet down the slope into shade. He was more ready for what was coming than he had been all through the day. He sat down, watching the earth pensively, feeling in his pack for a tiny notebook-pencil combination. He had a few technical notes to leave, and a few things to write to Stevie, and a few words for Mickey, very few, for she knew all there was to know about him, anyway.

A star sat alone on the black horizon, just below the earth. He noticed its brightness and began to write. His pencil stopped.

He looked up. The star was gone.

His pulse began to race. He started to count, for he could not tear his eyes from the dark horizon to look at his electric watch. At the count of fifty-three the light appeared again. Now he forced his eyes to the watch, his hand shaking. At eight seconds he looked up.

Two more seconds and the light blinked out. He very quickly checked his oxygen. Four hours left. And if the light on the shelter capsule was blinking, the shelter had landed erect; if it had landed erect, it was operable. The shelter might be two, three, four hours beyond the horizon, but he knew with absolute certainty that he would make it if he had to crawl the last mile on his hands and knees. He moved down the slope. Passing the wreckage he paused for a moment, looking up at the man.

Then he struck out across the eternally quiet dust of the Ocean of Storms.